AU\!

FACTS

Fun & Interesting

Australian Facts

&

Mini
Slang Dictionary

Sharks are immune to all known diseases.

91% of the entire country is covered by native vegetation.

Australia's national anthem was 'God Save The King/Queen' until 1984.

The longest fence in the world (The Dingo Fence) was originally built to keep dingoes away from fertile land and is oddly known as "The rabbit proof fence."

Dingoes are more closely related to the Indian wolf than dogs and do not bark. Instead, they howl.

Kangaroos and emus cannot move backwards easily. Whilst they physically can go backwards, they rarely do.

Melbourne has the largest remaining tram public transport system in the world.

Perth is the only city in the world which can have aircraft land in its Central Business District.

Saltwater crocodiles are found around the northern areas of Australia from Broome in Western Australia to Rockhampton in Queensland.

You will find more kangaroos than you will humans in Australia.

A retired cavalry officer, Francis De Groot stole the show when the Sydney Harbour Bridge officially opened. Just as the Premier was about to cut the ribbon, De Groot charged forward on his horse and cut it himself, with his sword. The ribbon had to be re

Sydney Harbour Bridge took 1,400 labourers to build over eight years.

Texas is the largest state in the continental United States, but the largest state in Australia, Western Australia is more than 3 times its size but Texas has 13 times as many people.

The common wombat is nicknamed the "bulldozer of the bush."

In the wet tropics of the Queensland rainforests, you can find the highest concentration of primitive flowering plant families in the world.

There are over 60 different types of kangaroos.

Canberra was decided as the capital city of Australia because Sydney and Melbourne couldn't stop arguing who should get it.

In 1932, an "Emu War' took place in Western Australian when a deployment of soldiers armed with Lewis Guns tried to reduce a population of 20,000 which was threatening he wheat crop. Despite many emus being killed in various battles the humans lost a war

Camels are not native to Australia, yet Australia has the largest number of feral camels worldwide with over one million of them roaming around.

Australia does not have any active volcanoes on the mainland continent. However, there are 2 active volcanoes in the Australia Antarctic Territor - one on Heard Island and one in the McDonald Islands.

No part of Australia is further than 1000 kilometres from the sea.

There is no official language in Australia although English is spoken as a first language in 80% of homes and is used as the primary language of government.

The oldest daily newspaper in the southern hemisphere is the Sydney Morning Herald (1831).

Melbourne was the capital city of Australia for 26 years between 1901 and 1927, before the capital shifted to the purpose-built city of Canberra.

The Box jellyfish has killed more people in Australia than stonefish, sharks and crocodiles combined.

There are more than 140 species of land snakes and 32 species of sea snakes in Australia .

Out of the top 25 deadliest snakes in the world, 75% are found in Australia.

When threatened, wombats make loud hissing sounds and kick backwards like a donkey. In retreat, they dive headfirst into their burrow leaving their bum exposed.

Female quokkas will expel their offspring from the pouch when threatened by predators.

Many Australian words are derived from Aboriginal languages such as yabber, wallaby, kangaroo, kookaburra, and wonga.

The Mountain Ash tree found in Tasmania and Victoria is the tallest hardwood tree in Australia and the tallest flowering plant in the world. It can reach heights up to 114 metres tall (375 feet).

Between 1838 and 1902 in Sydney it was forbidden to swim between 6am and 8pm. Sharks temd to feed at dawn and dusk so the hours in the midst of the day are the safest for swimming.

The Great Ocean Road is a 243 kilometre road that was built between 1919 and 1932 by soldiers who had survived the First World War and returned home.

Australia is the world's only continent located entirely in the Southern hemisphere.

The Australian emu is a large, flightless bird that can run as fast as 45 kilometres per hour (28mph).

Bert Appleroth invented Australia's famous Aeroplane Jelly who began making jelly crystals in his bathtub in 1927.

The Great Victoria Desert is larger than the whole of the United Kingdom and is just one of Australia's many dry areas.

The secret ballot box, the most prized symbol of democracy, was pioneered in Victoria in 1856.

Australian termites are known to have evolved from cockroaches.

Melbourne was briefly called Batmania, after John Batman the city's founder and you can still visit Batman Park in Melbourne's CBD.

Over 300 different languages and dialects are spoken in Australia including 45 Indigenous languages.

The Great Southern Reef is a series of golden kelp forest reefs that extend around 8,000km of Australia's southern coastline, covering a total area of 71,000 square kilometres.

21% of Australians don't speak English at home.

The Australian Aborigines are ethnologically most akin to Caucasians.

Australia is the fourth largest exporter of wine globally, totalling 760 million litres of wine that is shipped overseas each year.

The termite mounds that can be found in Australia are the tallest animal-made structures on Earth.

Bondi Beach is the most popular beach in Australia. It sees more than 2.9 million visitors per year.

The world's largest rock is Mount Augustus in Western Australia.

When running at top speed emus do flap the wings, using them to help balance and change direction. They also flap their mini wings to help cool themselves down.

Australia is the most obese country in the world as of 2012 with a 26% obesity rate despite being a sport-loving nation.

The Daintree Rainforest found in Far North Queensland, is the world's oldest surviving tropical rainforest. It covers 1,200 square kilometres and is thought to be 180 million years old.
Granny Smith apples originated in Sydney in 1868 in the orchard of Maria Smith in Ryde.

Western Australia is home to what is believed to be the oldest evidence of life on Earth - the Stromatolites.

Australia is the only English-speaking country to have made voting compulsory in federal and state elections. It results in a voter turnout of 95 percent.

Australia was one of the founding members of the United Nations.

Australia exports it's camels to the Middle East.

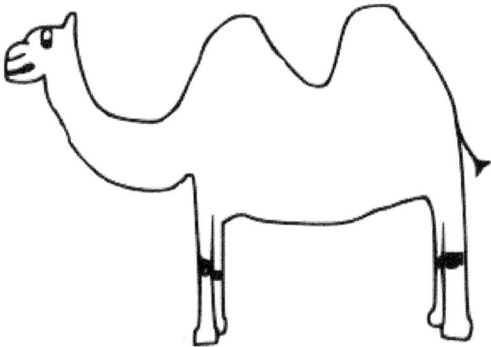

In 1856, stonemasons took action to ensure a standard of 8-hour working days, which then became recognised worldwide.

Lady Elliot Island in the Great Barrier Reef is kept together by three things - dead coral, tree roots, and guano (bird poo).

The last tram ran in Sydney on 26 February 1961. Trams still run in Melbourne.

Australia has the highest electricity prices in the world. Due to the iniquitous carbon tax.

Quokkas are known as the world's happiest animal after being shown smiling in thousands of selfies with humans.

An Australian election TV debate was rescheduled so it didn't conflict with the finale of reality cooking show Masterchef.

There are ten deserts in Australia and the largest is the Great Victorian Desert.

People from Sydney are typically referred to as Sydneysiders, while a person from Melbourne is called a Melbournian.

Over a trillion bottles of wine are produced in Australia every year.

Australia is a big country! The distance from the most easterly point of Australia to the most westerly is 4,000km. From the most northerly point to the most southerly point in Tasmania the distance is 3860km.

No part of Australia is more than 1000 km from the ocean and a beach.

Mount Augustus is actually twice the size of Uluru.

Before the arrival of humans, Australia was home to megafauna: three metre tall kangaroos, seven metre long goanna's, horse-sized ducks, and a marsupial lion the size of a leopard.

Crocodiles kill at least one person every year in Australia.

An Australian man once tried to sell New Zealand on eBay, with a starting price of A$0.01.

AFL (Australian Rules Football) was invented to keep Cricketers fit in the off season.

The bearded bushranger, Ned Kelly, has had more biographies written about him than any other Australian.

The first television station in Australia opened in 1956 as TCN Channel 9, Sydney.

The Chiko roll was invented by Frank McEnroe in 1951. He originally called it a Chicken Roll even though there was no chicken in it. The shape was based on the Chinese spring roll, and the filling is vegetarian.

European settlers in Australia drank more alcohol per capita than any other society in history.

The oldest Australian chocolate bar is the Cherry Ripe which was first created in 1924 by the Australian confectioner MacRobertsons and later sold to Cadburys.

A gay bar in Melbourne won the legal right to ban women from the bars, because they made the men uncomfortable.

There are an estimated 40 million kangaroos in Australia.

The cleanest air on earth is recorded in Tasmania but only when the wind is blowing from the west across the Roaring Forties. Air from a northerly wind brings pollution from Melbourne.

Mount Augustus is often said to be the world's largest monolith but this is incorrect, it is in fact the world's largest monocline which is a fold in rock strata.

Canberra became Australia's capital to resolve disputes between Sydney and Melbourne which both wanted to be the country's administrative centre.

Australia Day takes place every year on January 26 and is a celebration of different cultures, races, religions, beliefs, and views.

The Great Barrier Reef is the world's largest living structure. It can be seen from space and is considered one of the seven natural wonders of the world.

There are more than 2,000 species of spiders in Australia but only a handful are dangerous.

There are 63.8 million sheep in Australia and so outnumber humans 2.5 to 1.

The average Australian can expect to eat during his or her lifetime: 17 beef cattle, 92 sheep, 406 loaves of bread, 165,000 eggs 8 tons of fruit, half a ton of cheese and ten tons of veggies.

Wombat poop is square and helps aid communication between them and other wombats and to mark their territory.

Australia is a biodiversity hotspot with 200,000 species of plants, fungi, animals, fish, insects and other organisms already named.

Sydney Tower, at Centrepoint, is the highest building in the southern hemisphere, 324.8 metres above sea level.

Many of Australian's Indigenous nations played ball games, often using a furry ball made of possum skins. The Wurundjeri people played a game called marngrook which seems to involve a high kick now seen in Australian Rules football.

Aboriginal culture is the oldest culture on Earth.

Ningaloo Reef is home to whale sharks, pelagic fish like tuna and billfish, humpback whales, dolphins, manta rays, dugong, and turtles such as green, loggerhead, and hawksbill turtles.

Emus are huge flightless birds which have very tiny wings.

Saudi Arabia imports camels from Australia, mostly for meat production.

The world's largest cattle station is almost the same size as Belgium at 30,028 square km.

Australia is home to 150 volcanoes but are all extinct or dormant. None of them has erupted in 5,000 years.

The Gold Coast's canal system is so large, it's bigger than Venice and Amsterdam combined.

Camels were historically used to help with construction and other labor around the country, but now there are more than one million wild camels in the deserts.

The Tasmanian Devil has a jaw strength similar to a crocodile, but its jaws are much smaller!

The Melbourne Cup is a horse racing event that takes place every November. It's a public holiday in Melbourne and a busy day throughout other parts of the country.

Aboriginal and Torres Strait Islanders make up roughly 3.3 per cent of the Australian population.

The biggest property in Australia is bigger than Belgium.

The largest producer of gold in the world is located in Australia. Rather than being found in one of the large cities, its home is a small town named Kalgoorlie.

Tasmania has the cleanest air in the world.

Sydney's Opera House was designed by Danish architect Jorn Utzon in 1957. Construction began in 1959 and it was officially opened by Queen Elizabeth II in 1973.

Australia holds the Guiness World Record for the most amount of Christmas lights on a house with over half a million lights.

If you visited one new beach in Australia every day, it would take over 27 years to see them all.

It does snow in Australia during the winter, and can often have even more snow than Switzerland.

Kangaroos belong to the family Macropodidae which means big feet.

There are hundreds of dinosaur footprints fossilised in the rock in Lark Quarry and they are around 95 million years old. The Dinosaur Stampede National Monument at Lark Quarry Conservation Park is in outback Queensland.

There are 1 million Camels that roam wild Australia's Deserts - the largest number of purebred camels in the world.

Prime Minister Kevin Rudd mentioned the Iced Vovo biscuit in his speech on the night of 24th November 2007. After this, Iced Vovo sales spiked.

The second tallest tree in the world, the Huon pine, grows in the rainforests of southwest Tasmania.

Highway 1 in Australia is the longest highway in the world, spanning around 9,000 miles in total.

The World Surfing Championship was first held in Sydney, in 1964.

Kangaroo meat can be purchased from the supermarket, butcher and available on restaurant menus as a leaner and healthier alternative to beef or lamb with a 1-2% fat content.

There are over 300 mines in Australia mining minerals such as coal, zinc, silver, and gold.

Once, Tasmania was part of Australia's mainland. 12,000 years ago, when the ice age ended, ocean levels rose and drowned the landbridge.

Ningaloo Reef is home to over 450 different species of marine life and 250 species of coral.

90% of Australians live less than 50km from the coastline.

You won't find Burger King in Australia, but you will find it under the name of Hungry Jacks.

The oldest skeleton found in Australia was at Lake Mungo in New South Wales. It is believed to be 38,000 years old and is the skeleton of a female.

Given that most of the population lives near the coast, Australia's inland offers plenty of spots for stargazing, including Winton, Queensland which is certified as a Dark Sky Sanctuary.

Marsupials like koalas, quokka and kangaroos can be found nowhere else in the world.

You can fly from Perth to Melbourne faster than you can fly from one end of Western Australia to the other.

Snakes flick out their tongues so that they can detect chemicals in the air which helps them to track prey.

Australians put beetroot on their hamburgers.

More than 70% of the Australian population participates regularly in some form of sport, although over 25% of the country is considered to be obese.

Australia's Capital city, Canberra, meant "woman's cleavage" in Aborigine and was named that because the city is cradled between two mountains.

The actor Russell Crowe is often mistakenly thought to be Australian. He was actually born in New Zealand but moved with his family to Australia when he was just four years old.

On average, each Australian farmer produces enough food each year to feed 600 people for that whole year.

Australia has a larger population of camels than Egypt.

The Nullabor Plain is the world's largest single piece of limestone bedrock, a staggering 200,000 square kilometres. At its widest point, it runs for it is 1,100 km (684 miles).

Australia has 20 world heritage listed sites including historic townships, cities and landscapes and the Sydney Opera House.

Tim Tams are a popular Australian biscuit, approximately 35 million packets are sold annually meaningevery person in Australia eats 1.7 packets of Tim Tams each year.

The original Freddos invented in Australia were shaped more like real frogs than the cartoon-like character we know today. The creators of Freddo Frogs initially considered creating chocolate mice instead of frogs.

When Freddo Frogs were invented at MacRobertson's chocolate factory in Melbourne in 1930, Australians went so crazy over them that people were jailed for stealing Freddo Frogs.

The emu, Australia's national bird, is the second-largest bird in the world by height, after the ostrich.

The wine cask (Goon) was invented in Australia.

Magnetic termite mounds are only found in the Northern Territory. The mounds are aligned north-south to the earth's magnetic field.

Australia is very sparsely populated: The UK has 248.25 persons per square kilometre, while Australia has only 2.66 persons per square kilometre.

The Great Ocean Road is the largest war memorial in the world.

Melbourne is considered the sporting capital of the world, as it has more top level sport available for its citizens than anywhere else.

Uluru is the largest single chunk of rock in Australia and the largest monolith in the world.

Not only is Australia the flattest continent on earth, but it's also the largest island on earth.

Tully, in Queensland, is the wettest town in Australia with an average annual rainfall of 355.6 centimetres (11 ft, 10 inches).

The cleanest water on earth can be found in Tasmania.

Wombat poo is cubed shaped so that it doesn't fall off rocks but stays on top which aids in communication between wombats.

The four huge granite-faced pylons at each end of Sydney Harbour Bridge don't support the bridge. They are there for aesthetic reasons only.

The first ever Australian police force was a group of 12 of the most well-behaved convicts known as The Night Watch and then as the Sydney Foot Police.

Australians drink 1.7 billion litres of beer per year. That's about 680 bottles of beer for each adult.

Of the 100 snakes that are venomous only 12 species can kill humans.

Of the approximately 26 million people who lived in Australia in 2023, more than 25% of all Australians were born in another country.

Tasmanian devils may look small, but they have the strongest bite per body mass of any mammal on earth.

The average person in Australia swallows three spiders a year.

There are more than 1000,000 saltwater crocodiles in the Northern Territory of Australia.

Australia is home to 21 of the world's 25 most venomous snakes.

Wombats have the largest brains of all marsupials.

Kangaroos and emus were used on the coat of arms to symbolise constantly moving forward.

Roughly 25% of Australians were born outside of Australia.

Melbourne was briefly called Batmania. You can still visit Batman Park in Melbourne.

The capital city of Australia, Canberra, has a population of around 300,000.

The longest river in Australia is the Murray River which runs for 2,508 kilometres (1,558 miles) through New South Wales, Victoria and South Australia.

The Australian 50-cent coin was once round like other coins.

Qantas once powered a flight with cooking oil.

There is a Boomerang Association of Australia. Other countries have boomerang associations too and a World Boomerang Championship is held in a different country every two years.

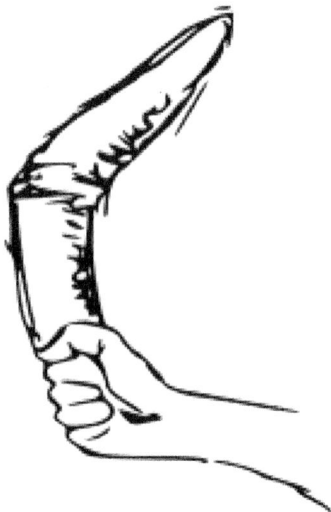

Australia is the largest continent occupied by one nation and is the least populated.

The Australian Alps actually receive more snow each year than Switzerland.

If Melbourne had stuck to its original name, you could have told people you lived in the city of Batmania.

The Australian Alps is the only area on the Australian mainland that receives deep snow every year.

Australia's richest woman Gina Rinehart earns $1 million every 2 hours.

Quokkas are considered the friendliest animal in the world and can only be found in Western Australia.

Australia invented the world's first waterproof polymer banknotes in 1988. They are both long lasting and hygienic as they are resistant to dirt and moisture.

Aussies love their sports. This includes cricket, golf, tennis, swimming, and four codes of football, to name just a few.

Aboriginal culture is the oldest on Earth. It's estimated that the continent's original inhabitants have been in Australia for 60,000 years.

Australia is home to the Boulia Camel Races, an annual event that features the longest camel race in Australia, along with camel tagging competitions, children's games and fireworks.

Australia is home to around 4,000 types of ants and 350 types of termites.

Australia has the highest rate of gambling in the world with over 80% of adults engaging in gambling.

Wombats are notorious for digging alternate exits to their burrows when traps are placed at the entrance.

The first Australian born governor-general was Jewish.

Australia is almost the same size as mainland USA.

Ayers Rock is a red granite monolith, with a circumference of 8.85 kilometres.

It is a known fact that Wallabies like to break into Opium crops, get high and run around in circles to create a crop circle.

The population of Australia around the same size as the city Shanghai, in China.

The highest jump recorded by a kangaroo is 9 metres (30 feet) in a single leap.

Fraser Island, also known by its aboriginal name K'gari, lies off the Queensland coast and is the largest sand island in the world.

Australia is a BIG country!

In 1880, Melbourne was the richest city in the world.

The Australian magpie is a skilled mimic and can copy the songs of around 35 other bird species and even make some horse and dog noises.

A termite colony can have between a few hundred to a few million termites and the queens can live up to 50 years.

Australians invented notepads, dual-flushing toilets, the pacemaker, the cochlear implant, spray-on skin for burns patients, black box flight recorders, baby safety car capsules and the Hills hoist rotary clothes hoist.

In Australia, Maltesers were originally marketed as a weight-loss food.

The world's longest stretch of completely straight railway is found on the Nullabor Plain and runs for 480 kilometres.

Sydney is the largest city in Australia with over 4.5 million people.

Australia has three national Frisbee teams.

Melbourne has the world's largest Greek population outside of Athens.

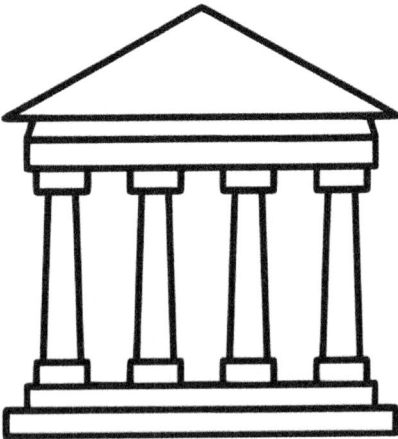

Taxonomists believe that they have only discovered 30% of the biodiversity species in Australia so far.

Australia has the world's longest golf course, a unique 18-hole par 72 golf course along the Nullabor Plain encompasses 2 states (WA & SA) and is 1,365 km (850 miles) long.

Australia is as wide as the distance between London to Moscow.

Christmas is in summer in Australia, which means that many families like to spend it at the beach. Seafood is common for Christmas dinner.

There were over one million feral camels in outback Australia, until the government launched the $19m Feral Camel Management Program, which aims to keep the pest problem under control.

The highest recorded temperature of 53.1 C was at Cloncurry, Queensland, on 16 January 1889.

There is a Napoleon Pear tree in a garden in Hobart which is more than 120 years old and continues to produce 1.5 tonnes of fruit annually.

The largest cattle station in the world is located in Australia and it's bigger than Israel.

Moomba, Australia's largest free festival held in Melbourne, means "up your bum' in many Aboriginal languages.

If you visited one new beach in Australia every day, it would take over 27 years to see them all.

Australia is home innovations including the black box flight recorder, the electronic pacemaker and Wi-Fi technology.

Australia has the world's longest golf course measuring more than 850 miles long.

65% of Australians are overweight.

There are more than 150 million sheep in Australia, and only 24 million people.

Australia's record 24-hour rainfall of 907 mm (36.28 inches) occurred at Crohamhurst, Queensland, in 1893.

The closest American state in population to Australia is New York, which has 19.6 million people, yet Australia is more than 53 times its size.

Vegemite was created by left over Yeast used to create Beer.

Volcanoes can be found in various parts of the world, but Australia is the only continent that does not have an active volcano.

The Great Barrier Reef in Queensland is the largest coral reef system coral in the world with 2,900 coral reefs and a total area of 348,000 square kilometres.

Australians consume chicken above all other meats and poultry. It averages to 47 kg per person per year.

Violet Crumbles were given that name as the inventor's wife adored violet flowers.

Indigenous Australians represent the oldest continuing living culture in the entire world. It is estimated that the continent's original inhabitants, the aboriginal people, have been in Australia for between 40,000-60,000 years.

The red kangaroo is the biggest species of kangaroo in Australia. The largest "big red" ever seen was 2.1 metres tall (6ft 9in) and weighed 91kgs (200lbs).

Even as recent as 2018, politicians discussed the Australian flag design and whether it should be changed. The flag still incorporates the Union Flag of the United Kingdom.

In some parts of Australia, up to 90 per cent of the koala population is infected with an STI.

The Blue Mountains get its name from the blue haze you can see around it from the plains below. This blue haze is caused by oily droplets evaporating from eucalyptus leaves and mixing with water vapour and dust. These scatter short wavelength light rays w

From 1897 to 1905, Kings Cross, Sydney, was called Queen's Cross.

In 1832, 300 female convicts mooned the governor of Tasmania. It was said that in a "rare moment of collusion with the Convict women, the ladies in the Governor's party could not control their laughter."

Melbourne has the world's largest Greek-speaking population of any city outside Greece and Cyprus.

The world's largest electorate (2,255,278 km2) is Kalgoorlie, Western Australia.

Koalas sleep for around 20 hours per day.

The Great Barrier Reef is the largest organic construction on earth.

The Northern Territory has just 1% of the Australian population.

The deadliest marine animal in Australia is the box jellyfish.

Ugg boots, made from sheepskin, originated in Australia and became popular in the 1960s when surf champions wore them to keep their feet warm when waiting on the beach.

Fifty percent of the continent has less than 300 millimetres of annual rainfall.

Brisbane holds the World Championship of Cockroach Racing each year.

The amount of fish fingers sold in Australia each year could cover Tasmania.

Cathedral termites in the Northern Territory, Western Australia and Queensland build mounds up to eight metres in height.

The first radio station in Australia was built near Pennant Hills, Sydney, in 1912.

Marble Bar, Western Australia, recorded the longest period of extreme heat above 37.7 Celcius for 160 days from October 1923 to April 1924.

1 million wild camels roam the Australian deserts. They were originally brought over to help with railroad construction.

Many deserts in Australia have thunderstorms. However, given the heat, the rainfall evaporates before it hits the ground.

Of the seven continents, Australia is the smallest, at 3 million square miles. However, if considered an island, it is the largest in the world.

Lake Eyre in the southern outback is the lowest point in Australia and is 15 metres below sea level.

The Australia Eucalypt or gum tree has over 500 species and is the toughest hardwood in the world.

After China, the largest number of sheep can be found in Australia. This also means that Australia is one of the world's leading producers of wool.

According to a survey conducted in Britain, around 10% of the population believed that the moon was closer than Australia.

As a land of extremes, the highest temperature recorded was 50.7 degrees Celsius and the lowest recorded was minus 23 degrees Celsius.

The Pinnacles Desert within Nambung National Park in Western Australia has hundreds of limestone pillars rising from the desert sand with the tallest aound 3.5 metres high.

Australia is the 6th largest country in the world after Russia, Canada, China, the USA, and Brazil

Australia is the driest inhabited continent on earth. Only Antarctica gets less moisture falling on its landmass.

Former Prime Minister Bob Hawke set a world record for sculling 2.5 pints of beer in 11 seconds. Hawke later suggested that this was the reason for his great political success.

Most countries do not eat the animals which feature on their coast of arms but Australians eat do eat emu and kangaroo.

You can fly from Perth to Melbourne faster than you can fly from one end of Western Australia to the other.

The creators of Freddo Frogs, invented in Australia, initially considered creating chocolate mice instead of frogs.

Australia invented the world's first seat belt law in 1970.

Australians use classical music to fight crime. In 2013, Knox Council in Victoria decided to blast Bach and Beethoven from speakers at shopping centres at night to deter teenage loiterers.

While kangaroos are considered a national icon, with over 40 million estimated throughout the country, they can also be considered a pest in some locations.

Indigenous people settled on the land for around 50,000 years before the British arrived.

Ningaloo Reef gets its name from the Aboriginal Wajarri language word Ningaloo meaning deep water or high land jutting into the sea.

The world's oldest fossil, which is about 3.4 billion years old, was found in Australia.

Moomba is the name of an annual festival held in Melbourne. In some Aboriginal languages, it means "up your bum."

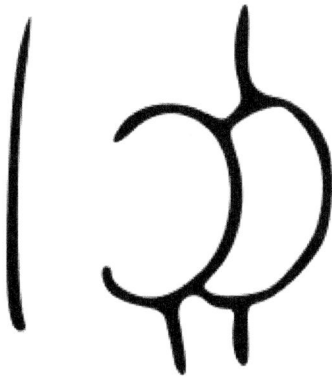

The national floral emblem is the wattle, a flower that was selected in 1912.

The low humidity, low air pollution and lack of population make the Australian outback one of the best places in the world for stargazing.

The Memorial Arch at Eastern View marks the start of the Great Ocean Road and commemorates the returned servicemen who laboured to built it.

Australia is almost the same size as mainland USA (North America).

The wombat deposits square poos.

Other dangerous (usually venomous) animals to avoid include the blue ring octopus, the stone fish, funnel web spider and the cassowary; one of the world's largest birds that when provoked attack with their sharp claws.

Around 80% of the 162,000 convicts shipped to Australia between 1788 and 1868 were thieves. Robert Scattergood had stolen two live geese.

The only two mammals in the world that lay eggs are native to Australia - the echidna and platypus.

Koala bears are popular in Australia, although there are 10 times as many camels as koalas.

It used to be legal to hunt and kill Aborigines.

There are 250 distinct Aboriginal language groups throughout Australia.

Australia's native plants include species of eucalyptus, acacia, evergreen trees, orchids, and ferns.

More than 80% of Australia's plants and animals are unique to Australia and are found nowhere else in the world.

There are 60 wine regions in Australia.

Australia's Aboriginal people are estimated to have occupied the mainland for at least 65,000 years, forming one of the oldest continuing living cultures on earth.

The health service in Australia includes doctors who will visit remote areas by helicopter. For many Australians, this is their only access to urgent medical assistance.

Australia has the world's 9th largest road network with 356,000km of paved road and over 466,000km of unpaved road.

Australia's federal Parliament in Canberra banned security guards from calling people "mate" in 2005. It lasted one day.

Australia has one of the world's lowest population densities, with a landmass only slightly smaller than the USA, yet a population of around 26 million compared to 332 million in the United States.

The Great Barrier Reef has a mailbox. You can send a postcard with the only Great Barrier Reef stamp.

The Tasmanian devil's head and neck are so huge, they make up 25% of its body mass and give it a powerful bite.

Kati Thanda-Lake Eyre in the Flinders Ranges of South Australia is Australia's biggest salt lake measuring 144 kilometres by 77 kilometres and covering 9,500 square kilometres.

Mount Disappointment was named by British explorers who were disappointed that they couldn't see Port Phillip Bay from its summit.

Wolf Creek, Western Australia, has the largest meteorite crater in Australia, measuring 853.44 metres in diameter and 61 metres deep.

It would take around 29 years to visit one new Australian beach every day. There are 10,685 of them.

The Australian thorny devil can live for up to 20 years. It has one of the longest lifespans of lizards of its size in the world, likely due to its amazing camouflage abilities.

Around a quarter of all Australians were born overseas.

Melbourne has a population of 4 million.

Each week there are an estimated 70 tourists that overstay their visas.

Australia is home to the over 10,000 beaches.

Western grey kangaroos are knowns as "stinkers" because they have a strong body odour caused by the types of plants they eat.

The elusive 'drop bear' is a fake animal that was created to scare tourists. The bear apparently dropped from trees and other areas but is entirely fictional.

Ugg is a generic name for sheepskin boots and is not trademarked in Australia but UGG is trademarked in 100 other countries by the American company Deckers Brand.

Wombats have tiny eyes and poor vision. They make up for it with excellent hearing and smell.

In 1880, Melbourne was the richest city in the world.

There are no Bills of Rights in this country, making it the only Western country to omit this from its governmental system.

Tasmania is home to one of the oldest plants in the world, King's Holly, believed to be at least 43,000 years old.

The annual Australian Day Cockroach Races held at the Story Bridge Hotel in Brisbane are a popular event, featuring a steeplechase and a sprint for the cockroach participants.

Locals call the Sydney Harbour Bridge "The Coathanger."

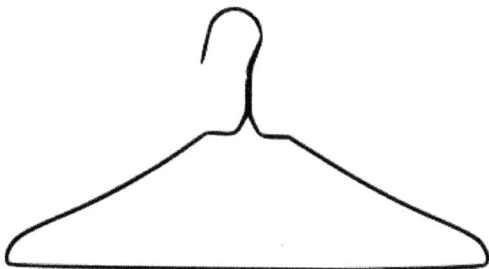

In 1854 a large meteorite was found at Cranbourne, Victoria, weighing more than 5 tons.

When Australia was first colonized, 160,000 convicts were sent in boats from England to Australia. The survivors were kept in prison camps, while many others died en-route.

Saltwater crocodiles have roughly 68 sharp teeth and can exert two tonnes of pressure from a single bite. These crocodiles are found around the northern areas of Australia from Broome in Western Australia to Rockhampton in Queensland. There are more than

New South Wales is the most populated state with 31.8% of Australia's population living there.

91% of the country is covered by native vegetation.

A baby kangaroo when born is only about 2 centimetres long.

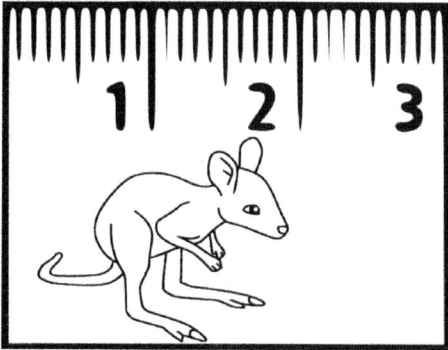

Mount Kosciuszko's mean monthly temperature is often below freezing for eight months of the year.

The Australian Dollar is considered one of the most advanced currencies in the world. It's waterproof, made of polymer and notoriously hard to counterfeit.

Australia ranks 56th in the world in terms of broadband speed.

Sir John Robertson, a five-time premier of New South Wales in the 1800s, began every morning with half a pint of rum.

Almost one-fifth of Australia is considered a desert despite being surrounded by water. 70% is classified as arid or semi-arid meaning it gets less than 500mm of rain annually.

Australia boasts an incredible diversity of birds, including parrots, pigeons, magpies, finches, black swans, and the iconic laughing kookaburras.

Australia and Antartica are the only continents wholly located in the southern hemisphere.

The Dingo Fence runs over 5,530km through Queensland and South Australia. It is the longest fence in the world and is 3 times the length of the Great Wall of China.

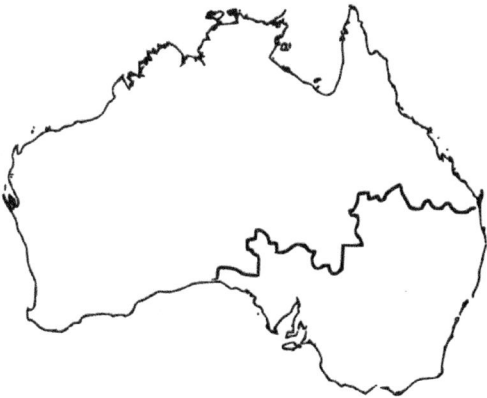

In Canberra it's legal to film hard core porn and selling the end-product has been made legal in the city.

Uluru is 348m tall, higher than the Eiffel tower, the Great Pyramids and the Statue of Liberty.

Western Australia is home to a number of Pink Lakes such as Lake Hillier.

One of Australia's favourite sweet treats is the lamington, a cube of sponge cake rolled in melted chocolate and then in coconut.

60% of food produced in Australia is exported and feeds a massive 40 million people around the world each day.

Sydney hosted the Olympic Games in the year 2000.

The Great Barrier Reef is the planet's largest living structure.

The hairs on Australian spiders might look hairy but they are actually sensory setae which spiders use to collect information about their surrounding environment.

Female flies seek humans in search of proteins that they need to make eggs. The sweat on human bodies is an ideal source.

Before finding fame as an actor, Paul Hogan from Crocodile Dundee worked as a painter on the Sydney Harbour Bridge.

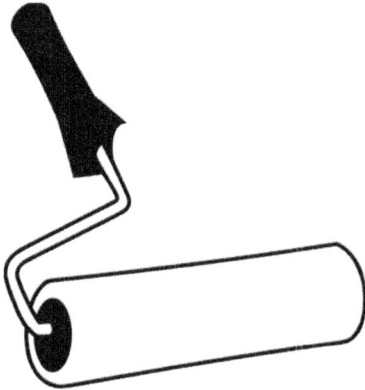

Australia is ranked second on the Human Development Index which takes into account a long and healthy life, knowledge and a decent standard of living.

In Australian slang, if someone has done a 'Harold Holt' it means they have disappeared quickly after the 17th Prime Minister of Australia, Harold Holt, who disappeared while swimming off the Victorian Coast in 1967.

Western Australia is three and a half times as big as Texas.

Despite being a huge continent, 90% of Australia's population live on the coast, due to the majority of the country's interior being a vast desert, commonly referred to as the Outback.

An Australian radio station called Joy Radio was established in 1993 and became the world's very first gay and lesbian radio station.

The first photos from the 1969 moon landing were beamed to the rest of the world from Honeysuckle Tracking Station, near Canberra.

The original estimate to build the Sydney Opera House was $7 million. It cost $102 million.

Around 1.3 billion litres of wine are produced each year in Australia.

It is estimated that Australians eat over 270 million meat pies annually.

Platypuses are highly poisonous and have enough venom to kill a dog or make a human seriously ill.

The koala has the smallest brain in proportion to its body size for a mammal.

There are more kangaroos and sheep in Australia than there are people.

Lake Eyre, 15 metres below sea level, has the lowest elevation. It is also the driest area.

It took 272,000 litres of paint to paint the Sydney Harbour Bridge before it opened on the 19th March 1932. Nowadays it takes 30,000 litres of paint to touch up and repaint the structure.

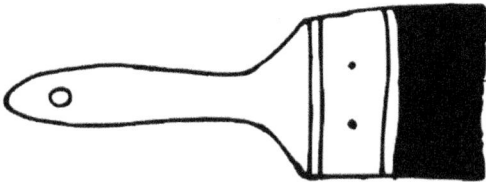

Perth in Western Australia is one of the most isolated cities in the world. The closest Australian city is Adelaide which is 2,200 kilometres away.

The peak of Mount Kosciuszko is the highest point in Australia at 2,228m (7,310ft) above sea level.

There are around 200 different types of races and cultures within Australia, making it one of the most multicultural nations in the world.

The Great Barrier Reef is the only living structure on earth that can be seen from space.

Australian Slang Words & Phrases

A

A Cold One	Beer
Accadacca	How Aussies refer to Australian band ACDC
Ankle Biter	Child
Arvo	Afternoon
Aussie Salute	Wave to scare the flies
Avo	Avocado

B

Bail	To cancel plans
Barbie	Barbecue
Bare	Barbecue
Bathers	Swimsuit

Beauty!	Great! Most often exclaimed as "You Beauty"
Big Smoke	The City
Bikkie	Biscuit
Billabong	A pond in a dry riverbed
Billy	A tin used over a campfire to boil water for tea
Blocking cattle up	Generally refers to mustering on horseback when the cattle are first approached and held in one spot for a time until they have quietened down enough to move forward.

Bloke	A guy, man
Bloody	Very. Used to extenuate a point
Bloody oath	Yes or its true
Bludger	Someone who's lazy, generally also who relies on others
Bogan	A person whose speech, clothing, attitude and behaviour are considered unrefined or unsophisticated
Booze Bus	Police vehicle used to catch drunk drivers

Bore Runner	A person who drives around the station usually 2 or 3 times a week checking the water for the cattle.
Bottle-O	Bottle Shop, a place to buy alcohol
Brekky	Breakfast
Brolly	Umbrella
Bruce	An Aussie Bloke
Brumby	A wild horse
Buckleys Chance	Little chance
Budgie smugglers	Men's bathing shorts/costume
Buggered	Exhausted

Bullock	A castrated male cow
Bush	In the countryside away from civilisation

C

Cab Sav	Cabernet Sauvignon
Cactus	Dead, Broken
Carrying on like a Pork Chop	Making a great fuss about something for little or no reason
Choc A Bloc	Full
Choccy Biccy	Chocolate Biscuit
Chook	Chicken
Chopper	Helicopter, usually used for mustering cattle

Chrissie	Christmas
Ciggy	A Cigarette
Clean skin	An unbranded and unearmarked heifer, cow or bull
Clucky	Feeling maternal
Cobber	Very good friend
Coldie	Beer
Copper	Policeman
Coppers	Policemen
Crack the shits	Getting angry at someone or something
Crikey	An expression of surprise

Crook	Being ill or angry
Cruisie	An easy job or affirmative
Cuppa	To have a break for a cup of tea

D

Dag	Someone who's a bit of a nerd or geek.
Daggy	Uncool, not fashionable
Daks	Trousers
Deadset	True
Defo	Definitely
Devo	Devastated
Digger	Soldier

Donkey	Usually a drum of water with a fire underneath stoked up when hot water is needed for showers
Draft / Drafting	Usually refers to separating cattle into different catorgories for branding, trucking or treating. Can be done on horseback or in a yard. Can also refer to the sport of campdrafting
Drongo	A Fool, 'Don't be a drongo mate'
Drover	An experienced stockman, who moves livestock, usually sheep, cattle, and horses on a horse over long distances

Dunny	Toilet
Durry	Cigarette

E

Esky	An insulated container that keeps things cold (usually beers)

F

F*ck Me Dead	That's unfortunate, that surprises me
Facey	Facebook
Fair Dinkum	Honestly
Fella, Fellas	A guy, a group of people
Flannie / Flanno	Flannelette shirt

Flat out	As busy as a bee
Float	A horse trailer
Footy	Football (AFL / Aussie Rules)
Fresh horse	A horse that hasn't been used for a while.
Frothy	Beer
Furphy	Rumours or stories that are improbable or absurd

G

G'day	Hello

Galah	An Australian cockatoo with a reputation for not being bright, hence a galah is also a stupid person.
Gnarly	Awesome
Going off	Busy, lots of people / angry person "he's going off"
Good On Ya	Good work
Goon	The best invention ever produced by mankind. Goon is a cheap, boxed wine that will inevitably become an integral part of your Australian backpacking experience.

Grazier	A farmer who is in the business of raising cattle or sheep for the market
Green horse	A horse, broken in but with not much training or experience
Grub	Food

H

Hard yakka	Hard work
Heaps	Loads, lots, many
Heifer	A female animal that has never had a calf

Hobble	To join the front legs of a horse with two straps and a swivel chain (usually at night) to stop them going too far from camp
Holding the cut / cutting	When cattle are drafted on horseback it is often referred to as cutting and the cattle that have been separated from the mob are called the cut
Hoon	Hooligan (normally driving badly!)
Horse plant (or just 'plant')	The group of work horses kept ready for work at any time

I

Iffy   Bit risky or unreasonable

J

Jackaroos and
Jillaroos   Usually young station
                   workers

K

Killer   One of the stock to be
                   slaughtered for eating
                   on the property

Knickers   Female underwear

Knock it off   Stop that nonsense
Knock off   Finish work for the day

L

Lappy   Laptop

Larrikin	Someone who's always up for a laugh, bit of a harmless prankster
Legless	Someone who is really drunk
Lollies	Sweets

M

Maccas	McDonalds
Manchester	Sheets / Linen etc
Mate	Friend, companion, colleague

Micky bull	A young bull, usually up to about 18 months of age, which should have been branded and castrated but has been missed in previous musters.
Mob	A group of cattle, horses or sheep running or mustered together. Can also be a description of a family or station grouping or group of people
Mongrel	Someone who's a bit of a dick
Mozzie	Mosquito
Muster	Round up sheep or cattle

N

No Drama	No problem / it's ok
No drama	Forget about it (in forgiveness) or Yes, I'll do it (it will be no problem)
No Worries	No problem / it's ok
No Wucka's	A truly Aussie way to say 'no worries'
Nuddy	Naked

O

Offsider	Assistant, who is usually younger or less experienced

Outback	The interior of Australia, "The Outback" is more remote than those areas named "the bush"

P

Paddock	Fenced area
Pash	To kiss
Piece of Piss	Easy
Piss	To urinate
Piss Off	Go away, get lost
Piss Up	Most social occasions
Pissed	Intoxicated, drunk
Pissed Off	Annoyed

R

Rack Off	The less offensive way to tell someone to 'F Off'!
Rapt	Very happy
Reckon	For sure
Rellie / Rello	Relatives
Ringer	A male or female stock worker on an Australian cattle station
Ringing	A term for someone who is a ringer
Ripper	Fantastic

Roo	Slang for 'jackeroo' or 'jilleroo'. A term often used for a person who is inexperienced or meaning that the person is not very skilled. Also short for kangaroo
Roo Bar	A stout bar fixed to the front of a vehicle to protect it against hitting kangaroos (also cow bar)
Rooted	Tired or Broken
Runners	Trainers, Sneakers

S

S'Arvo	This afternoon

Saddle Bronc	The sport at a rodeo in which a rider attempts to ride a horse that in inclined to buck
Salties or Freshies	Crocodiles, saltwater or freshwater crocodiles
Sanger	Sandwich
Servo	Service Station / Garage
Shark biscuit	Kids at the beach
She'll be apples	Everything will be alright
Sheila	A woman
Shoot Through	To leave
Sick	Awesome
Sickie	A sick day off work

Skull	To down a beer
Slab	A carton of beers
Smoko	Cigarette break
Snag	Sausage
Stoked	Happy, Pleased
Straya	Australia
Strewth	An exclamation of surprise
Stubby	A bottle of beer
Stubby Holder	Used so your hands don't get cold when holding your beer, or to stop your hands making your beer warm

Stuffed	Tired
Sunnies	Sunglasses
Swag	Single bed you can roll up, a bit like a sleeping bag

T

Tailing	To contain a 'mob' of cattle or horses while they graze
Tea	Dinner
Thongs	Flip Flops
Tinny	Can of beer or small boat
Too easy	Similar to 'No drama' or 'No worries' - I'll do it, it will cause no problems

Top End	Far North of Australia
Tracky daks	Sweatpants (tracksuit pants)
True Blue	Genuinely Australian
Tucker	Food
Two Up	A gambling game played on Anzac day

U

Up Yourself	Stuck up
Ute	Utility vehicle, pickup truck

V

Veg, Veggies	Vegetables

W

Weaners	Young steers or heifers, usually six to eight months old, recently weaned from their mothers

Y

Ya	You
Yard	A structure used to hold and process cattle and sometimes horses
Yarn	To have a chat, a discussion, generally very informal
Yous	Plural of you
Yarded	Put in the yard

Printed in Great Britain
by Amazon

58126217R00069

If you want to be on our confidential mailing list for our Readers' Club Magazine (with extracts from past and forthcoming titles) write to:

SILVER MOON READER SERVICES

The Shadowline Building
6 Wembley Street
Gainsborough
DN21 2AJ
United Kingdom
or
sales@babash.com

or telephone
01427 816710
(UK office hours only)

NEW AUTHORS WELCOME

Please send submissions to
Silver Moon Books Ltd.
PO Box 5663
Nottingham
NG3 6PJ
or
editor@babash.com

First published 1996 Silver Moon Books
Second Imprint 2004
ISBN 1-897809-36-0
© 1996,2004 Mark Slade

S S

ISLAND OF SLAVEGIRLS

BY

MARK SLADE

1: CELLMATES

The girl was naked; her wrists tied high above her head to a meat-hook. Her feet barely touched the dusty floor and she hung, slumped against the cracked wall-plaster, in the musty Singapore cellar.

She was blindfolded, her head turned sideways, her half-masked features erotic to him. Her sexy mouth was soft, full and quivering; her body firm, her bronzed flesh shiny with the sweat of fear, the slight glow emphasised by the long black hair. But most erotic of all, the centre of his attention, were her rounded unblemished buttocks, contracting and relaxing as her terror mounted, and her fearful shaking and her moans of protest; entreaties, in a tongue foreign to him, but one which he interpreted correctly and ignored anyhow.

He suddenly had a fierce erection, surging, pulsing, unlike any he'd known before, as the brothel Madam handed him a short dog-whip.

Lying in his cell, that was what Nick Keane was remembering...

Recalling a time when he was free.

Able to satisfy his sexual urges.

That doe-eyed, almond faced beauty.

A prostitute, yes, but he had so much wanted her. In a room up the rickety stairs the Madam had shushed him with a wave of her arms. "Hey no Johnny. You too drunk. And we got better." She'd smiled, a Hellish smile showing black teeth. "We got girl here," she said, "she no want fucky-sucky. Bad slut. You punish? Hey Johnny?"

Bewildered, in drink, and urged on by older worldly-wise mates, he'd agreed. Mainly, he remembered, so as not to lose face in front of his shipmates.

So, he had taken the whip.

Swallowed the nerves and had begun the beating.

Not because he really wanted to.

5

And he didn't have to hit too hard, did he?

Christ! Who was he trying to kid?

Her screams. Her delicious screams. How he'd relished the sound of those screams. That and the sound of the leather upon her buttocks and thighs; the erotic sight of the flaming welts which appeared as if conjured up; the struggling, defenceless body twisting this way and that, bumping into the plaster, the chalky distemper smearing itself over the sweat-run skin, her hair whipping about as she shook her head, writhing, trying to escape.

But all in vain.

Keane remembered the surge of ecstasy; the feeling of utter power, as the leather had landed again and again and again. He remembered his wanting to hurt the girl, lash the bitch until she passed out. Jesus! He simply had not wanted to stop: wanted it to go on and on, savouring the delicious screams of agony. They had just let him get on with it; in fact the old crone had urged him on. "Hey! Johnny! That no good! Hit harder! She very bad girl!"

Then half-forgotten smells came back to him, the spicy tangs of the Orient, the dry smell of that basement and the sharp acrid flavour of the Madam's French cigarette; then the sudden pungent odour as the girl's bladder let go and urine ran unheeded down her shapely legs.

That was when they had stopped him, untied the near-unconscious girl and dragged her from the room. That was when he realised that he had ejaculated all down the inside of his trousers.

And, in the depths of his mind he'd known what he was...

Suddenly his cellmate, Zach Miller, broke into his reverie. "Ever whipped a woman's bare arse, Nick?"

"Huh!" Jerked back to reality, Keane lifted his head and shoulders from the mattress to look across the cell. Zach Miller was lying on his back, staring at the ceiling, his arms pillowing his head. He shifted his gaze to look at Keane, an enquiring frown on his high forehead.

"Well, have you?"

"Christ Zach!" Keane wondered if the man was telepathic. "You get some funny ideas sometimes." This was true, though not particularly unusual. Like most Sundays, or 'Sindays' as Zach liked to call them, they crashed out, on top of their beds, to talk. Invariably, the subject was women. And sex. Then women and sex; and more sex.

Some of the things Zach came out with.

Bit way out? Way out!

Although, to Keane, of course, sadism wasn't way out.

But this was the first time Zach had mentioned the subject, and to mention it just as Keane was thinking about it seemed real weird. Or had he fallen asleep, had a dream and said something? No! Not him. Too discreet. Had to be. It must be pure coincidence. Keane shook his head in bewilderment, and tried to steer Zach away from the subject.

"Weird sodding question!"

"Come on Nick!" Zach coaxed. "Don't tell me you've never thought about that sorta thing." He sniffed. "We're both in for indecent assault offences and you're an ex-Navy man."

Keane leaned forwards, his eyes bright with anger. "Don't make it sound like I just had a pathetic grope, Zach. I shagged the arse off the bitch and she was as willing as I was. It was her old man who decided I'd raped her!"

"At least you had your end away," Zach shrugged. "Me, I got put away just for sticking my hand up a bird's knickers."

Keane grinned. "Just console yourself, thinking of all the ones you got away with." He looked at Zach. "Anyway, what's all this got to do with whipping female arses?"

Zach rolled over onto one elbow. "Well, you know! You been around. You seen some things, eh? An' you look kinda well... domineerin', know what I mean?"

Keane gave him an incredulous frown.

"Come on Nick! You're just the sort of bloke some women

juice up for. Tall an' dark. You look hard." He shrugged. "Inside, I mean." He appraised Keane carefully. "Fact, I'd say you're a cruel lookin' bastard!"

Keane had never considered that before, but maybe with his sexual preferences and at six-foot two, without any fat, and with thirty-eight years of life in his face, he might have looked a bit intimidating. He'd even got through the initial bullying all sex-offenders suffered.

Got through!

Bloody Hell!

He'd beaten one guy senseless; they'd been forced to drag him off. He'd had no trouble since. Prisoners tended to avoid him.

"Maybe Zach, but that don't mean..."

"You musta thought about it though!" Miller insisted.

"About what?"

"Whippin' a bird's arse, pratt!" Zach made a circular motion in the air with his hands. "A smooth, round, young, female arse!" He made a whooshing sound. "One stripe, diagonal, right to left." He repeated the pantomime. "Then another, the opposite way!" He grinned, "That's the right sorta kiss to smack on a girl's behind!" He let out a long sigh. "Oh! Yeahhhh!"

Keane sighed deeply, turned onto his back.

He wanted Zach to shut up, but Zach persisted. "I reckon you would if you had the chance!"

Keane groaned, inwardly.

Tried to stifle the memories and the beginnings of an erection. Then he thought. Why not tell him? Zach probably wouldn't believe it anyway, but if it helped him get his rocks off, well it was doing him a favour. "I wouldn't kiss anyone's arse Zach, let alone a female's." He grinned wickedly. "But, whipping a female, well, that's different!"

"So you know then?" Zach became eager. "You bloody have, haven't you?"

"Yeah!" Keane admitted. "I was a kid Zach. Maybe

seventeen." He gazed at the floor. "Shore-leave, in Singapore it was. Got real pissed-up on brandy. They had a girl who wouldn't do what they called 'Fucky-sucky'. They asked me to do the making!"

"Oh Christ Nick!" Zach let out a frustrated groan. "You jammy bastard!" Zach was actually grinding his thighs together and, though Keane wouldn't normally have taken any notice, he could see there was a hard-on bumping up the guy's jeans. He wasn't alone as the dam burst and, for the second time in a few minutes, the erotic memories came flooding back.

So, Keane told him.

For the first time, in detail, he told someone else about the one event in his life that had made him realise just what he was.

Throughout, Zach had been gazing at him intently, then, he blurted straight out. "Hey Man! What was it like? How'd it make you... You Know! How did it FEEL?"

Something in his voice warned, and Keane frowned at him. "Are you just curious Zach, or comparing notes?"

Zach sucked his teeth. "Could be!" He shrugged, "But how DID it make you feel?"

He wasn't going to let it go. Keane tried to be offhand. "I was drunk Zach!"

"Ever done it since?" Zach probed.

"Expensive luxury!" Keane grinned, trying to make light of it.

"Would you if you got the chance?"

"Come on Zach." He stood up and stretched. "Naughty girls are in short supply in England." He looked around the cell; pulled a face. "And they're non-existent in here."

Zach lapsed into silence then and, rolling back onto his bunk, gazed back at the ceiling. "Yeah! Thinkin' and talkin' about it is about all we can do in this place."

"Come on Zach." Keane tried to cheer him again. "Our time's near done. We'll soon be able to do something about a hard-on!"

Zach rolled over to face him again, a slight smile on his face. "And I'll tell you something else Nick. It'll be OUR kind of hard-on. You been good to me Nick! Let's stick together, eh?"

"OK then Zach, it's a date. I can use you. I'm in on something that will make us some real money. Our way!"

"Yes?"

"Yeah—when we get out!"

2: A Club Called 'Shackles'

England was sweltering its way through a hot summer. Soho was no exception. Even by night. It was even hotter in this weird nightclub.

Tristie had drunk far more Southern Comfort than was good for her and, at the moment, that was a dangerous thing for her to do. Not that she couldn't take the stuff. She could manage her drink, but this was a nightclub called 'Shackles' and nubile young amber-blondes such as Tristie shouldn't have been in the place, drunk or sober.

'Shackles' was full of perverts and kinks.

Precisely the sort of place her parents, God rest their souls, had always warned her against.

Tristie was beginning to feel sick and wished Lisa hadn't agreed to bring her. Tristie had a photo-date next day for the magazine 'Busties'! Big money! Top of the range glamour stuff. Couldn't afford to mess that one up.

"Oh God, Lisa!" she murmured, "Hurry up!"

But Lisa was taking her time in 'Cell One', as the ladies' powder room was called, and this smoky cramped box of a place was becoming boxier as it continued to fill. The whole atmosphere was getting to Tristie and she shuddered.

Some of the customers were not particularly careful about personal hygiene and the place was thick with the smells of unwashed bodies, overlaid by the cloying scent of cheap perfumes and boozy beer-breath. And the language! They threw four-letter words around like confetti.

That didn't particularly bother Tristie, but it could get tiresome after a while. It was as if they needed the bad language as an accessory; to suit their macho image, prop up falling egos.

And did some of these men need propping. Ughh! Not at all the sort of man she associated with. Then she smiled slightly. As far as she was concerned, most men were there for a free meal, or a nice show, or a complimentary drink;

11

at least until Mr. Right came into her life.

Tristie sipped at her current drink and, for the umpteenth time, looked about her. All in all the atmosphere was rather dismal. It was also a bit over the top, even by modern standards. The place was lit by imitation flaming-torches of low wattage, casting dull shadows on the plastic stone-effect wall-panels. All around this imitation dungeon there were pictures of men and women in bondage of every imaginable sort. In Tristie's experience anyway. She couldn't think of many more ways to tie or chain someone up. And some of the people in the photographs had been ugly, butt UGLY! In the photographs? God some of the people here were out of Star Trek's alien cupboard.

She swirled her Southern Comfort around the glass and looked around again. In each corner of the room there was a cage containing a naked woman, collared and in chains. The cages and the chains were supposed to be of iron, but they hadn't been very well done. Anyone could see they were cheap plastic. As for the manacles, the girls had to hold onto them to prevent them slipping off, for God's sake.

And, clearly, they needed acting lessons.

It was all supposed to be a turn-on, of course, but now that Tristie had got used to the smells, the sights and the sounds of the place, it was beginning to seem a bit comic. And the funniest touch of all was the ridiculous four-figure price tags tied around the girls' waists. Presumably, these were a 'humorous' touch, to be taken tongue in cheek, because a hastily scribbled card in front of each cage said: 'In your Dreams!' Which, even if the girls had been good, would still have taken the edge off the effect. And, although Tristie had no idea if women anywhere were ever really sold, none of these girls would have been worth a four-figure price.

So Tristie thought, anyway.

And here she was.

Slightly tipsy.

The S&M scene here seemed to attracted all sexual types. She was glad of only one thing. With the possible exception of her friend, Lisa, Tristie was easily the best looking woman in the room.

That wasn't just because at twenty-one, she was one of the youngest girls present. Mainly it was because of her pale Irish features, a genetic bequest from her mother, and her statuesque Arian figure handed down by her Germanic father. But above all, there was her hair.

What hair!

A literal cascade of coppery-blonde locks which streamed down her back, to finish just below the hem of her mini-skirt. Tristie was proud of her locks and she knew that here, in this dim place, every time she moved her elegant head, the orange glow danced like fire in her hair. So, just to show off, especially down here with all these uglies, Tristie tossed her head a lot. Well, they were supposed to like being tormented weren't they?

Anyway, they really were uglies. Most of them.

She smiled to herself, then. She had heard it said. Cute sexy blondes had far different expectations of what they would get out of life than the uglies.

Tristie was one of the cute sexy blondies!

She was special, wasn't she?

So, her expectations were high!

And the uglies? Well, bad luck!

She could use what she'd got.

Life was better that way and if a few of the uglies got bruised along the way well, so what? She hadn't asked to be born beautiful.

Tristie, although she didn't realise it yet, had some growing up to do.

Then, to her relief, Lisa came back.

Her friend had on a dark coloured leather dress herself, but there was nothing particularly kinky about it, though it was tight, showing off her tight bum and slim waist nicely, hugging her feminine curves and emphasising the lightness of her flawless skin. Tristie was pretty sure she herself wasn't a lesbian, but if she had been that way inclined, then Lisa was the sort of girl who would have attracted her. Years before, when they were both at the same school, she had wondered, vaguely, what Lisa's smooth skin would feel like against her own; well, to be honest, she still did fantasize about that, occasionally.

But it had mostly been in her adolescence, when Tristie may have been even more unsure of her own sexuality. One thing Tristie had known though, was that Lisa was a little sadist. Lisa had been a Prefect and, as was the way in most Public schools, had been given great licence to punish wayward girls.

Tristie had never fallen foul of her, but she knew girls who had, who all confirmed that Lisa had a strong arm, really enjoyed thrashing them; found the slightest excuse to do so and favoured a length of rubber cable as a whip.

And that it hurt.

Terribly.

Tristie shuddered and pushed the thoughts aside. Despite all this, for some strange reason Tristie liked Lisa. Lisa had never harmed her, or even suggested she might like to. They were friends, Tristie accepting Lisa's nature as a mere foible. Just Lisa's way. No problem, Tristie was well aware, she was flirting with danger, but this was the nineteen-nineties, for God's Sake. Lisa wouldn't dare!

Lisa floated up to Tristie in her usual sexy way and slipped an affectionate arm around her waist, giving her a slight squeeze.

"Had enough?"

Tristie nodded, once again causing her hair to spark with dancing light. "I ought to be going. It's time I..." Her voice trailed off as a man came into view across the room.

What a man!

He stood out. Oh Lord, did he stand out!

For two reasons.

One, because he was dressed straight, in a lounge suit. Two, and most of all, he was tall, six-foot two at least, with doorway-wide shoulders. Also, as far as Tristie could see in the gloom, he was quite handsome in a heavy-set way. He towered over everyone else in the cramped room and the weird set of people made respectful way for him. Very respectful, actually. Sensible of them.

Tristie couldn't keep her gaze off him. Her heart suddenly jumped as she realised he was coming over towards them. She dug Lisa in the ribs. "Lisa! That man! He's coming over to us!" She drew in a gasp. "Oh God, Lisa! He's gorgeous!"

Lisa giggled. "Silly! That's Nick Keane. He's a friend of mine." She wrinkled her nose. "In fact I want you to meet him." She gave a small shudder of excitement herself. "He is a bit special, I agree." She flicked Tristie's hair back from her face. "And he likes girls with long hair." She hugged Tristie slightly. "Especially if it's the colour of yours."

Tristie felt her heart lurch again, and she was suddenly very aware of her glorious mane of hair, feeling it brushing against the backs of her knees.

Nick Keane came up to them and smiled, a slightly crooked grin. "Lisa! I take it this is Tristie?"

"Oh yes!" Tristie blurted out, breathlessly, then blushed, immediately regretting her impulsiveness.

He appeared not to notice her embarrassment and held out his hand. "Nick Keane." He showed his lop-sided grin again. "How are you, Tristie?" His eyes glinted as they flitted quickly up and down her fine figure, then he smiled. This time, a different sort of smile. "Very well, it seems." His dark eyes burned in the dim light.

Tristie felt another shudder course through her. God! She had just been undressed by his gaze. She actually felt naked; vulnerable; and she had to admit to a burning wetness down there. She ground her thighs together, hoping they wouldn't notice, and shivered again as nervous excitement ran through her. What was it about this man? A definite, overpowering air emanated from him and she detected a slight cruelty in his smile...

She kicked herself mentally.

With his size and clear heterosexual air, what other sort of man would she expect him to be, in this place? But God, did it matter? He was a hunk and a half. She knew she'd be like play-dough in his hands.

Then a drink appeared and soon another Southern Comfort was sliding down her throat.

What the hell, she thought, looking at Nick Keane.

Wasn't this what she'd really come for?

To satisfy her curiosity?

Nick Keane looked like a man who could certainly do just that. Like a man who could be satisfying in other ways too. She stilled the nervous pounding of her heart. If she had to lose anything tonight, she wouldn't complain if it was to this man. So, she may as well enjoy the rest of the night. She didn't have to come here ever again, did she? She sipped at her drink, then tossed her hair slightly.

Keane knew he'd found a good one as her hair wafted spicy perfume his way. He smiled to himself. She certainly knew the tricks. Or at least she probably thought she did. She would soon find out that there were other tricks for her to learn. When she reached the Island and the General got his hands on her. But, for now, this sexy little piece of merchandise would be at Keane's own disposal. He looked at her, his eyes gleaming.

"Are you a well-behaved sort of girl, Tristie?"

"Well, I'll be good for you Nick!" She smiled, then added brazenly, "if you've made up your mind, that is."

"You did that for me. When you tossed your hair, just now." Keane winked at her. "And what's the perfume you wanted me to smell?"

"You don't miss much do you?" A thoughtful expression

on her face, she gazed at him for a moment, then smiled. "It's called Poison!"

"Smells a bit like cannabis!"

She chuckled. "Not my bag, Nick."

Keane shrugged. "Nor mine," he grinned. "So what do we do afterwards?"

"We'll do it again."

"Looks like my boat'll be rockin' tonight, then?"

"Oh! A boat." She grabbed his hand, a slight frown. "It's not a rubber dinghy is it?" She wrinkled her nose, then smiled.

He chuckled and shook his head. "Bit bigger than that!"

"Oh good!" she giggled. "It's just that I can't stand the taste of rubber!"

There was no real answer to that. As for the kind of rubber she meant, the General didn't use those.

Keane put his empty glass on the bar. "So. Let's go and mess about in boats!"

"You're in charge." She traced her lips with her tongue, then leant towards his ear. "And I'm all yours." she whispered.

For a moment, a smattering of irony. If only she knew! She wasn't his, not for long. She was about to become the General's property. Then Keane felt a glow of satisfaction. The girl was a natural submissive. Convenient, but unimportant. Sooner or later she would be whatever the General wanted her to be. It just meant he wouldn't need to improve her too much. She was halfway there. Keane smiled to himself. There might even be a bonus in her hide.

Tristie knew she was smiling at this gorgeous man, but somehow she didn't feel like smiling. Suddenly, his face had gone all funny; sort of blurry at the edges. She felt herself sway then.

They grabbed hold of her arms, Lisa taking the drink from her. "Oops! Tristie." Lisa's voice seemed to be coming from far away, echoing in her ears, like a buzz-drill. Lisa increased her grip.

Tristie had a vague awareness. They were ushering her through the crowd. Curious stares. Giggles from some and knowing looks from others.

Tristie was suddenly frightened.

Knowing exactly what was going on.

Wondering why Lisa was doing this to her.

She wasn't drunk for God's sake!

She had to tell the people!

They would help her!

She shouted at the swimming sea of fish-eye faces. "I'm not drunk, for God's sake! I'm being abducted!"

One or two in the crowd may have connected that this sort of thing had happened before, when the tall guy was in the place.

But if anyone did, no one said anything.

Anyway, they'd seen plenty of pissy-arsed immature females taken away from 'Shackles' for a night of fun and games.

Come on! That's how they got their jollies!

This was just another silly inquisitive bitch.

So drunk, she couldn't even talk intelligibly.

Hey, man! Lucky tall-guy!

***

Zach Miller was waiting in the Merc, parked in the side-alley.

The girl climbed into the back of the car, showing a yard of thigh as she did so. She seemed to have forgotten what had just happened. Her brief reluctance was over and she snuggled up into the corner of the seat...

As he leant towards her, Keane caught a brief glimpse of Zach's wide, cheerful smile in the driving mirror. "Traffic's heavy tonight!"

He understood the code. No games tonight. Straight to

18

Brighton, get the boat moving and set course for the island.

The girl still hadn't opened her eyes and Keane picked up the syringe.

Her eyes remained closed.

It was just too easy.

He plunged the needle into her thigh and squirted pentathol into her blood stream.

The girl gave a sudden jump, and her eyes opened wide, in a brief expression of alarm.

Zach half-inclined his head backwards. "All done Nick?"

"All done!"

The little cockney turned his head briefly. "General has two more for us to collect. Wants us back soonest." He grinned into the mirror. "No time for shaggin'."

"Get some on the island then."

Zach nodded, then glanced backwards and grinned. "Well there's plenty of it there!" He turned away again. "An' we got an overnight stop. There's some stock for Sheik Malik. General wants us ready 'case we have to take 'em across the Channel."

"Some more? Not suit the General then?"

"Yeah! Shame eh!"

"Shame!" Keane grunted. "Well, let's get this little lovely to the 'Kukri'."

Twenty minutes later they had stripped the doped girl, settled her into the bunk and made a quick search of her handbag. This revealed nothing more alarming than a canister of American Mace, and a packet of three.

Zach pointed to the two contradictory items. "Can't seem to make her mind up Nick."

Keane grinned. "Probably choosy!"

"Smart-arse!"

The girl rolled her head sideways with a sloppy smile on her face. "It's all gone wrong Nick! All wrong." She giggled. "Now I'm for it!"

"Sweetie, you don't know the half of it," Zach chuckled,

and shut her up by slipping a perforated ball-gag behind her teeth, and tightening it around her neck. He patted her cheek. "No Nick for you tonight." Then he chained her wrists and ankles to the specially provided rings at each corner of the mahogany bunk.

Nice touch, those rings, Keane thought.

Looked just like design extras.

Keane took a last glance at the naked, half-conscious girl. She lay stretched out, a tasty offering, but in her drugged state she wouldn't have been much good. "Well little Tristie," he murmured, "it would've been nice, but we can't always have everything."

Her moans were quiet behind the gag, and her gaze rolled towards him, her eyes still dreamy. As he turned to leave the cabin he noticed the glistening droplets of her juices on the frizz of her delicious sex-mound.

She seemed to be enjoying herself.

A natural, he thought.

May even enjoy the General!

3: ON THE ISLAND

Tristie moaned to herself as she woke. Then her heart jumped as she realised she was in half-darkness, naked and freezing, facing a fierce draught of cold air whistling past her exposed flesh. She gasped out loud and stared in terror into the gloom, her panic growing.

She was in a small square cage and her arms were stretched upwards and outwards, her wrists fastened to the top of the cage. Tight metal bands around her ankles fastened her feet to the floor. Thin chains were wrapped around her slim waist, and had been taken down between her thighs, back between her tender sex-lips and then pulled up between her buttocks. The ends were secured to the back of the collar about her neck and each time she moved they cut deeper into her.

As if that wasn't enough, there was a vile taste of rubber in her mouth and her stretched lips were sore, forced wide open by a ball-gag. The ball had been rammed behind her teeth and secured behind her head, with tight straps digging into her face.

She felt degraded, dirty and ashamed. Her nostrils were full of the stink of dirty oil and of her own unwashed flesh. Through the battered bars of the cage she could just make out the rough stone walls of a tunnel and a set of metal rails stretching out before her. Her mind was very muzzy, but she was aware enough to realise that the cage was in some kind of truck.

Her heart leapt again and her stomach churned as the whine of machinery sounded in her ears. The truck started to move forwards, down a steepening slope, picking up speed. Through the bars, Tristie saw the rocky sides of the tunnel merging into a grey-black blur as the truck gathered momentum.

On and on the truck sped, through the gloom, seeming as though it would never stop. Her ears popped as the pressure changed with every yard of the rapid journey as they went deeper and deeper into the gloomy tunnel.

Her heart was racing, her mind was in turmoil, and she screamed into the gag. Futile struggles against her chains merely caused more agony as the truck continued its descent. Chained as she was, Tristie was able to do nothing. The manacles cut into her wrists and ankles as the engine pitched into a demonic wail and the truck hurtled on.

At last it began to slow and, still panting with fear, Tristie felt her senses returning. There was a stronger smell of oil now, and as the whine of the motors began to fade she could see a glow ahead and hear the murmur of men's' voices floating along the tunnel towards her.

There was a slight jerk as the truck stopped and she cried out as her weight was thrown against her chains. The front of the cage was pulled aside with a clatter, and the gag was unfastened and jerked roughly out of her mouth. She had just enough time to draw in a longed-for gulp of air, and see the four sweating half-naked men who stood in front of her, when one of them stepped forwards and there was a sudden smell of leather as a hood of some sort was thrown over her head. The hood was fastened tightly about her neck so she could barely see through the eye-slits. Coarse hands mauled her naked body, hands which prodded and probed, trying to enter her vagina and anus, and roaming over her breasts.

Strong fingers unfastened the tight chains about her body and finally invaded her sex; pinched and kneaded the flesh of her buttocks and thighs, dug into her breasts; twisted her nipples; took cruel handfuls of the soft flesh of her belly. These animals were laughing as they tormented her.

Her struggles were automatic but futile, and as her ordeal went on she realised that the chains were also being removed from her arms and legs. She heard a man's voice, strangely familiar, as someone unshackled her from the cage.

Then she was thrown to the floor, to sprawl defenceless

on her back, wincing as rough stone scraped her skin. Strong hands pinned her down, and she moaned as once more she felt metal bands being fastened around her wrists and ankles.

As she lay trembling and terrified, she wondered what on earth was going to happen to her. Then she gasped as she felt something cold and hard being placed about her neck. There was a noisy fiddling just below her right ear, a series of metallic clicking noises. Then she jumped in shock as a loud clang sounded, almost deafening her, then a tattoo of smaller tapping noises.

She realised what had been done to her as she felt the weight of the circle of iron around her neck. God! They had riveted a collar on her! Her shaking increased and her heart was racing in mad panic now. Oh God! What was happening to her, how had she got into this terrifying nightmare?

But it was no nightmare!

The hood was wrenched away and replaced with another, this one wringing wet and stinking of sweat. The hood was without eye-slits, the stench too much to bear, and she gagged.

She groaned as the hood was buckled tight about her neck. She prayed she would be able to breathe, then realised that air was coming into the hood from slits in the side.

She had no time to ponder as she felt her wrists and ankles being released, and she gasped in terror as she realised a chain was being clipped to her newly acquired collar. Someone prodded her buttocks with his toe and sneered, "On your knees bitch! And move yourself!"

Bewildered, terrified and shaking, Tristie obeyed as quickly as she could. Then she screamed into the hood, as searing, burning pain slashed across her buttocks, and she knew she'd been struck with a whip.

Then the voice again. "Crawl! You're going to the lower levels!" Then she felt one of the men sit astride her back, and she squealed out in agony again as, once more, a whip cut into her buttocks. She felt the man's heels dig into her thighs, and sobbing her fright into the hood, but knowing she had no option, began to crawl forwards.

Still in a stupor, Tristie moved as best she could; blind, wondering, and groaning, as the man's weight forced her downwards, so that the loose shale on the floor dug into her hands and knees. Her mind was in turmoil. What was going to happen to her? Was she to be raped? Killed? Or was she to be tortured? Or was all this a vivid nightmare? Or maybe...!

Her terrified thoughts were interrupted then, as she was pulled up by a savage jerk on the neck chain, and the man riding her got off her back. She heard someone say, "To heel, bitch, and turn left!"

Even in her state of bewildered despair, Tristie knew she must obey or be whipped. So she crawled; crawled like a submissive dog towards the man until she felt his leg against her right side.

The stinking hood was unbuckled and as it was dragged off her head, a rising stench of stale body odours hit her nostrils like a wall and she heard the buzzing of flies darting towards her filth covered body.

Then someone pushed her sideways into a pile of filthy wet straw. More flies swarmed about her as she was dragged to her feet again. The man was shaking her and growling. "Stand in the archway!" She struggled again, but could do nothing as she was herded into the centre of a stone arch; part of the vaulted ceiling. Her arms were pulled outwards and her wrists were tied to rings set in the pillars to each side of her. Coarse hands began rubbing a hot, greasy substance all over her body and she struggled against her bonds. Then she started to shiver as the sticky mess began to cool.

The man chuckled. "This is just body grease slut! Makes your skin look nice." He caressed her breasts and belly, gazing intently at her body. "Helps keep you warm down here." He giggled then. "And it makes the whip hurt even more." Another slash of the whip stung her belly and he laughed as she cried out. Then, lapsing into silence, the man continued to apply the grease to her skin.

Moments later he stepped back. "Nice and shiny!"

And then another voice: "Now for the finishing touch!"

Tristie frowned as she looked up and saw the man in front of her. He was holding something that looked like a heavy net. Then she realised it wasn't a net, but a Basque, a strange looking one, made of coarse rope, woven into a diamond net-pattern.

She could do nothing but whimper as the strange garment was placed about her body and adjusted so that her nipples were pushed right out through the wider holes in the bra-cups. Then they began to lace up the Basque. She could feel her soft flesh being squeezed. She could feel her nipples pushing out further as the stiff wire frames of the bra-cups were forced upwards beneath her bosom, forming a platform for her well-rounded breasts; breasts which soon became piled high, until her cleavage looked like the cleft between the globes of a baby's bottom.

Despite herself, she knew her nipples were becoming turgid as they were stimulated by the pressure.

Then, finally, the tightening was over and one of the men ran his hands over her tightly encased belly and breasts. "Looks good on you," he said, his hands roving over her at random.

There were no suspenders on this Basque. Just a length of thin chain hanging at the front and rear of the hem. The men spread her legs, then pulled the rear chain forwards through the vee of her thighs and jerked the links tight between her labia, laughing as she yelled out in her discomfort. Then they clipped the chain to the front of her collar. They did the same with the front chain, taking it between her legs and clipping it to her collar at the back of her neck.

She started to scream as the cruel chains dug into her, but then another ball-gag was forced between her lips and secured tightly about her face. Her arms were released from the rings in the wall and her wrists were bound behind her and pushed high up her back and secured to the rear of the collar.

Next, two of the men lifted her, like a side of beef, and hooked the mesh of the Basque, between her shoulders, over a hook in the wall.

Tristie grunted into the gag as she felt her weight coming on her bent arms and the chains cutting deeper into her crotch.

Then she heard the sound of a whip cutting through the air just before fearful pain filled her mind and she gurgled her agony into the gag. She wriggled and bucked against the confining Basque, in a futile attempt to avoid the lash, as time after time it ripped into her body.

Finally, the whipping ceased and she heard the man again, "Welcome to the Island! That's just to remind you to obey us at all times! Understand?"

Hardly aware of what she was doing, Tristie nodded dumbly and winced as she felt herself being lowered to the filthy floor. Then there was the cool kiss of another chain, as it was shackled to the side of her collar. Another blinding hood was slipped over her head and buckled around her neck. A clean one, this time.

The whip cut into her buttocks once again and she was ordered to stand.

Trembling, she struggled to her feet, then screamed into the gag, arching her hips forwards as another stroke of the whip slashed into the soft rounded globes of her buttocks. Again the whip cut into her flesh, this time across the backs of her thighs.

"Walk on!"

Sobbing, Tristie stumbled forward, unable to see, just able to stand, with only her legs free to move. She tried in vain to evade the vicious slashes of the whip which came each time she slowed. Submissive now, Tristie sobbed into the gag, wondering what was to happen to her.

She was halted by a sharp tug on the neck chain and she was pushed to the floor, where immediately she felt the sting of another needle in her upper arm. More drugs! God! How much more could she take?

She tried to shake her head, but it was hopeless. Her mind drifted into half-awareness, and as she hovered on the brink of unconsciousness, she had a moment's recall; enough to remember again, the club in Soho and the giant called Keane. Keane! That was it! The voice she half recognised. It was Keane!

4: THE GENERAL

General Evan Brice was the typical ex-Army type. Tall, upright, and sporting a clipped grey moustache below a hooked nose. Over a high forehead, his hair was thick, badger grey. Keane had never seen him without collar and tie.

Shame he wasn't a real General!

Brice wasn't short of brains though.

He'd made several fortunes from ex-Army surplus, which included the island. Complete with a disused monastery, built into the side of a rockface, the place had been ideal for his purposes. The island had a long and chequered history and since the Monks had left it had been used as a nineteenth century quarantine hospital, an asylum, and as an Army Prison during the Crimean War. It had last been used by the Government as an Army explosives depot, and when it came on the market the General had bought it for himself.

The Government had done most of the work for him.

The Monastery had been used by them as offices and living quarters, and on the other side of the island they had used the old cells as storage bunkers, the detention quarters having already been connected to the Monastery by a long tunnel. Brice had renovated the half-ruined offices to make a luxurious home, and utilising the ready-made cells and tunnels, had built what he called the Pleasure Palace, linked to his home by the subterranean tunnel.

As befitted his self-appointed rank, he lived well.

A high life-style.

An unusual life-style.

Unusual for an Englishman, at least.

Maybe there were those in the Middle-East who lived like he did, but how many British men kept a harem of young female sprites?

That's what the General sometimes called his girls.

Sometimes, but not often.

He usually called them sluts or bitches.

Call them what he would, they were no more than slaves; amusements who must please him. Those who didn't please him and the ones he just plain didn't want, he spread around the world as merchandise. They were the means by which he made further money to fuel his grandiose appetites. In short, the General was big in the so-called white-slave trade, although not all the girls finding their way through his hands were white. To the General, any nice bundle of female genes between the ages of twenty-one and thirty was money in the bank, wherever she came from.

Give the General his due, he ran things well.

Like a Military operation.

Real smooth.

Everything done as and when it should be. No mistakes.

Just like Keane and Miller, he couldn't afford mistakes and discipline was tight, although he would never treat Keane and Miller as other ranks. Harsh discipline was reserved for the girls.

That was why Keane sometimes felt sorry for Ruth.

The General had taken a particular liking to her.

That meant pain for the girl.

It had been three months now since Keane had acquired her for the General, and in that time it was clear that the sadistic General had beaten all rebellion out of her. She had quickly become one of the most subservient girls Keane had ever supplied.

She was in the room now.

Naked, she was kneeling beside the General's chair, her upper body stiff, upright, and her knees spread about eighteen inches apart, displaying her smooth thighs and the rounded swell of her rouged and shaven sex. She was half-facing the door, but she couldn't see anything, because of the half-hood she was wearing—only the lower part of her face was visible beneath the leather visor.

There was just a trace of colour on her lips and around

her neck there was a golden collar with a slave-bell attached at the front. Her slender arms had been secured high up behind her back and her wrists were clipped to the back of the collar.

Just below her navel a golden ring pierced the flesh of her abdomen. Sometimes the General would have a length of chain attached to this and stretched tight, up to the front of her collar, to pull her sex upwards, displaying her labia and clitoris. Today, though, the chain led downwards, to disappear in the slit between her sex-lips. Keane knew that the other end of the chain would be secured to her wrists and pulled taut, the links cutting deep between her labia and her buttocks. This had the effect of pulling her body even further backwards, the better to display her curvaceous form.

Her long ash-blonde hair streamed from beneath the hood, to fall each side of her gorgeous breasts, and her erect nipples, each pierced with a gold ring, were brought into further relief with black lipstick. Between the rings a gold rope-chain depended in a graceful arc, brushing the skin of her tight belly.

As he walked into the office, Keane caught his breath in admiration, feeling a spasm in his loins. She really was a gorgeous animal, and he wanted her.

The General looked up. "Ah, Nick. Good to see you, m'boy."

Keane noticed then that Ruth was wearing earphones and that they were plugged into the stereo-system. Was the General going soft on the girl? Keane smiled and pointed to Ruth. "In-house entertainment now General?"

"Oh no," the General laughed. "Not for the slut, at least." He leaned back into his chair. "A little idea I had last week. All she can hear is static." He grinned, and picked up a long, flexible quirt. "Now, watch her perform." He leaned forward and gave a light tap with the quirt on the slavegirl's head.

Ruth's response was immediate. She turned to face away from the General and spread her thighs even wider, wincing as the chain between her labia bit deeper. She began to inch her upper body towards the carpet. Her soft rounded buttocks were now being forced high into the air and her hair fell downwards, to cover the back of the half-hood. She was trembling with the effort of preventing her upper body from falling forwards, but was managing it.

Keane grunted his approval. "She's got good control."

"Two weeks ago she couldn't do this without falling flat on her face." The General chuckled. "But the exercise has soon toned up her stomach muscles." He flexed the quirt. "And the whip helps, of course." He tapped the back of her head twice more.

Gasping a little, Ruth pushed her upper body even closer to the floor and she wriggled her hips, obviously trying to ease the cutting chain now pulling deeper into the depths of her sex-lips.

The General scowled at that and his wrist jerked so that the quirt cut into the flesh of the girl's offered buttocks. The crack was muted in the plush surroundings. Ruth squealed, but her hips stopped moving as, whimpering, she finally got the whole of her upper body flat against the carpet.

The General leaned back, smiling. Then he tapped his slavegirl's taut buttocks three times.

She began to sway her upper body from side to side like a snake, her gorgeous firm breasts brushing the deep pile of the carpet. Keane could see her nipples becoming even more turgid as the strange performance went on. Ruth began to lift her upper body in a slow, sinuous writhing, like a cobra, until she had raised herself back to the kneeling position. Then, still gyrating her body, she started to bend backwards, opening and closing her mouth, her tongue darting in and out, as if licking an imaginary penis.

The General tapped her breasts once, and Ruth began

moving forwards again, making her way back down to brush the carpet with her front. A few moments of brushing herself against the pile again and the performance started over.

After she had reached the laid-back position for the third time, the General tapped her right shoulder with the whip. Obediently, she forced her torso back as far as possible, and remained still, holding her mouth wide open, licking her soft lips, allowing her saliva to well up, clearly inviting him to enter her mouth.

The General leaned forwards and covered her mouth with his hand. Ruth straightened up to the full kneeling position, turning to face her Master once more, and lowered her head in total submission, the links of the gold breast-chain and the slave-bell tinkling softly with her movements.

"And all without one word of command," the General said. "She was difficult at first, but she's becoming a most pleasing little beast." He grinned, and tapped the girl's head again.

The obedient slavegirl turned away and began her snake-like dance all over again.

The General watched her for a moment. "She'll carry on until I stop her. Or until she drops with exhaustion." He licked his lips as the girl writhed before him. "I'm going to call her Chu'mana. That's Hopi-Indian for snake-girl, d'you know?"

"I didn't General." Even if he had known, Keane was aware the General wanted to hear him say otherwise. Vain old bugger.

The General stood and went across to his huge desk, reaching for the decanter of whisky. "A drink?" He didn't wait for an answer, just poured two good slugs and dropped ice into them. He handed Keane a glass. "I like the girl you sent me last week, by the way." He snapped his fingers, searching his memory. "Ah, yes, Tristie." He made a small circle with his finger and thumb. "Excellent. Good flesh. Well shaped. And my God, that beautiful hair!"

Keane sipped his whisky. "She is a bit extra, isn't she? Are you keeping her?"

"Oh yes. She'll make a good pony-girl."

"That might be a waste, General. I reckon she's promising for bedroom games."

The General chuckled and pointed to the girl still gyrating up and down. "Like little Ruth?"

"Like little Ruth," Keane agreed.

"You have a soft spot for little Ruth?"

That was true, Keane reflected. The sight of any beautiful woman in bondage had always done something for him; to see Ruth like this was particularly erotic. He looked at the girl, bound in her misery, still swaying her upper body, but becoming tired as more small gasps began to issue from her mouth.

There was a twinge of remorse.

Brice was the quintessential sadist.

Then Keane let the stirring in his loins take control, as he relished the thought that he had only to ask and Ruth would be his for the night. He shrugged. "She's desirable General. And... Well..." He shook his head, and pointed to the girl struggling to keep her upper body moving. She was mewling softly now; quivering with physical effort; clearly trying to bear her agony without complaint. "She's in a lot of pain General. Why not let her rest?"

The General sat down. "There you go again," he sighed. "I sometimes wonder if you are really cut out for this work." He sucked his teeth. "You do it well, but you can show pity for these bitches." His expression made it sound like a question, as he pointed to Ruth again. "For this little animal especially."

Keane sat on the edge of the desk and sipped his drink.

"Maybe she didn't really deserve all this, General." He took a large slug of whisky, but it didn't entirely bury the remorse.

"They all have it coming," the General sneered. "Sluts!"

He finished his drink. "So don't let pity cloud your judgement, there's a good fellow... I'll just switch off the earphones." He leaned forward and tapped Ruth's gyrating buttocks with the quirt.

She immediately stopped her hypnotic swaying and struggled upright again, panting slightly.

The General pressed a small switch on the side of the half-hood, and put his fingers beneath her chin. "I shall give you to a guest tonight. Make sure you please him, or it's the whip again."

Still trembling from her exertions, the girl's head moved in a submissive nod. "Yes Master." There was no hesitation in the way she addressed him; no shame, degradation or embarrassment. To her, the General was clearly the Master.

Now he leaned forward and gave her a light kiss on the lips. In a conditioned response, the girl's tongue flicked out, searching for the General's mouth, but he chuckled and pulled away. He switched the earphones on again and turned to Keane. "Would you ring for Sheena please, Nick?"

Keane nodded.

Sheena was the housekeeper; sort of.

In fact, she was the house Madam.

She was good with the whip.

Damn good. Any excuse to use it was excuse enough.

The girls were terrified of her and she made damn sure they stayed in line.

But Keane liked her.

She also liked him.

She was also a switch-hitter, although they had enjoyed more than one good night together once she got the message Keane liked to be in control. Which was good; because Sheena was able to turn on the slavegirl bit herself, when she felt like it. Or, as she had put it, "for the right guy."

Keane went across to the large marble fireplace and pulled the bell-rope.

Sheena came in within a minute, dressed in her working

outfit, as she described it; a skin-tight, lamé jumpsuit, a gold one this time. The white leather belt around her firm waist nipped her shape even more, and there was a white leather dog-whip tucked in at her side. She almost floated across the room, her wide hips swaying, one foot placed in front of the other; model-girl style. Her thick golden hair, hanging down almost to her waist, framed her sensuous form. Her blue eyes sparkled in her pretty but slightly harsh features. She smiled at the General.

"You rang, General?"

"I'm afraid you will have to do without Nick tonight." He pointed to Ruth. "Take this animal to his rooms. Feed her. See she bathes properly, then replace the hood. Chain her to his bed, where she will wait on her knees."

"I take it the earphones are to remain on?"

"Oh yes."

Sheena looked at the bound girl. "First, I'll have some things to say to her when we're alone." She shook her head. "Taking Nick off me." She chuckled. "Bad girl." She taunted the temporarily deafened and unsuspecting Ruth.

Then she came close to Keane.

The waft of her female smell surrounded him.

A primitive, animal scent, devoid of all perfume.

A clean, healthy smell, signalling 'come and get me'.

She pressed her taut body against him and her hand reached for his loins. "Nick," she pecked his lips. "It's been too long since I saw you." She squeezed his penis. "And this too," she whispered, pulling a doubtful expression. "Are you sure you prefer this little trinket Nick? I can be a good girl too you know."

He grinned at her. "She can't bite back, Sheena."

Sheena grinned. "Well, if you get fed up with her, you come to my room." There was no jealousy there. Just acceptance that Keane wanted Ruth that night.

The General had been watching in amusement and now he grinned. "Never mind Sheena. There'll be other times,

35

I'm sure. Are you ready to run the new girl?"

"She's on her way to the Parade Ring now, General." She licked her lips. "I've had her dressed for the occasion. The slut will give us some good entertainment." She went towards Ruth. "But first I'll deal with this one." She grabbed the exposed locks of Ruth's hair, pulled her upright, and dragged the whimpering hooded slavegirl from the room. Just as the door closed on them, Keane heard the slash of the dog-whip on flesh and one squeal of pain from Ruth as she was hurried away along the corridor.

The General turned to Keane again. "Nick. Why don't you come with me to the Parade Ring? See if your judgement is still good, eh?"

For a moment Keane wondered. Was there anything sinister behind the General's last remark? Then he shrugged, mentally. Probably. Maybe a bollocking threatened? But what the hell? That was later. For now, pleasure. The running of a new slave—especially one supervised by Sheena—always got him in the mood for serious action.

It would be an appetiser, before he went to deal with Ruth.

5: THE PARADE RING

The new slavegirl still wore the netted Basque, but now they had removed the ties from the hem, and at the front of her collar they had fitted a six-inch diameter metal disc, so it rested on the soft rounded platform of her jutting breasts. On the disc, painted in red, there was a figure seven.

Her arms were secured in front of her with manacles, and about a foot of chain held her slim wrists together. A piece of hempen rope was attached to the centre of the wrist chain, and jerking on the rope without ceremony, Sheena dragged the protesting slave into the centre of the sawdust covered ring.

Unable to resist, the weeping girl staggered into the glare of the stage lights, almost losing her balance, trying in vain to pull her hands downwards to hide the glorious swell of her exposed sex. Sheena took a riding crop from her belt, and jerking on the rope again, pulled her charge to a standstill. The bewildered slave blushed deep red beneath the gaze of fifty or so pairs of eyes.

They saw a young woman with a fine figure and long copper-gold hair, which, although somewhat matted at the moment, added to her overall prettiness, a foil for her wide, bright, brown eyes and full sexy lips. The tight-fitting Basque and the glowing oils on her skin told them that this lovely creature was a new acquisition.

There was sudden comment from someone who must have noticed the frizz of fine pale coloured hairs in the vee of her delightful thighs.

"Hey folks! A genuine blonde!"

There was an appreciative murmur from the rest and Keane nodded in satisfaction. He had made a good choice.

From the girl's general demeanour, he could also tell she was beginning to learn; although fading welts on the tanned flesh of her firm well-rounded buttocks and the backs of her soft thighs suggested that her first lessons had not been

37

easy.

She remained still, except for the slight nervous trembling, obviously wondering what was to come next. Then the chain between her wrists jingled as again she tried to cover herself. She looked towards Sheena. "Please! Oh Please! Let me go!" She crouched down, almost kneeling, trying to hide her nakedness, but the posture only emphasised her delicious curves, as the Basque displayed her oiled flesh.

A gasp of admiration rose from the small audience, and then growls of approval as Sheena silenced the girl by cracking the crop against her palm. Grabbing the long hair and ignoring the squeal of pain, Sheena pulled her upright.

"On your feet, slut!"

Sobbing, the girl dropped her hands to cover her sex once more, but Sheena merely loosed the rope and pushed her towards the back of the ring, where a large ringbolt was set in the stonework.

Beside the ring there was a wooden rack, festooned with whips, chains, collars, and other cruel bondage devices. Sheena nudged the well-rounded buttocks.

"Stand over there, facing the wall."

Still shivering, the frightened girl lowered her head obediently, and stopped, her nose pressed close to the stonework.

"Turn round!"

Head down in submission, she obeyed, pushing her chained wrists even lower, trying again to cover her naked sex.

"Arms above your head! Our guests want to see what you have to offer."

With another gasp of pain, the helpless girl obeyed, shame and degradation showing clearly in her lovely face as she lifted her chained arms.

"Get those arms higher! Reach!"

The hapless girl stretched, automatically standing on tiptoe, reaching as high as she could, her face straining with the effort. Her lithe body was now stretched taut, emphasising her well-conditioned figure. There were more excited mutterings and groans of pleasure as the audience took in the delightful show.

Sheena turned towards the seating area, just visible beyond the stage lights, and tapped the steel disc at the girl's throat. "As you can see, Number Seven is new, but of the usual high quality." She smiled and slid her fingers between her captive's labia. "Not a virgin, but then it wouldn't have lasted long here anyway." Sheena ran her hand down the girl's shapely flanks. "And she's beginning to learn how to behave." Again, she caressed the cringing body. "She's been difficult, but the marks should fade." Sheena smiled coldly. "We thought you would like to watch us run her."

There was a sudden burst of loud, enthusiastic chatter and stray comments floated about.

"Use the wire whip Sheena!" a high, piping voice rang out.

Then another, deeper, voice: "Let me try. I'll show the bitch!"

A fat balding man in the front row pointed to the girl's genitals. "The slave needs a shave!"

The chant was taken up, quietly. "The slave needs a shave! The slave needs a shave! The slave needs a shave!"

All the time, the girl's terror was clearly increasing as her body began to tremble violently.

Sheena just grinned and motioned the audience to be quiet. "Patience, Ladies and Gentlemen, patience!" She stretched a hand out to the rack and took down a length of rough baling cord. She went to the girl again and prodded the vulnerable sex-mound.

"Hands on hips!"

Meekly, the girl lowered her arms obediently. The chain between her wrists was only just long enough. She made no resistance as Sheena crooked her elbows, forcing the chain to press into the soft flesh beneath the Basque at her abdomen. Then Sheena threaded the baling string through her bent arms and wound the stuff around a couple of times, before tightening it with a savage wrench, forcing Tristie's elbows together.

Sheena grinned as the slave grimaced in pain and arched backwards, pulling herself into a more upright and revealing posture which pressed the manacle chain deeper into the slight swell of her stomach. Sheena knotted off the baling string, forcing the lovely head back slightly, so that the breasts were forced even higher in the Basque, the nipples swelling towards the audience, which elicited fresh murmurs of delight.

Sheena gave a satisfied grin and caressed Tristie's left nipple. "Now, Number Seven, don't get too worked up, will you?"

There was a burst of laughter as Sheena turned the girl around again, showing her arched back. Reaching from behind, Sheena took the hempen rope, pulled it back through Tristie's thighs, and upwards, between the rounded globes of her soft buttocks, to wrap it around the baling string. She tightened the rope and then gave another tug, pulling the rope up towards the girl's collar. The blonde head went back even further as Sheena secured the rope to the back of the steel band.

Next, a savage downward tug on the rope and Sheena tied it off around the baling string. The sadistic woman ignored the yelp of pain as the rope cut deep into the girl's sex-lips, and stood back, admiring her sobbing victim.

An expectant hush fell over the audience as Sheena reached to the rack and took a six-foot coach-whip. She cracked it, for effect, raising a cloud of sawdust from the floor.

The terrified girl began to shake, and her sobs echoed around the room.

Sheena chuckled, and prodded the exposed buttocks with the handle of the whip. She pushed the helpless body forwards, urging her into a trot. "Run around the circle! I want a moving target!"

Sheena cracked the whip in the air again and laughed with the audience as the frightened girl jumped nervously, obviously expecting a slash from the leather. The whip snapped across the laughter again.

"Faster! Show them what you can do!"

Now the leather struck home across the jiggling buttocks, wrenching a tortured scream from the girl. She began to move faster, her breath coming in loud gasps, the sweat beginning to start all over her body, the netting of the Basque displaying her perfectly. The friction between her thighs was turning the sweat and body-oil into a foamy mess, reminiscent of the pre-race sweating-up often seen on a racehorse.

Sheena laid another slash into the tormented slave, this time across her thighs, almost entangling her legs, causing her to stumble. Another slash of the whip and the girl crashed to her knees, raising fine sawdust which began to coat the film of body-oil and sweat on her skin.

The whip landed across her defenceless shoulders and the screaming girl staggered upright to continue running the gauntlet of cheering spectators. Above it all was the strident sound of Sheena's voice: "Come on, slut! Faster! Let's see those buttocks jiggling!"

And so it went on, until the girl was moving in a blind stumble, gasping in near exhaustion. Then Sheena seemed to tire of her sport. "Right, Number Seven! Finished!" She gave one more slash of the whip, this time curling it around the girl's calves, and tugging to bring the helpless captive to the sawdust, where she rolled to a halt against the edge of the arena, her sweat run body coated with a fine covering of sawdust, her lungs heaving and straining.

The tortured slavegirl rolled into a submissive huddle as Sheena walked over to her. Raising her whip hand high, Sheena slashed it into the exposed buttocks three times.

The girl screamed once and straightened up, her body arching in pain, before she collapsed into a senseless heap.

Sheena looked down, contemptuously. "No stamina!" She turned towards the stage entrance and clapped her hands.

Two more young girls, naked but for their steel collars, came running into the small circle. One of them had a thick wooden pole which she pushed through the crooks of Tristie's elbows. Then they each grabbed an end of the pole, and dragged their unconscious burden backwards from the arena.

The General had been watching the whole performance with an intense expression on his face. He turned to Keane. "Congratulations Nick. That is a fine specimen. I think I may decide to keep her for myself." He smiled. "Now, shall we have her in my office and welcome her to her new life as a slavegirl on our island?"

6: A Welcome for Tristie

There was a small commotion from outside the door of the General's office. Zach Miller's gruff voice; bullying. The sounds of a squealing girl being given the rope's end. Then silence until Miller, dressed in tatty motorcycling leathers, dragged in a sobbing hooded figure. He was pulling her along by the hank of hair which stuck out from beneath the hood that blinded her, moving her backwards, so she could find no purchase on the floor, her heels scuffing along the carpet, as she struggled to keep her feet.

The girl was naked now, bound in the usual fashion for a new slave—hands manacled together, the steel chain between the wrists threaded through the ring at the front of the iron collar, still riveted around her lovely neck. The chain was long enough for delicate hands, at breast level, to reach a man's thighs and scrotum and caress them.

Zach slammed a foot into the back of the girl's knees, so her legs buckled and she dropped like a sack, forced to kneel in front of the General.

The frightened girl's body was shaking. Her breath came in panic-stricken gasps. The sweat of fear was beginning to pump out of her pores, sheening her smooth pale skin, forming droplets on the oil which had been smeared over her naked form.

Zach unbuckled the hood and pulled it away. Her golden hair fell free, pouring down her back in a torrent of silken strands. Zach growled; part pleasure, part annoyance. He grabbed her mane of hair and pushed it over her shoulders, so it fell forwards, covering her breasts and brushing against her tanned thighs.

"All yours General." Zach's eyes gleamed as he tucked his rope whip into his waistband. With a last contemptuous look at the kneeling girl he strode from the room.

Keane, standing beside the General, took his dog-whip from his belt and looked down at Tristie, reappraising her.

Young.

Twenty-one at most; and so nubile!

With that waterfall of amber-blonde hair.

When she stood, it would reach to the backs of her thighs.

She was a dolly: a real stunner.

Definitely one for the General's collection, Keane reckoned.

Another new slavegirl to learn her place.

And she would learn!

The whip would see to that.

He turned to the General. "Ready when you are."

Brice smiled, then took a thin leather-bound cane off the desk. It was a switch of about thirty inches long, with three or four fine chain filaments at the thinnest end. He whacked the switch down hard into a sheaf of papers on the desk. The crack reverberated about the room.

The girl jumped, squealing in shock as she looked at him, her face contorted with fright. She shrank back, shaking, as he walked softly over to her. With a gentle tap, he bounced the switch off the top of her buttocks, just hard enough to make a small slapping sound. He chuckled as she cowered, sobbing in terror, her frightened gaze alternating between his face and the leather switch.

The General looked down at her.

"Lower your head!"

Mutely she obeyed, still trembling; still sobbing.

As if caressing a lover, the General allowed the switch to slip through his left hand, caught the tip and bent the cane almost double, before allowing it to spring back straight, the air whistling as the leather cut through it.

She jumped, and again gasped with fright, but remained with her head bent low.

The General chuckled.

"Nervous little bitch, isn't she?"

There was a cruel twisted grin on the General's face as he looked down at the trembling captive. Then he sighed and half-turned his upper body to the right, away from the kneeling figure. He took his arm back in a low wide arc and then spun, fast, like a tennis player, to swing a full-bodied blow, underhand, into the soft underpart of the girl's buttocks.

Her agonised shriek cleaved the air as the blow propelled her forward in an involuntary dive. She rolled away from him, onto her back, frantic now, heaving her hips upwards, trying to ease the searing pain.

Keane drew back his arm, but the General stopped him.

"Wait Nick. She isn't yours just yet." He flexed the leather switch again, making it whistle as it sliced through the air. He sauntered over to the terrified girl, and for a few moments caressed her shapely buttocks with the supple cane. He spoke, softly.

"On your knees."

But of course, the girl was new.

Frightened.

She didn't understand and merely shuddered, remaining on her side, sobbing into the carpet. Maybe she hadn't even heard the General.

No excuse! The General slashed the whip into her again, and then, ignoring her wails, grabbed a fistful of her hair to drag her back onto her knees. Then he sat down again and leaned forward.

"Do you know what has happened to you?"

The girl shook her head slowly. Then her head began to loll and she started mumbling to herself. "No! No. No. They can't do this to me. No! No." She suddenly hauled herself upright and screamed at them. "I won't stand for this." She was glaring. "You'd better let me go, you bastards!"

The General sighed and glanced at Keane. "Such stubbornness, Nick!" He glowered at the slavegirl.

"Damn you!" She pulled a face. "You're just sad perverts and I'm nobody's slave!"

The General looked down at the sobbing girl. "You really

45

are being difficult." He sighed deeply again. "Still, as you seem unwilling to accept your position, I'll explain it in detail! Perhaps then you may see sense!"

The girl seemed not to hear. Her shoulders heaved with her crying.

"You have been here for a week, more or less. Heavily sedated and in a constant state of semi-consciousness. Your food intake has been controlled, and you have been kept clean. You have lost a little weight!" He grinned at the cowering slavegirl. "Now your figure has fined down, you will be in great demand here!"

The girl was quieter now and the expression on her lovely face had changed to one of bewildered half-acceptance, her confidence gone. She gave a slow shake of her head. "It just can't be!"

The General flashed a casual smile. "You know it's true!"

Frowning, she shook her head again.

A sudden whoosh!

The whip slashing into her bottom.

She screamed out, cowering away.

The General leaned over her.

"Was that real enough for you?"

The whip slashed into her again, and again she screamed.

The General spoke quietly. "You call me Master! Now, what have you to say?"

The girl seemed to accept now that she had to submit. "What are you going to do to me... Master?"

"Whatever I wish!"

She lowered her head, groaned, and tried again. "Please! Let me go!"

The General chuckled. "Let you go? I don't think so." He placed the handle of the whip under her chin, lifting her head, and spoke as if explaining to a child. "For one thing, I had to pay a lot of money for your body! For another, if you were in my position, would you let me go?"

"But I won't tell anyone!" The whip slashed into her body

again and she wailed out in pain.

The General grabbed her throat. "Once more slave. If you were in my position, would you let me go?"

Miserably, the slavegirl shook her head. "N-no, I suppose not!"

"No what!"

She trembled. "No, Master."

"Better!" He tilted her head up with the handle of his switch and looked into her tear-streaked face. "You are beautiful. You have the sort of looks and figure which men so desire. That makes you of great value to us."

The girl trembled and moaned. "Oh but please, please let me go!" Then clearly, still self-conscious, added, "Master!"

The General gave an evil chuckle. "Come now. You should be happy! You can fulfil your sole purpose in life. You will become a plaything, a toy to satisfy the desires of extremely rich men and women. People who have to suppress their urges because of old-maidish social attitudes. Here they can indulge themselves and you will help them realise their fantasies."

The girl shook her head, moaning, in clear distress. "Oh No! Please! You can't do this..."

"We've been through all that." The General drew in a deep breath. "You will stay," he said in a matter-of-fact way. "You will submit. You will be kept naked and in bondage at all times and you will satisfy whatever demands are made of you!" His evil smile flashed again. "You will learn to give pleasure to men and women alike! In fact you will learn to do *anything* we demand of you! And I mean *anything*!" He sneered at her. "As for you, I think you are a natural. You will soon be acting as a slavegirl should and you'll be enjoying it!" He examined the leather switch closely. "In the end, it doesn't matter. You will either obey or be whipped and tortured. If that doesn't work, well…" he broke off and shrugged, slowly "we have plenty of guests who prefer unwilling slaves to play with. Only their idea of

47

play won't be the same as yours!"

The girl stifled a sob and looked down at the floor. "Oh no!" She looked up at him. "I want to go..."

Casually, the General slashed her across the shoulders with the switch. "Silence!"

The girl screamed in agony and fell over again, rolling into a protective huddle, clearly expecting a further beating. She shook her head, terrified. "No! Please! Oh, please! *Let me go! LET ME GO!*"

"How she pleads, Nick!" The General chuckled as he shook his head and lifted his arm.

Her scream battered about the room, her voice cracking as the fine leather lash cut into her. "Leave me alone! For God's sake! Stop hitting me! Please!" She rolled over onto her side and away from him.

He stood up and followed her. "You are trying my patience!" He shook the switch, holding it over her cringing body. "And you call me Master!" The switch cut into her flesh three more times, extracting more screams of agony.

"Damn you! You Bastard!" Once more the switch attacked and she screamed.

"Will you never learn?" He gave a deep sigh. "This painful little interview will last as long as it takes for you to learn your first lesson in obedience!" He leaned back again and gently stroked the switch across her breasts.

There was a terrible air of finality about his words and the girl shuddered with obvious disgust and fear. She gave another shiver, as though realising the import of his words and then she hung her head in defeat. Her voice was tremulous, but still she pleaded. "Please Master! Please! Let me go!"

"You are wasting your time." The General turned to Keane. "This slut may be difficult." He sighed, "But not impossible, eh Nick?"

"Not impossible General, not impossible. Just more fun!"

The girl, blinking in the light, looked up at him, her young face wet with tears and screwed up in terror and bewilderment. "Please!" she said, "please don't hurt me any more."

"Whip her," the General said curtly.

She screamed as Keane's whip landed across her buttocks and cowered away from him.

The General bent forward and said in a soft, patient voice: "You must learn, girl. Only complete submission and instant obedience will save you from the whip." He lifted her chin and smiled. "Most times anyway." Then he lifted her head by her hair. "I am the General and you are now one of my sprites." He flicked her thighs with the switch, barely touching her skin, and chuckled as she flinched.

"Whip her!"

Keane slashed into the girl's buttocks, feeling the surge of power as the leather bit her flesh. He clamped a hand over her mouth to stifle her cries of agony. When she had quietened down, he released her and pushed her head to the floor once more.

The General continued, looking down impassively. "You are a slavegirl and you will obey us."

The girl shook her head. She was frantic now, but through her pain she still pleaded. "No! No! You can't..."

"Whip the slut."

Again Keane's dog-whip lashed into the defenceless body. Once more the girl screamed in pain and shock.

"You will obey," the General said.

She still resisted. "Please. No. Please let me go. I won't tell..."

"Whip her."

Keane extracted further screams of pain and she fell to her side.

The General leaned towards the beaten girl. "How much longer?" He grabbed her hair and pulled her head up. "Submit, and the beatings will stop."

The girl looked up at him, but still she seemed not to

understand. "Oh Please, no! You can't do this..."

"Whip the slut. Properly."

Keane began a careful, calculated whipping. Not vicious, but hard enough, picking his targets carefully, now a buttock, a thigh, then a breast, then the belly, each blow dragging wails of pain from the tormented girl. Sweating slightly with exertion, Keane followed her writhing form around the floor as she tried to escape the lash. He kept at it, the whip slashing into her body, until her screams reached deafening pitch.

"ENOUGH!" the General's strident tones rang out. He stood, crossed to the whipped girl, and leaned over her. His voice went quiet, but was all the more menacing for that. "This isn't make-believe! You will learn to obey or be whipped to shreds!" He pulled her upright and dragged her over to his chair again. Dumping her on her knees, he sat down.

"Someone will be looking for me," the girl said.

"You have no one!"

"My friends!"

The General interrupted. "She is either stubborn or stupid, Nick! Whip her again!"

The whip slashed into the girl's thighs once more and she screamed.

"You call me Master!" The General grinned at her. "Now, did you say something?"

They were breaking her. She lowered her head. "No, Master!" She was hesitant, the word clearly still alien to her.

The General smiled with satisfaction. "Better. Not perfect, but better." He stroked the whip across her back. "Such a simple word, yet so hard to say, but you'll get used to it!"

The girl closed her eyes in defeat. "Yes, Master!" Suddenly, she was beginning to sound subservient.

"Good! Now where was I? Ah, yes! We need a name for you, but for the moment you are just Number Seven." He

50

grinned at her. "That is on your disk, I think?" He leaned towards her and she pulled back.

He glared at her, and she trembled. She swallowed and closed her eyes, remaining still, rigid almost, as the General began to fondle her breasts. "Yes, Number Seven. That will suit you well!"

The girl shuddered and pulled away slightly. Obviously she wasn't quite ready, for she looked up, and shook her head. "I'll escape!"

The General smiled evilly. "Use your intelligence, Number Seven, and realise how remote that possibility is!"

The girl was not so sure of herself now. "But you can't keep me here." Out of the corner of her eye she saw his whip hand rising. "Master!" she added, quickly.

"Whip her!"

The whip slashed into her tortured buttocks once more and she screamed. "No!"

"Slavegirls do not answer back." The General grabbed her shoulders and shook her. "For the last time, you have been abducted and no one knows where you are. You are now a slave and I will use your body for my pleasure, as and when I feel the need." He shrugged. "In that respect, you will do whatever I ask of you." He leaned back into his chair. "And when I don't need your body, I have guests who are always ready to use you instead. Now, do you understand?"

Tristie looked utterly crestfallen, clearly understanding the awful truth. She couldn't escape. She really was a slave. She looked up at him. "Y-yes Master." She even seemed to be finding it easier to call the man 'Master'. Her sad expression told all.

Suddenly, she slumped in front of the two men and began to sob. She raised her head. "Please don't hurt me anymore. I'll be good."

Keane understood.

There was something about Brice that commanded

51

respect. He might well have been a real General. Even without the whip he seemed to intimidate.

Keane grunted to himself.

She had been easy.

It usually took days to get a girl this far.

But then she was young.

At twenty-one, schoolday discipline was only a few years behind her; no time for her to develop much character.

Or maybe she was a submissive anyway.

All the better.

Just the sort the General liked.

An adult, but young enough to mould as he saw fit.

The General prodded his girl's buttocks with his switch. "Offer yourself."

Panic-stricken, sucking in deep draughts of air, the new slavegirl shivered, her face a mask of bewilderment, clearly confused; no doubt trying to remember what she had been told. Like all new arrivals, she would have been weaned off the sedatives, and her training would have begun. She would have been told so many things, shown so much. It was doubtful if she would remember all that was expected of her.

She shook her head. Then she seemed to remember, as the General's switch whistled through the air to land on her buttocks with a loud crack. Squealing, she obeyed, and almost in a conditioned response, crawled towards the General.

Keane flicked the offered buttocks with his whip again, and pushed her on. Then another flick of the whip. "Stop!"

The girl obeyed.

"Offer yourself, Number Seven!" Keane snapped.

Obedient now, she turned around, lowered her head to the floor, submissively touching her nose to the carpet, forcing her buttocks upwards, spreading her knees to expose her genitals to the General.

"I offer myself to you, Master!" she quavered, her lips

trembling uncontrollably, clearly having to fight with the words.

The General grinned. "She is learning Nick, thanks to your efforts."

"And the whip!"

"Yes!" The General nodded, standing up. "Of course, the whip. Always the whip!" He placed his foot on the back of her neck and grabbed her hair. Then he stooped down to begin a none too gentle examination of her body, running his hands over her exposed flesh, sliding strong fingers casually into her vagina and her tight little anus. He looked down at her and traced the switch across her back.

Suddenly the girl seemed to capitulate completely. "I am yours, Master!"

Keane smiled.

He had seen it before.

A girl being broken.

Finally accepting that she was a slave.

And not just because she feared the whip.

Admitting, in the heart of her, she was finished.

Except this time it had been so easy.

Too easy. She was acting up to them. He nudged her with his toe. "Number Seven is playing games with us, General!"

The General tilted her chin upwards and sneered at her. "You act quite well, Number Seven. Almost convincing!" He shrugged then. "No matter. Soon you really will submit." He grinned at her. "And the sooner the better, for your sake." He looked at Keane. "I think she'll do for the moment, Nick." He stood up. "Now, I wonder how well she rides." He leaned forward, and taking a bunch of keys from his pocket, undid the manacles about the girl's wrists.

"Fetch me the riding tack, please Nick."

Keane nodded, went to the rack and took down leather reins and a small bridle. He also collected a vicious looking crop, and a pair of long pointed spurs. These he handed to the General, who slipped the bridle over the slavegirl's head.

He dropped the reins. "No need for these with hair like hers, eh Nick?" Still grinning, he fitted the spurs to his boots and then sat astride the girl's back. He filled his left hand with a hank of hair and kicked into her thighs with his heels. With a sadistic swipe of the quirt he hissed: "Forwards, mare!"

Screaming her agony, Tristie began to crawl forwards, wailing, as each blow of the General's quirt urged more speed from her. Soon she was crawling as fast as she could, being obliged to lift herself off her knees, so she was up on hands and feet. As the General rode her around the room, he was continually applying the crop to her buttocks. "Faster mare! Faster! Show me how you gallop!"

Bucking and screaming each time the crop slashed into her flesh, sweating with the effort of carrying the General about the room, the poor girl staggered on, crying.

The sadistic General showed her no mercy, and six or seven times he rode her around the room, using savage jerks on her golden locks to guide her. Finally, he stopped her by the door and dismounted.

Gasping and spluttering, she collapsed into an exhausted heap as the General stood up. His face curled into an expression of fierce anger and he laid the crop across her rounded buttocks, wrenching yet another scream from her.

"On your knees!" he shouted, leaning over the terrified girl. "I'll tell you when you can lie down!"

In mad panic, she scrambled to her knees once more, to remain quiet, but quaking, her pain-wracked breathing filling the room.

The General looked at Keane. "She runs well." He ran his hands softly over the trembling body, allowing his fingers to stray into the crease of her buttocks, before straightening up. "Stay on all fours mare! Yes, you could make a good pony-slave." He smiled cruelly and bent, once more running his hands over her abused flesh. "A few weeks in front of a trotting-gig will bring you round to the right

54

way of thinking, but first it's the Discipline Suite."

He glanced at Keane. "A whipping Nick. Then she can be branded and pierced." He paused. "After that, give her a few days in the cages. That should bring her around." He sneered at the slavegirl. "Before long, you will be begging to see me, or he'll have the hide off you!" He caressed her right flank. "Such a pretty hide, and one for which we can charge our patrons a great deal." He squeezed her throat again, then pushed her away from him. "Understand?"

Tristie nodded, panic widening her eyes as she glanced at the quirt. She remained on all fours before the General, crying quietly. There was another slash of the whip, and she squealed and cowered as he stalked from the room.

Keane nudged her with his toe, and in moments had removed the leather tack and had re-shackled her wrists to her collar. Then he clipped a length of chain to the collar and pulled savagely. "Come on then, we've work to do. Move that pretty little arse of yours!"

Still panting from her exertions, Number Seven, the General's latest slavegirl, bowed her head and allowed Keane to lead her from the room.

Within a few yards Keane shouted: "Halt and face left."

The girl obeyed, to stand in front of a heavy pair of green plastic flap-doors. There was the strong smell disinfectant in the air and there were pieces of straw sticking out from beneath the doors. Keane prodded with the whip and herded her through.

The room was small and square, with a low ceiling and solid rock walls. There were a couple of wooden stalls built against one wall, and these were filled with straw bedding. Each stall had a large iron ring in the wall and a trough of water.

Nothing more than a stable.

Keane pushed the girl towards one of the stalls and dumped her bodily into the pile of clean straw. He clipped the chain to the ring. He pointed to a small shelf in front of the trough. "There's meat, fruit, bread and milk. It's good and fresh, like all the food you'll get here." He bent down to look into her eyes. "So I should eat it, if I were you." There was a sudden touch of tenderness in his voice, and he cradled her chin in his hand, tilting her head. "A body like yours needs looking after." He placed a soft kiss on her lips and then, as if realising he was showing a chink in his armour, stood up. "Anyway, there'll be nothing else, unless you fancy the straw!"

7: The Walk!

Tristie had eaten the food, and was surprised that Keane had told her the truth. It had tasted so good. Then she thought about Nick Keane. God! What a fool she'd been. She had made it so easy for him, back in that awful nightclub. She had accepted the doctored drink, like a baby taking milk. He was to blame. He had abducted her, brought her to this awful place against her will. He really was the one to blame, wasn't he? She ought to hate him, but much as she hated what he had done to her and would delight in seeing him sent to prison, she realised that, somehow, she didn't hate him. In fact, if there was anyone here she could perhaps trust at all, for some strange reason she felt it was him. There was definitely something different about his approach. It was as if he was forcing himself to do the things he did.

For a brief moment she brightened. Perhaps she could use her looks to advantage, even persuade him to help her...

She shook her head. Who was she trying to fool?

Then she shuddered and pushed a terrible thought aside. A slight inkling that there was still the lingering desire to feel his hard muscled body...

She shook her head violently. Damn them! It was something they had given her again! Surely. In the food perhaps...

That was when her thoughts became confused and she knew she was falling into a natural sleep.

Her dream was a nice one.

Keane was definitely there.

***

The dream was shattered, it seemed only moments later, as a strap landed on buttocks, jerking her into awareness. Zach Miller was standing beside her, grinning, as she shook her head, trying to wake herself fully. She backed away, huddling in fear against the wall.

Dressed in jeans and a heavy white sweater, he had a strap in one hand and a canvas grip in the other. He placed the bag on the floor, and bent close to her face.

"It's time for a walk!" He poked her in the ribs. "On your knees!"

Still shaking with terror, Tristie knelt and began to sob, quietly, too frightened even to dare to turn her head as Miller went behind her.

He bent to the bag and fished out a vile ball-gag, which he stuffed in her mouth. He lodged the thing behind her teeth and fastened the straps around her neck, beneath her hair. He took a short iron bar from the bag and fastened it between her ankles, as a hobble, forcing her legs about two feet apart. He took the rope that was still attached to her collar, and with a savage haul, pulled her into a backward bow, before fastening the rope to the centre of the hobble. Then he pulled her even further backwards and secured a wrist to each ankle.

"Crawl, bitch! Forwards, out of the room, turn left and wait."

She tried to move, but it was agonising. The backward bend of her body filled her with pain, and her spine felt as if it would snap. She pushed her hips back and sagged forwards to take the strain off her spine, but, immediately, she began to choke as the metal collar became tighter, almost throttling her. Her head began to swim. She settled for the lesser of the two evils and remained bent backwards. Gasping with pain and effort, she began her agonising crawl, out of the room and into the corridor, wincing as the rough concrete snagged her knees and shins.

Shaking with apprehension, she stopped in the corridor and waited obediently, looking fearfully around her. Her mouth dried as she saw there were whips, ropes, leather belts and chains hanging at regular intervals all long the rough stone walls. There was even a heavy metal Basque, and Tristie could make out the tiny hooks lining the inside of the contraption.

She shuddered as she took in the full import of the thing. God! That netted Basque had been torture, but this! She trembled again as she looked at it, hanging there, mute, yet giving out a clear message: 'Behave, or else!'

Suddenly Tristie realised she was looking at the Basque with more than a little fascination. She was already experiencing severe bondage, but she couldn't help wondering. What would it feel like to wear that thing?

Miller emerged from the room and grinned at her. "You'll find out soon enough!"

Tristie started and grunted in surprise.

"Oh, I know what you're thinking! Like all natural slaves, you're juicing, wondering what it'd be like in the Iron Lady!" He smiled cruelly. "Misbehave too much and you'll find out!"

Tristie shook her head, desperately trying to ignore the sudden warm moistness inside her vagina, as she thought of being placed in the iron Basque. Why should she feel like this? Come on girl, she thought, you've been abducted and if you don't get away, you face a life of abuse and torture! And you look forward to that?

Something must have shown in her eyes, for Miller grinned at her. "You're a natural. You enjoy flaunting yourself. I knew it!"

Tristie was surprised to feel she was blushing, but not from shame or embarrassment. She had actually felt the nervous thrill of sexual excitement before, during hours spent in front of a camera, flaunting herself, just as he said. She really had enjoyed it, mostly because it meant she could taunt men, even if only by proxy. She swallowed, trying to hide it from him.

He chuckled. "You know what it's all about, don't you? It wasn't just the money was it?" He stretched an arm out and took down a long rod from one of the hooks. He showed her the stick and pulled a sadistic smile. "A cattle goad. Shocking little thing." He laughed at the feeble joke. He was still taunting her and now he spat on his hands and rubbed his saliva over Tristie's left nipple.

Then he touched the goad to the moist patch.

The tortured Tristie screamed into the gag. Her eyes bulged and the veins stood up in her neck as a jolt of electricity seemed to set her breast on fire. Then the goad touched her moist sex-lips and she arched backwards, her screaming agony even breaching the gag and echoing about the corridor.

Miller stood over her as she recovered. "I said you were getting wet!" He nudged her with his foot. "Now, it's time to move, so don't dawdle, or it's the goad."

Tristie gurgled through the gag, understanding fully, knowing she must avoid the goad. She nodded her head frantically.

"Right then," Miller ordered. "Crawl!"

Hating herself for submitting, yet knowing she had no other option, Tristie responded to the prodding from Miller, and began to make her painful way along the corridor.

Before long, however, as even Miller had to acknowledge, they were too slow. After a few yards he pushed her to the floor and released her bonds. "Stay still while I re-bind you, so you can walk properly. Okay?"

Tristie nodded dumbly, and then screamed into her gag, as the goad was pushed into the vee of her thighs again. He didn't switch the thing on this time, but just sniggered before removing the goad. "Answer me!"

All that came through the gag was an unintelligible gurgling. Her tortured body continued to shake as she cowered from her tormentor.

"Gurgle, gurgle, gurgle!" he mocked her. He grabbed her hair and yanked her head back. "It's a good job I know you're trying to say Master!" He grinned into her contorted face and took more nylon string from his pocket.

Tristie was totally submissive now. In moments her hands had been bound together behind her back once more, her elbows pulled tight into each other and the ball-gag removed.

Then Miller reached out to a rack on the wall and took down a leather hood. He held it up to show her. The hood was just like the others she had been made to wear, except this one had a wide hole in the front. Inside, she could see the four-inch long tube, stitched into the leather, and she began to tremble as she realised how the hood would be worn. Then darkness enveloped her, as he slipped it over her head.

Tristie almost vomited from the stink of stale sweat which filled her nostrils. Then she stopped worrying about it, as the tube inside was forced into her mouth. The stiff rubber pushed at the back of her throat, pressing her tongue down, forcing her mouth to open wide. Then the hard ring around the outer end of the tube was lodged behind her teeth and she almost choked as the hood was secured by a tight strap, buckled about her slender throat.

"On your feet, bitch, and walk!"

Obediently, Tristie staggered to her feet, staring in wild fear through the eyeholes in the hood. She screamed into the gag as another electric shock jolted her body. She walked along the corridor as fast as she could, praying the evil Miller wouldn't prod her with the goad again. She was wasting her time. Whenever she exhibited even the slightest sign of stumbling or slowing the goad went between her soft buttocks, causing her to stagger, screaming and gurgling through the gag.

The corridor was no more than a circular tunnel with a floor built in. In this area, the arched walls and ceiling were covered in white glazed tiles, and even through the narrow eye-slits, the bright reflected light was hurting her eyes.

The passageway seemed endless, the way forward

disappearing in a haze of light. Every so often doors led off to the sides, and there was the slight hum of machinery, and a none too gentle draught of cold air.

Occasionally Tristie's eyes widened in horror as she saw other girls—obviously captives like herself—being subjected to the most severe bondage and whippings by cruel looking men and women who were all dressed in similar fashion to the perverts she had seen at that night-club.

From time to time, they also met men and women in heavy, warm overalls, who took no more notice of Tristie's predicament than they would have taken of a beast being led along a country lane. It seemed as if, to them, Tristie was nothing, a mere piece of female flesh being moved about the place. Good God, here she was, naked and bound, wearing a ridiculous hood and a cruel gag, being herded like a beast in full view of complete strangers.

How could they just ignore such a spectacle? How could these people take her predicament for granted like this? Then she shuddered. Of course. Even from what little she had seen so far, she knew this place, wherever it was, would require staff to run it. These people then would be the staff. Which meant they were probably as perverted as Miller and the demented General. A bound naked female being herded about would be a familiar sight to them and would mean nothing, except perhaps to give them a thrill.

Then, suddenly, there was a tiled wall and a wide metal door in front of Tristie and she stopped as Miller stepped in front of her and opened the heavy door and pushed her through.

The cold air of the passageway beyond made her shiver as Miller prodded her on down the dim corridor. She felt her flesh rise into goose-pimples as her captor shut the door behind them with a heavy clang. Here the passageway, although still circular, was rough cast concrete and there was no proper floor. It sloped downwards, interminably it seemed, and the lighting was now infrequent; just a necklace of white bulbs casting harsh shadows.

Progress was slower, for Tristie kept tripping over the uneven surface, and soon her feet were bleeding, her toes stubbed and bruised, and she was shaking both from the cold and the constant attentions of the electric goad. She also had pressure pains in her ears as they went deeper into the hillside.

Now the cold was really taking a grip on Tristie and her naked body shook as if she had the ague. In her misery she sobbed, wretched heavy sobs, as her hands began to numb, from both the cold and from the tight bindings about her wrists.

Eventually the slope levelled out again and after a few more yards the whip cracked and the leather cut into the soft globes of her buttocks again, shattering her thoughts.

"Turn left! Through the red door."

They were in front of a side corridor, this time with a stone wall sealing it off. The door was made of iron, with a rectangular grille at eye-level. Through the grille, Tristie could hear the moans and sobs of other women and her heart raced in fear as she read the notice beneath the grille: HOLDING AREA—KEEP DOORS LOCKED.

Locked! Tristie shuddered and her heart raced. Was she going to be imprisoned and left?

The whip shattered her thoughts again and she screamed her anger and pain, almost falling over once more. Recovering her balance, she stepped through into the room.

Then the stink of unwashed human flesh.

She gagged, but resisted the urge to vomit. Her nervous gasps bubbled through the tube-gag as she gazed fearfully around. The room was similar to the one they had just left. It was dim, smelled musty, and it was freezing. Her heart dropped like a stone as she saw three square, iron cages. One of them was occupied by another naked and chained girl.

Miller opened an empty cage and prodded Tristie forward once more.

Shivering, her stomach heaving and fluttering, Tristie tried to ignore her desperate need to pee. She stepped into the cage, and Miller cut the nylon cord from her wrists, then he unshackled her arms and removed the hood and gag. A length of chain was hanging from the top of the cage, and Miller shackled the chain to Tristie's steel collar. Then he shoved her bottom down onto the rough wooden seat fixed across the rear of the cage, before lifting her arms, to chain them to the top of the cage. Finally he wound another piece of cold chain tightly about her waist and secured it to the back of the cage.

"Just to stop you from hanging yourself… you're here to learn how to give pleasure to our guests. You won't be leavin' this area until I think you're fit; until you're ready to submit. Then, when it pleases the General, he'll assess you again. The General isn't a patient man, so you better learn quick… I'll leave you to think about things. Someone will be here shortly, to give you a shower. No doubt you'll need it after a while!" He pointed to the grating in the floor of the cage. "You want to pee, you just pee!"

He locked the cage and walked out of the room, slamming and locking the heavy door behind him. His footsteps faded and Tristie began to sob quietly, as the lights went out and plunged her into lonely darkness.

8: A Slavegirl Serves her Master

Ruth was kneeling in darkness, trying to ignore the roar of static in her ears. Her half-hooded face was almost touching the floor and she could smell the dust in the carpet. She wanted to sneeze, but if anyone was in the room, she might be beaten if she did so.

She moaned to herself, trying to ease the discomfort of being bent almost double, her hands still secured tightly up her back. For once, Sheena had not whipped her. She had given her food, then, telling her she was to wait for a guest, had turned up the volume of the awful noise in the hood, and left her chained like this.

But wait! Had something gone wrong with the earphones?

The howling had suddenly stopped. For a few moments, her ears still rang with the noise, but gradually this went away and she realised someone had switched off the noise, someone was in the room with her.

Her spirits plummeted. One of the attendants probably, no doubt coming to 'tender her up', as they put it, for the guest. That was what usually happened. Then she felt herself being unchained from the floor, and her wrists were released from her collar, although her hands were left tied together.

Then the hood was gone and she gasped in surprise as her eyes adjusted to the light. Blinking, she looked up, not really believing what she was seeing. It wasn't an attendant. It was Nick! Oh God, Nick! But it couldn't be! Ruth's mouth dropped open and her eyes widened in amazement. Then she found her voice. "Nick! Oh Nick! You've come for me!" Then she began to laugh, almost hysterically. "You're too late Nick. I don't want to leave here now!"

Nick, her one-time lover, shook his head. "You won't be leaving." He cradled her head in his hands. "And it's my fault!" There seemed to be sadness in his voice. "It was me who brought you here in the first place."

"But Nick, I..."

He silenced her with a finger on her lips. "Shush! I'm not here to hurt you, Ruth."

She was suddenly battling with her emotions.

Part of her mind tried to tell her this was her Nick, but at the same time she knew he was not the Nick she had known. Neither did she need to be told why he had brought her here, recalling how her father had bullied her into giving evidence against the man she loved. However, that had been over three years ago, two and a half years before she had even been abducted. In fact, she hadn't known Nick was out of prison. She was still puzzled. "Then why Nick! If you arranged for me to be brought here. Why? To get even with me?"

"No!" he snapped. "Mainly to get back at your old man."

"But me as well."

"Yeah. Maybe. In a way."

"It doesn't matter now anyway." She gazed up at him— as a slavegirl. "I've been here too long. I know my place and not all of the guests are cruel. I even like some of them." Then she remembered. Whatever they had once meant to each other, whatever Nick had done to her, he was her Master now. She had to obey him, and she knew how she must address him. "Master, I'm sorry, I was forgetting..."

"Shh!" He placed his hand gently over her mouth. "I know. And maybe it's me who should apologise... Ahh, the hell with it. What's done is done!" He spread her knees wide. "Stay as you are, Ruth!"

"Yes Master!" She kept her head low as he began to undress. Then he nudged her with his toe. "Kiss my feet, Ruth."

"I am called Chu'mana, Master!"

"I've no time for that bullshit. You're my Ruth!"

Ruth smiled slightly then and suppressed a shudder of excitement. Obediently she leaned forward, and began to kiss his feet. In the months since she'd arrived, all resistance, any shame or embarrassment, had been beaten out of her.

But she still wanted to cling to the memories of what she and Nick had once had. Even though she was a slave now, if anyone was to be her Master, she hoped it would be Nick. She was strangely relieved—happy even—that it had been Nick who had caused all this in the first place.

"What does my Master wish of me?"

"Just remember that to everyone else here you are my slave! At least for tonight"

"I AM your slavegirl, Master."

"Yes. All right then." He began to stroke her hair, and she moaned to herself as she saw his erection was already beginning to thicken.

Ruth's juices began to flow; she felt the hot tingling inside. If Nick was to take her it would be wonderful. As a lover he had always been the best. She hadn't known about this side of him. Or had she? She knew he had always been a robust lover, to put it mildly. Surely he would be expert in using a slavegirl. She shuddered in suppressed ecstasy as she noticed the dog-whip he carried at his waist.

Again Ruth began to nuzzle at his feet, kissing his calves and ankles.

He stood over her, then growled at her, smiling slightly. "They've worked wonders with you Ruth! You're just a hot little slave now, aren't you?"

"Oh yes, Master," Ruth breathed. "I am yours. Please take me Master! Please!"

He stooped and caught hold of her hair, to yank her upwards. "On your feet."

Ruth's desire welled and she felt her juices running from her sex. God! This was better. To have Nick treat her as a slavegirl should be treated. Shuddering, revelling in the act of submission, she obeyed.

"Master! What do you wish of me?"

Nick sighed. "You really have learned." He prodded her stomach with his finger. "Hope you haven't forgotten how to screw. I'll give you a bath and then we can find out." He caressed her cheek. "We're going outside, so it's got to be the hood and the lead again."

Ruth lowered her head and nodded. "Anything Master wishes!" She sank to her knees and remained still as he replaced the hood and clipped a chain to her collar. He jerked on the chain.

"Crawl!"

Like a dog, Ruth crawled after him, unseeing, as they went out of the room. Her heart hammered in anticipation. She gasped as the rough concrete scraped her skin. But she was not required to crawl very far. After a few yards Nick turned into a side passage and went to a blue door. He opened the door and the familiar smell of chlorine belched out with clouds of steam.

"On your feet and into the bathroom!"

He removed the hood again as she stepped into the large expensively tiled room and then paused at the edge of a marble-lined swimming bath. He unfastened her wrists and waited as she rubbed the circulation back into her hands.

Ruth remained at the edge of the pool. The water looked inviting and she wanted to plunge into it, but she knew she would have to wait for her Master's orders.

Nick ignored her, merely sliding down into the warm water, wading over towards a large, floating airbed. There was a sponge and a bar of soap on the bed.

"Bathe me!"

She climbed down into the bath, relishing the feel of the hot soothing water, smiling up at Nick, longing to feel his flesh with her hands, to feel his maleness in her body.

He threw the sponge and the soap into the water where it was deepest, and chuckled.

Ruth giggled. Suddenly it seemed so right for Nick to be teasing her with master/slavegirl games. She dived down and with some difficulty retrieved the bar of soap.

She began to soap his body, her fingers moving in languorous caresses as she lathered the soap into his skin.

She began to moan with desire as she teased his shaft to a fierce erection. Squeezing and massaging the huge penis she smiled at him. "Master is so big!" She felt her juices running as she remembered how it used to feel in her mouth, and she felt her lips opening, almost of their own accord.

She lowered her head and slowly took the whole shaft in her mouth. She felt her vagina burning as the bulbous head of his member nudged into the back of her throat. She allowed her tongue to twist around the shaft as she moved her head gently up and down, her fingers caressing his scrotum and the insides of his thighs.

Nick was squirming with pleasure now and suddenly he grabbed Ruth's head and pulled her away from him. "With your hands Ruth. Fetch me off with your hands!" He pushed her head away from him and lay back again.

Ruth groaned, writhed in the water, and clutched his member. Softly she slid her soapy fingers along the pulsing shaft, pulling his foreskin back, gently squeezing the glans at the end.

Nick roared out his pleasure and grabbed her hair. He pulled her face towards his, thrusting his tongue deep into her mouth.

Ruth began to wriggle, grinding her thighs together, longing for the penis to be deep in her body, but she began to masturbate him wildly as he delved his tongue deeper into her mouth.

His huge member swelled and pulsed as his sperm shot out to cover his belly, and he roared his passion.

Then he pulled Ruth away and chuckled.

"Clean me up with your tongue."

Trembling with suppressed desire, Ruth bowed her head again and began to lick the cooling sperm from his stomach, swallowing the creamy fluid like the sweetest nectar, until his belly was clean.

"Don't stop there. Lick all the soap off me."

"Yes Master!" Ruth bent her head to the task again, feeling

her juices rushing once more, as she relished in her submission to this man. Her heart leapt and she groaned in more ecstasy as she saw Nick's huge member beginning to swell once more. Then he leaned over the edge of the airbed and rolled off into the water.

"Out of the water. Lie on the floor!"

Puzzled, Ruth scrambled out onto the tiles, and obeyed him.

Nick climbed out of the bath himself and walked over to her. As he looked down at her, he smiled. "The floor's a bit hard, but then, so am I!" He knelt beside her, and began to caress her breasts.

She sighed, reached for him and pulled him down to her. "Oh Master! Take me!"

He growled, a softer sound, and spreading her legs. He entered her, his huge shaft sliding deep inside her warm, moist vagina. Again he growled his pleasure as Ruth, this submissive, luscious, soft-bodied slavegirl, responded; moaning in her passion; her hips moving against him; her tongue seeking the back of his throat. Ruth always had been good. At least, the General hadn't changed that. Except maybe for the better!

9: Tristie is to be Branded!

Tristie's awakening was abrupt and a scream was wrenched from her throat as an icy deluge of water shattered her slumber. It jerked her into wakefulness; to awareness that she had been moved. She was still in a cage, but this one was in the middle of a large square room. Her arms were now secured between her shoulders and fastened to her neck. Rawhide strips replaced the dog-collar.

She huddled into the corner of the cage, screaming as she saw the tall, well-formed blonde woman of about thirty-five who was showering her with the powerful jet. The woman was naked except for leather thigh boots, a wide leather belt nipping her waist, and a soft shiny leather cowl which covered the upper half of her face. She was laughing like a wild thing as she played the jet over the helpless Tristie. Despite the cowl, Tristie recognised the woman and she trembled.

Sheena!

Tristie tried to avoid the water jet, but there was nowhere for her to go. She gasped for breath as the icy water took the air from her lungs, chilling her skin until she felt the goose-pimples rising. She started to shiver and tried to huddle further into the corner, pressing her freezing flesh against the rough bars of her prison, miserable now, just waiting for her tormentor to tire of the sport. Gasping and spluttering, she clenched her teeth. Damn them! She wouldn't cry for mercy.

Then a more urgent need took over her mind.

The need to breathe, as the leather thongs about her neck began to shrink. She began to gurgle and choke, her legs thrashing about, her feet banging into the iron bars, and her lungs heaving for the air that would not come. Tristie could feel her cheeks beginning to bloat, her eyes beginning to bulge, and her swollen tongue starting from between her lips. She knew she was near to death as the rawhide strips cut deeper into her neck...

Tristie half realised that the hose had been switched off and Sheena was unlocking the door, taking hold of her wringing wet hair. Tristie heard Sheena curse again before cutting the thongs and then felt herself being pushed into the corner of the cage.

Still dizzy, coughing and spluttering, her throat feeling as though it was on fire, Tristie scrambled to her feet. She had vivid recollection of this woman parading her around that terrible sawdust ring. Tristie also remembered the woman's skill with the whip; and she had to avoid that whip! Obediently she got up and stood, panting, before Sheena. She lowered her head in submission, almost without thinking about it. Were they breaking her, or was it true what they said; that she was a natural submissive?

Sheena grinned smugly, and stretched out her right hand to caress Tristie's body.

"Kneel!"

Tristie still had her arms secured behind her back, but she sank to her knees, tottering a little and lowering her head again. It did suddenly seem natural to be subservient to this demented woman. And wasn't there the tiniest thrill running through her as she bowed her head; weren't her thighs really becoming wet with her own juices? This woman was quite lovely, in a harsh sort of way. There was something erotic in the way her nudity was emphasised by the scant leather which adorned her body; in the way her features were half-hidden; in the way her waist was nipped by the thick leather belt; and in the way the creaminess of her shapely thighs was enhanced by the dark leather of her boots, and the delicious swell of her love-mound.

And the whip! The ever-ready whip!

Tristie shuddered, her juices flowing ever more freely, as she gazed in fascination at the whip hanging from the belt...

Sheena sneered at Tristie. "You remember me? I'm Sheena. I ran you the other day." She chuckled as she removed the hood. "God, but you ran well!" She caressed Tristie's hair. "Soon, you'll really get to know and hate me!" She sniggered. "Not to worry, I'm going to teach you to give real pleasure! You probably think you're pretty good in bed, but you don't know the half of it!" she prodded Tristie with the handle of her whip, "yet!"

She took hold of Tristie's tethered wrists, pulling her arms upwards and over her bowed head.

"Kiss my feet!"

The thigh boots were covered in filth from the straw-littered floor, but Tristie obeyed. She bent forward, pushing her head down and thrusting her buttocks up, to kiss the filthy toecaps.

Sheena let go of Tristie's arms, so her captive could kneel upright again. Automatically Tristie lowered her head, as she knelt in front of Sheena.

"That wasn't too bad, but soon you'll be doing it as though you mean it!" She tilted Tristie's head up. "Now! You will remember to address me as Mistress at all times! And I mean at all times!"

Tristie looked up into Sheena's face. Best to play along with these monsters. "Yes, Mistress!" she murmured, and then waited obediently for the next command.

Sheena was smiling slightly. She grabbed Tristie's hair and pulled her close to her lower belly, pushing her face into the fine mat of hair at the vee of her thighs.

Tristie trembled slightly, but couldn't deny the quiet thrill she felt as she scented the musky odour of the woman's genitals. Quivering still, she tried to deny her feelings then whimpered as Sheena pulled her to her feet.

Sheena smiled at her. "You're going to make an excellent slavegirl!" She caressed Tristie's body again and seemed to pay a lot of attention to her left buttock and flank. Sheena kneaded the flesh there. "Just the right amount of meat, my pet."

Tristie shivered. Sudden loathing choked her. But she

knew she dare not show it. She offered a fierce prayer, hoping Sheena would not hurt her. But, reluctantly, Tristie was admitting to herself that she was in a desperate position. To these maniacs she really was no more than a slave and they could do as they wished with her.

As for now, well, Sheena still had the whip and Tristie had no illusions left. For the slightest transgression, real or imagined, Sheena would slash her flesh with the whip. Her punishment would cease only when she fell into unconsciousness.

Sheena smiled wickedly. "You're really beginning to learn, slave. I can see it in your eyes." She tilted Tristie's head up. "Isn't that so?"

Tristie knew she had to agree. "Yes Mistress!" Strangely though, she had barely thought about her response, had not even hesitated. The words had come out almost by instinct. But then, after all, she was a captive. Why shouldn't she behave like one? It was the easiest way out, at least until she could find a way to escape. Oh God! No! It wasn't really beginning to seem natural to her, was it?

Again Sheena grinned, patted Tristie's cheek and kissed her lips softly. "There's a good little slavegirl!" Her tongue traced wetly across Tristie's lips, then she went to the side of the room, to a square wooden chest. She reached inside and took out a heavy brass collar.

Tristie filled with shame as she tried to dismiss the thought of Sheena's lips on her own. The woman was a lesbian! Tristie shuddered, but stood in complete submission, in fear of the unknown, as Sheena came to her and fixed the collar about her slender neck.

Sheena looked at her captive, and grinned slyly. She felt Tristie's vagina, gently slipping her fingers into her warmth. Her fingers moved about gently and Tristie, much as she tried to resist, again found herself getting wet.

Sheena leered triumphantly. "You really are learning." She pinched the inside of Tristie's thigh, delighted as Tristie yelped in pain. "Or are you just playing along, hoping to escape?"

Tristie was filled with fear. Had this woman seen through her act! God, the whip! She had to convince this woman she was submitting. "No Mistress! Oh, no Mistress! I'm learning, Mistress, I really am!"

It seemed to work. "Of course you are!"

"Yes, yes, I really am, Mistress!"

Sheena grabbed Tristie's chin in a vicious grip and hissed into her face. "Speak only when you are told to!" Her grip tightened on Tristie's throat, turning her sobs into choking sounds. "And it's about time you realised that a whipping is something you'll have to get used to here. Anyone would think I'd really hurt you!" She pushed Tristie roughly against the wall. Then, reaching towards one of the wall-racks, she selected a long length of wicked toothed dog-chain. "This is just to remind you that you're a slave!"

Still sneering, Sheena threaded the thin chain through the ring at the front of Tristie's collar. "You'd better not be thinking of escape!" She centred the chain, and then fastened it with a padlock beneath Tristie's chin. Then she patted Tristie's cheek again. "It's impossible anyway, but we still punish those who try... One thing more," she squeezed Tristie's throat with her strong fingers, "you call me Mistress or Mistress Sheena!"

Incredulous, Tristie stared at Sheena. "But I did!"

Sheena took Tristie's left breast in her hand and squeezed viciously, pinching the nipple between finger and thumb. "I just told you slut! You speak only when told to!" The woman did not release the pressure until Tristie was on her knees, gasping.

Sheena laughed. "But of course, you did call me Mistress, didn't you?" She shrugged. "How silly of me. I never even noticed. It must be coming naturally to you!" Her grip tightened. "Except, from now on you say it as though you mean it! You understand me, slave?" She brandished the whip above the terrified Tristie.

"Yes Mistress!" Tristie wailed. "I'm sorry Mistress!" She lowered her head instinctively, and barely believing what she was doing, began to kiss Sheena's thighs, casting aside all shame, all pride, knowing anything was better than that whip! "Please Mistress," Tristie sobbed into the woman's scented flesh, "I beg of you. Forgive me! Don't beat me!"

Sheena pushed Tristie away. "Don't forget, then."

"No Mistress! I won't forget Mistress." Then she screamed as the whip cut into her body.

"Of course you won't forget, slave!" Sheena stood back then and meted out three more good slashes with the whip. "Just to remind you again! You do as you are told here. You are a slave. A mere animal. Do you understand?"

Cowering, Tristie sobbed miserably. "Yes, Mistress!"

Sheena pulled Tristie's shackled wrists up behind her back and secured them to the collar. She then picked up the two ends of the toothed dog-chain and bent towards her captive.

Tristie began to shake, trying to bear the strain of her arms bent high up her back and the chafing of the shackles between her wrists, knowing she had to suffer whatever was in store for her.

Sheena took the two lengths of chain down the front of Tristie's naked body and crossed them between her fine breasts, before taking them around her back, where she crossed them again, and wrapped them tightly around Tristie's waist. She led the two loose ends down through Tristie's crotch and pulled them backwards. The chain gouged into her tender sex. Tristie screamed as Sheena pulled, parting the fleshy globes of Tristie's buttocks, inching the chain into the lips of her anus.

Tristie screamed again. The chain bit even deeper into her labia as Sheena pulled it upwards, along Tristie's spine. Then came the click of another padlock as Sheena secured the ends to the back of the collar. Tristie groaned to herself. They seemed to be very fond of this particular form of bondage. If they did it to her much more, there would be nothing left of her genitals; nothing for anyone to enjoy, much less herself.

Sheena chuckled again and pushed a short iron bar between the two lengths of chain. Then she began to wind the chains until they were taut. Gradually the pressure of the chain between Tristie's legs became unbearable, and she began to struggle as the metal bit into her flesh. Her struggles were futile and Sheena just laughed as she wound the ratchet tighter and tighter.

She grinned into Tristie's face. "Come on, my little slave!" she said, "scream! Mistress Sheena wants to hear her little toy scream!

And Tristie did scream. Loud and long. In frantic agony as the chains bit deeper, until suddenly, just as she thought she would be cut in half, the torture stopped and Sheena wedged the iron rod between her elbows. Tristie heard the whip whistling through the air again and her hips jerked forward in an instinctive attempt to evade the lash.

But the whip didn't land.

Sheena chuckled and leaned close to Tristie's ear. "Just remember I have it!" Softly, she allowed the whip to caress Tristie's buttocks. Then, without warning, the whip slashed into Tristie's soft flesh and she screamed, falling to the floor. The whip cut into her defenceless body three more times and then, ignoring her screams, Sheena lifted her by her hair.

"Walk! We walk!"

Before Tristie could struggle, darkness engulfed her as a leather blindfold was strapped around her eyes. She began to panic. Then Sheena was forcing something between her soft lips. Tristie felt a hard ring being forced behind her teeth, stretching her lips wide, and she pushed her tongue through another vile tube-gag. The gag was secured behind her head. Tristie felt a bridle being fitted to her face and grunted in pain as her head was forced back again. She felt the straps of the bridle being tightened about her face and she trembled in fright as Sheena whispered a harsh warning into her ear.

"Don't bump into anything. If you do, you get the whip." She prodded Tristie forward with the handle of the whip. "Just a little game we play to make the walk a bit more interesting."

Sheena pushed Tristie towards the door. "Like all slaves here, you're just a beast and you have to be marked." Again she sniggered and pinched Tristie's left flank viciously. "Now!" she commanded, "WALK! You're going to feel the branding iron!"

Tristie felt her insides curl and her heart began to race. Branded! Oh God! No! They wouldn't! They couldn't! Surely they weren't that depraved! Pure terror forced her to swivel her hooded face towards Sheena. She tried to speak. Useless. The wide ring behind her teeth turned her protests to mere gurgles.

"It is useless to resist! You WILL be branded! Then maybe you'll realise you really are just an animal here. A piece of sex-meat!"

The whip slashed down again and again and Tristie screamed into the gag, twisting her hips away from the threat of the lash. Awkwardly, she stumbled and the whip descended again, slashing into the cheeks of her bottom as she tottered over. Tristie fell to the floor, shrieking in agony as the whip landed again and again. She almost blacked-out before Sheena ceased her demented assault.

Rolling herself into a ball, Tristie cringed against the rough wall of the passageway, unable to see from where the next blow would come. She trembled violently.

She heard Sheena mock her inability to resist.

Tristie could do nothing but gurgle, her saliva flowing through the ring-gag and over her naked breasts. She was still shaking with fear. If this mad woman said she was to be branded, then branded she would be. She had to accept it.

She began to walk blindly forward. Her arms screamed in burning agony, and the chain cut deep into her sexual parts with each step. She gasped each time Sheena prodded her buttocks with the whip-handle.

"Kneel!"

Tristie obeyed. Sheena had moved behind her. Tristie began to pant with fear as a chain was clipped to her collar, and her arms were released. The relief was delicious as the pressure came off her elbows and the chain between her legs loosened. But the respite was brief, and Tristie squealed as Sheena gave the chain a jerk.

"Heel!"

Shame filled Tristie's being, but she obeyed all the same. She crawled after Sheena. Sheena tugged on the chain, forcing her to keep up. The chain was pulled taut again and Tristie screamed into the gag as the rough concrete dug into her hands and knees. It seemed like an eternity before Sheena finally halted and moved behind her.

"Stand!"

Tristie struggled to her feet and stood waiting, wincing as Sheena shackled her wrists behind her back once again and clipped her wrists to the collar.

"Walk on!"

Tristie walked forward, behaving like the slavegirl she knew she was becoming; suffering the pain of the whip handle digging into her buttocks again and again. She staggered in her attempts to keep her balance. Then, a few steps later, Sheena slashed her yet again with the whip.

"Stop!"

Tristie sobbed as she halted. Then she drew in a nervous gasp as she heard the scrape of a heavy door opening in front of her.

"Walk!"

The submissive Tristie stepped forward, then wailed as the whip resumed its cruel lesson.

"Halt!"

The sound of the door being closed, then relief as the bridle, blind-fold and gag were removed. Tristie attempted to control the trembling of her legs and the fluttering in her stomach, as her eyes slowly adjusted to the new light.

One thought consumed her.

She was to be branded.

It would hurt... terribly.

Being burnt had always been the one thing she had dreaded more than anything; even as a little girl...

10: THE BRANDING ROOM

The room was big and square. Bright fluorescent light shone down, making harsh images of the discarded items of clothing strewn about the straw-littered floor. In the middle of the room there was a bunk where Keane stood, smiling slightly, and tapping his right thigh with the coiled dog-whip he held in his right hand.

He looked down at the bound slavegirl. Most of the fight seemed to have been well and truly beaten out of her. She was shaking, almost uncontrollably. Sheena stood over her: clearly she had been at work.

Keane smiled slightly. "Unchain her please."

When the girl had been unfettered and was completely naked but for her collar, he motioned to her. She swallowed, obviously trying to control her fear, and ever so reluctantly obeyed, crossing the room to stand shaking before him, head lowered.

He pushed the handle of his whip beneath her chin and lifted her head. "Are you learning?"

"Yes, Master!"

The girl's responses seemed instinctive now, but still she had some modesty, for she placed her arms in front of her body, crossing her wrists and covering her sex.

Keane growled at her and snatched her arms away, pulling them straight down her sides.

"You never, ever cover yourself! Understand?"

"Yes, Master!"

"Don't forget it." He placed his left hand around her neck, pushing the collar up to her chin. "Now, sit on the bed."

Her eyes widened and her cheeks went even paler. Keane pushed her shoulders down as she perched her buttocks on the edge of the mattress. He tilted her chin upwards, his smile cruel. "You are to be branded!"

The slavegirl began to shake all over then and her eyes widened. She made to speak, but Sheena's harsh voice cut in. "A whipping first, Nick!"

Keane held the girl's shoulders still, looking at the welts already to be seen on the white skin. He shook his head. "I think she's had enough of that, for now. Seems you had your fun already."

The woman shrugged. "Suit yourself Nick. But the General..."

"Stuff the General!" he said. "I'll whip the girls when I feel it's necessary, or when I really want to."

Sheena lifted her shoulders in a shrug. "It's your funeral Nick!"

"Not if you keep your mouth closed."

"There's one way to guarantee that Nick," Sheena said, licking her lips and showing him the point of her tongue.

He gave her a wry smile. "I don't want to kill you Sheena!"

She sulked. "You know what I meant Nick!"

"Later. Maybe!"

"I'll leave you to it then." She blew him a kiss and closed the door behind her.

Keane turned back to the girl and reached for a thick leather belt hanging over the bedhead.

"Hands on your head."

Mutely she obeyed, and Keane slipped the belt round her waist. There were two steel rings stitched into the leather and he adjusted the belt so that there was a ring just above her hips. Then he tightened the belt, forcing a gasp of pain from her as he fastened the large buckle at the front. He pulled her arms down and shackled her wrists to the rings and then, in one fluid movement, pushed her backwards to the mattress and flipped her legs up to swivel her body so she lay along the bed.

His gaze travelled along the shapely body and down the quivering thighs. He saw branding as blemishing fine goods, but that was how the General dispelled any illusions a slavegirl might have. It made them aware fully, even spiritually, that they belonged to him.

He was probably right, Keane reflected.

It was time to start.

"Stand!"

She sucked in a nervous gasp, but obeyed, swinging her legs to the floor and standing up, her movements awkward.

Keane turned her to her right and nudged her towards an alcove, where the room was darker. There was a low pillory here and she turned in panic when she saw it.

"No! No!"

"Do you want the whip?"

She trembled again. "No, Master."

"Then do as you're told." He pushed her towards the pillory and, shoving her to her knees, he opened the pillory and pushed her head down into the semi-circular opening. He slammed the top of the pillory down, imprisoning her, and fastened the bolt. Then he twisted her long tresses into a thick hank and draped them over her right shoulder, completely exposing her back and buttocks.

She was quivering, sobbing, her lungs heaving in air. Her fine toned muscles were jumping about in fearful anticipation; the knowledge of how vulnerable she was clearly added to the turmoil in her mind.

Keane could even smell the sweat of her fear.

Plain terrified.

She had good reason.

Going to a wooden rack on the wall, he took down a half-hood, went back to her and slipped the soft pliant leather over the top half of her face. He stood up to gaze down on that splendid body, now blind as well as helpless and naked.

His hormones were getting steamed up.

She was delicious.

A sadist's dream.

Which, on this island, was her misfortune.

Then the door opened and two naked collared girls came in, carrying a glowing brazier on two long steel poles.

"Put it down here." Keane pointed to a spot about three

yards in front of the pillory.

They hefted their burden over and set it down as they had been told. Then they sank to their knees before him, sweat glistening on their bodies; slicking their long hair, which touched the floor as they hung their heads in complete submission.

He had to admit that these two were both stacked. They were fit, lean and graceful, well tanned; although, at the moment, they were dirty.

No doubt they had just been taken from between the shafts of a pony-trap. He noticed the reddened patches around their shoulders, and the recent whip marks on their backs and buttocks. That explained their excellent physical shape. The General would have had them lifting weights every day and running naked around the island; training them to perfection.

Ready for sale.

Keane allowed himself a moment's idle wondering. Did these girls know they were to be passed on to Sheik Malik? Better for them if they didn't know. Save them a lot of stress. Christ! Those Arabs had things to perfection. They really knew how to treat a woman; especially white women. Sheik Malik in particular had a big thing about trap-racing; using white slavegirls to pull the gigs. That was if the girls were lucky. If not, they might find themselves chained, naked, to an oar in one of his heavy old-time so-called racing cutters.

The two slavegirls were panting slightly, and their pert breasts were gently heaving as they licked their lips seductively, virtually begging to be allowed to take him in their mouths.

But they were stinking a little.

Sweat and stink turned some guys on, but not Keane.

He liked his women clean. At least to begin with.

Any sweating, Keane wanted to be the one who made them sweat.

He made a circular motion with his hand.

Disappointment flickered in their faces, but, in silence, they turned from him.

A casual flick to their buttocks with his whip and they crawled from the room.

When they had gone, Keane turned back to the imprisoned Tristie. Her hooded face was bathed by the glow from the brazier and, already, the heat was getting to her. Sweat was beginning to run from beneath the hood, and the shakes were really taking hold, as the fiery coals made themselves felt, even through the leather. She gave an involuntary scream; obviously realising she really was going to be branded.

She shuddered. She wailed. "No. Please. No! Don't burn me please!" Her splayed thighs were wobbling from side to side as she shook and her body almost collapsed, prevented from doing so only by the pillory. She was gasping, panting, her whole body shaking with terror.

Keane stepped over to her, and kicked her knees wider apart.

The terrified girl sucked in another gasp as he fastened iron shackles, first to her ankles and then, heavier ones, just below her knees, pinning her shins to the straw covered floor.

She began to give out piteous sobs. "Oh God! No. Please. I'll do anything. Please. Don't burn me!" But she was wasting her time. She must know it. "Oh God, no!" she sobbed. "God help me."

"He's not a member of our Club," Keane said. "But you are." He gave her hair a sharp tug. "And what were you told to call us?"

She said nothing now, just whimpered.

Keane lifted the whip, whistling the vicious weapon through the air and slashing into her buttocks, wrenching a scream of agony from her.

"Does that refresh your memory?"

Then she remembered. Don't speak without permission.

She screamed out in terror. "Master. Please Master. Let me go. Please Master!"

"Do you want to come out of the pillory?"

"Oh please Master. Yes." She trembled. "Please, please don't burn me Master. Let me go. Please. I'll do anything."

At that moment the door of the room opened and Sheena entered. She came over to Keane and pulled him close to her leather-clad body. She raised her lips to his and gave him a soft kiss. Her hands slipped down the front of his jeans and she tickled his penis. "When is this monster going to make me scream, Nick?" She giggled and licked her lips. "Or shall I suck you dry?"

Keane smiled down at her, and shook his head, remembering. She'd almost bitten one guy's dick clean off.

In her passion.

So they said.

Keane was taking no chances. "You're too much woman for me just now, Sheena."

She shrugged, then smiled, mischievously. "I can wait." A brief kiss and she disengaged herself to step over to the brazier. She snatched the hood away from the girl's face and then sneered at her as she jiggled one of the irons in the glowing coals. She looked at Keane. "I'd like to brand this one Nick."

Keane shrugged. There would be others and he would get almost as much fun out of watching. Also, it might take Sheena's mind off his loins.

"Be my guest."

Sheena bent towards the girl and flashed an evil smile. "Are you ready for this?"

The veins in the girl's neck stood out and her eyes almost popped as she saw the white-hot coals in front of her. Her piteous screams began to reach fever-pitch.

Sheena silenced her with a slash of her whip. "Stop snivelling! You don't know what pain is, yet." She took the iron from the coals and held it up in front of the girl's face to show the white-hot leaf shape.

The girl's head lolled then as she almost fainted. She began to howl, becoming incoherent, and Keane admitted to a twinge of pity. But he stifled it and stepped back to watch Sheena brand the girl.

Give her the mark that said she belonged to the General.

A quarter inch deep, oak-leaf shape, burned into her flesh.

It was going to hurt the girl. Really hurt. But she was lucky.

She might have been sold to Sheik Malik.

Now, Sheena put the iron back into the coals and went around behind Tristie. She fastened a piece of dog-chain to the rear of Tristie's collar, before unlocking the pillory. Then, grabbing the golden hair, Sheena pulled her captive upwards from the pillory and right back against the leg shackles. She clipped the end of the dog-chain to a ratchet attached to a ringbolt in the floor and began to turn the ratchet.

Tristie's frantic screams echoed about the room, her voice cracking as she was winched backwards until she was lying almost flat, her legs bent in agony underneath her buttocks. Her folded thighs were splayed open, displaying her sex and her body was bowed upwards, stretching the skin of her breasts taut. Her arms were held tight against her sides, not even allowing her to support her own weight, and she gasped as she tried to move.

Sheena began to walk around the helpless girl, inspecting her from every angle. Tristie was breathing in ragged gasps and her body was trembling. Only her head was free to move about and she tried to follow Sheena about the room, her fearful gaze widening her eyes in terror.

Then Sheena stooped down and, with one final turn on the ratchet, patted the trembling thigh. Tristie began to shake as though she had the ague and her sobbing became irregular. "Oh my God NO," she screamed, "please No. You mustn't. Please let me go. Oh PLEASE, PLEASE LET ME GO!"

Sheena just laughed and went over to the brazier to take out the iron again. Frowning in concentration, she lowered the glowing iron slowly towards the glorious swell of Tristie's unshaven sex.

Feeling the blast of heat, Tristie screamed again. She tried to struggle but there was no free movement for her body at all.

Sheena allowed the iron to singe the downy pubic hairs, before drawing it away. "No. Not there," she murmured, patting the girl's stomach. "The guests might want to use that."

Tristie continued to beg. "Don't burn me. Please, don't!"

"I'll tell you just once more." Sheena held the iron in front of the girl's eyes. "You call me Mistress." She allowed the hot iron, now softening to red, to pass within a fraction of the girl's lips.

Tristie cringed. "Please Mistress," she sobbed. "Please don't do this."

"If you don't keep still I might burn you by accident." Again, Sheena let the iron pass within a hair of her helpless victim's skin, this time pausing as she reached the stretched breasts.

Tristie turned her head to the side, screaming, and her voice cracked, hysterical now. The iron moved downwards to the offered hips and Tristie let out one long piercing shriek of agony as the iron finally touched her left thigh and began to sizzle.

Sheena's breathing became heavy; almost ecstatic; groaning with pleasure. With a rapturous expression showing in her face, she pressed the fiery oak-leaf into the girl's skin, peering with intense concentration at the puckering flesh and the bubbling juices as the iron burned its way into the soft flesh. The stench of burning filled the room and the girl let out one more prolonged howl of anguish, before she fainted away.

Tristie's relief was short-lived, for she was revived with

a douche of cold water. Spluttering, she came back to full consciousness and immediately felt the pain on her thigh.

Sheena leaned over her and patted her cheek. "Now we have to fix you up with some pretty jewellery, so our guests will be interested in you." She turned to Keane. "You, Nick?"

Keane gave her a cold smile and nodded, stepping over to the wall rack. He took down a propane blowtorch and a stainless steel skewer, before walking back to the shackled slavegirl.

Tristie began to shake again as she watched him approaching her and her eyes were wide with terror, her gaze locked onto the blowtorch Keane was holding.

Keane smiled, then, with a casual glance at her, lit the torch, holding it close to Tristie's face as he adjusted the flame. Still smiling, he poked the end of the skewer into the blue flame and held it so Tristie could watch the metal turn white-hot.

Tristie's mind was a seething mass of terror and agony. What had she done to deserve all this? They were treating her like a beast. And as if the branding hadn't been enough, she knew that Keane was now going to pierce her body. She prayed. Prayed she would become unconscious again and stay that way, so she wouldn't feel anything.

Then she began to gabble, mumbling and whining, hardly knowing what she was saying as Keane bent towards her. She struggled against her bonds, but knew it was hopeless. She moaned and tried to move her head, but it was a mere waste of time and effort.

"Keep still," Keane said. "Struggling only makes things worse!"

Gasping for breath, Tristie felt her heart jump in sheer terror then as she felt her right nipple being pulled outwards from her breast. She shrieked as the skewer was pushed through her flesh, and a ring was fitted. She fainted, but, almost immediately, was revived with a bucket of cold water from Sheena.

Keane wasted no time, and again Tristie shrieked out as her left nipple was also pierced and a further ring fitted and squeezed shut. Her body was slicked with blood-fluids as her natural defences came into play against the burns, and she wriggled against her bonds, screaming in her torment. But they hadn't finished yet. She howled her anger and agony as Keane grabbed each of her ears in turn, to pierce the lobes and pinch further rings in place.

Then the worst agony of all, as Keane pulled a vertical fold of flesh out from just below her navel. The skewer did its evil work again, but this time Keane wriggled the hot metal about, enlarging the hole.

Tristie bucked and heaved her hips, trying to ease the burning pain, and yelled her agony to the uncaring walls as the hot steel burned a large hole in her flesh. Then the ring was fitted into the hole and clipped shut. Tristie was beside herself with agony now, and her head was whipping from side to side as she tried to drive the searing pain from her body.

Ignoring Tristie's struggling and screaming, Sheena bent to release her from the chain which was holding her body flat on her back, and pulled her up into a kneeling position. Then she went to the rack again to collect a number of fine silver chains.

She held the chains up for the tortured girl to see. "Beauty chains, for a beautiful slavegirl." She shook the chains, just enough to make them jingle; an almost musical tinkling. "The guests love them. Especially on a slavegirl like you!"

She clipped one chain to each of Tristie's nipple rings, then secured the two ends to the ring in Tristie's belly. The bright metal rested alluringly against the slight swell of Tristie's belly, shimmered as her abused body shook with pain and fright.

Sheena stepped forward, unfastened Tristie's arms from her sides, and pulled them in front of her, to snap her wrists in manacles, separated by about a foot of chain. Sheena grinned at Tristie. "Now we see how you perform for a guest," she sneered, as she fastened a long piece of hempen rope to the centre of the manacle chain. She walked towards the door, pulling on the rope.

Tristie had no option but to follow, sobbing and trembling, wondering what was to happen to her now.

11: Riding the Pleasure Saddle

When she regained her senses, Tristie could still feel a burning sensation on her thigh. Then she forgot all about the branding for a moment as she became aware of herself. She frowned, wincing as she felt rough stone against her back, chafing her skin. There was a harsh smell of leather and a tough unyielding skin enveloped her nose and mouth. She had been gagged, this time with a tube-gag. The hard rim lodged behind her teeth. She could feel her arms, stretched upwards and outwards to the limit, her wrists manacled, tight against the stonework, and her buttocks scraping against the flinty surface.

Her legs were also stretched outwards, pulling her crotch apart, and her ankles were shackled to the wall. Most of her weight seemed to be taken in the vee of her thighs, where she could feel something spreading them apart; something which felt like...

Like a saddle!

Opening her eyes, she blinked in the strong light bouncing off the white tiles which covered the vaulted ceiling and the continuous wall of the circular room. As her vision returned, she glanced down. She was suspended, her feet about six inches above the floor. She could also see the end of the saddle protruding from between her thighs. The saddle was made of a soft plastic material and was about the size and shape of a man's thigh. She shifted slightly. Her gasp of pain gurgled through the tube gag as she moved, and she caught her breath. God! Her vagina was being stretched wide and she could feel something enormous and hard inside her, something which was pushing deep inside her body.

She groaned, wondering what these monsters would do to her next, then jumped, nervously, as a door in the wall opposite opened and a woman came into the room.

The woman was dressed in a tight-fitting yellow Lycra suit which emphasised her fine figure, but her features were hidden behind a silken hood, and all that Tristie could see were her large brown eyes, her full lips, and the strands of blonde hair peeping from beneath the hood.

Sheena!

Sheena walked over to her and looked upwards. "High, but not so mighty, eh bitch!"

Tristie moaned slightly, trying to speak through the gag.

Sheena merely slashed her whip into Tristie's left thigh. "Silence!" She caressed the red wheal on Tristie's thigh. "And when I let you speak, you call me Mistress. Got it?"

Tristie nodded, gurgling her answer through the gag. She was under no illusions at all by now. She knew that to these perverts she was just a slave and, despite her abhorrence of the situation, she knew she had to submit.

Sheena patted the saddle. "I'm introducing you to the pleasure saddle. The General's latest idea. A good one, don't you think? You're wriggling already, you sexy little bitch, and the dildo isn't switched on yet." She grinned. "A demonstration?" She smiled evilly. "Unless you'd prefer to be taken down now, for discipline?" She reached out and grabbed a handful of Tristie's soft buttock, squeezing sadistically, wrenching another gasp of pain from her. "I think so, yes! But first, I want to watch you squirm." Mistress Sheena grinned and leaned forward to press the switch on the saddle.

Tristie gasped as she felt a sudden tingle in her vagina. The tingling became stronger and soon she was forced to squirm, trying to deny the pleasure she knew was mounting. But she was unable to conceal her ecstasy as the pulsations of the dildo excited the sensitive membranes inside her body. As the imitation cock swelled, the vibrations thundered through her body and, despite herself, Tristie began to moan as her juices began to flow.

Soon she was writhing on the saddle and mewling her passion through the tube-gag, as sheer ecstasy took hold of her. Involuntarily, she grabbed hold of her short wrist chains and began pulling on her shackles, lifting herself upwards, before ramming her hips down, deep and hard over the huge dildo. Grinding herself down onto the saddle, she writhed her hips and belly, her lovely head drooping in sexual abandon, her golden hair, wet with perspiration, flicking about her naked breasts like a bead curtain, as she wriggled her torso, squealing and moaning in her pleasure.

Her juices ran from her body, slicking between her soft white thighs and the saddle. Her thighs clasped the saddle in a woman's love grasp, the wetness slopping, her flesh sliding against the plastic as she jiggled her hips around until she felt her orgasm mounting. Arching her hips forwards, again she let out soft sounds of passion; the warming feeling wrenching her soul, going through every fibre of her body.

Then the pulsating suddenly stopped and Tristie sagged, gasping with the efforts she had been making.

Sheena's breathing was ragged, as her gaze wandered over Tristie's shining sweat-run body. "You're a gorgeous little slut," she said. "A real package of sex!" She took her quirt from her belt and gazed upwards, her expression hardening.

She reached out to switch on the saddle again. Then she raised the quirt. Viciously, she began laying the lash into Tristie's chained body, extracting screams of agony as it cut into defenceless flesh.

Tristie didn't know what to do with herself. The kiss of the whip was agony, but at the same time intense pleasure was being wrung from her by the surging of the huge pulsating dildo inside her body. She ground her hips down onto the saddle, feeling the dildo tingling deep inside her vagina. She felt the pain of the manacles digging into her wrists and struggled in her agony as the whip landed on her body.

The experience was becoming deeply erotic as her struggles to avoid the pain caused her greater pleasure on the saddle, and her squeals turned to whimpers of perverse delight as the pain and the pleasure went on.

Then Tristie sagged as Sheena tired of her sport, stopped the whipping and switched off the pleasure saddle. She gazed up at the tortured Tristie. "You really are a gorgeous little peach! I'm looking forward to playing with you this afternoon!"

Half aware that Sheena was unshackling her, Tristie trembled, docile now, and she allowed herself to be lowered to her knees on the tiled floor.

With her lips twisted into a cold smile, Sheena grabbed Tristie's hair. "Come on, slut! Time to clean you up a little." She ran her hand along Tristie's right flank. "Oh yes! Am I going to enjoy you!" She dragged Tristie to her feet and undid the tube-gag. "I won't need this thing. I've got nothing to shove in your mouth!" She giggled and then pushed Tristie towards a doorway. "Now, move that pretty little arse!" She cracked the whip. "Keep out of my range, or those buttocks will feel the whip."

Tristie drooped her head and moaned, but she allowed Mistress Sheena to herd her through the door and along the passageway. Then a crack of the whip on her buttocks reminded her to run. Still whimpering, she broke into an awkward jog.

12: KEANE INTERROGATED

Keane's world fell in on him at eight-thirty, next morning. Of course, he didn't appreciate the exact time. Just as he stepped aboard his yacht 'Kukri' for the daily checks, something just hit him over the head.

When he recovered, he was sitting in a Windsor chair, nursing an almighty headache. As full awareness returned he realised his arms and legs were bound to the chair, and that his leather coat had gone. His shirt was still on, but it was open to the waistband of his jeans.

He blinked in the harsh light.

He was in the General's bedroom.

What the hell? He looked about him, bewildered.

The General was there.

Sheena was there.

Ruth was there, on the bed, lying on her back, naked, with her slim wrists tied to the bedposts. Her legs had been hoisted up and pulled backwards by chains, attached to ringbolts in the wall behind the bed. The bed was well away from the wall, so that Ruth's body was folded over backwards, her legs wide apart, displaying her gorgeous sex-mound, her soft, creamy inner thighs and her tight rounded buttocks, all exposed to the whip.

Sheena, her face a mask of sadistic pleasure, was standing near the bed. In her right hand a short dog-whip swung gently, with Ruth's exposed parts well within range.

Keane shook his head, trying to clear the fog of pain, trying to think, to understand what was going on. Hopeless.

He tested the ropes.

As he had guessed, also hopeless.

He was in trouble.

But the worst of it was he couldn't see why.

He sure as Hell wanted to know why, and when he got free of these ropes, somebody would...

"Are you with us Nick?"

Keane looked at Brice and vaguely wondered why he had ever regarded this creep as a General. But it was second nature after all this time. He cleared foul tasting spittle from his throat and spat. "What is this?"

The General ignored him. "Liven him up, Sheena!"

Sheena's hand twitched, and the end of her dog-whip slashed out towards Keane. The tip of the leather cracked right in front of Keane's chest, the end of the whip just touching his skin.

It hurt: burned.

Not much, but bad enough to raise a small red wheal.

Keane pulled away. "You bitch Sheena!" He was getting angry, and again he struggled against the ropes.

"I warned you yesterday Nick. I think you're getting soft," the General said. "We can't have that! Sheena!"

Again the whip slashed towards Keane, this time contacting his chest with more force. Keane exploded a gasp of pain, "Bastards!" He struggled against the ropes again. "Get these ropes off me, or so help me, when I do get free..." Despite the bravado, he was more than a little scared and his mouth had begun to dry.

He was well aware of what Sheena could do with that whip.

He'd watched her work the girls often enough.

And he knew he wouldn't like it one bit more than they did.

He licked his lips. "When I get out of this chair, you little bitch..." His words ended in a roar of pain as the whip struck with full force, shredding the front of his shirt, searing its way into his chest. He heard Ruth scream out too, as he hung his head, grimacing, hiding his pain, trying to hold back genuine tears.

But Ruth hadn't been touched.

Her cry sounded more like sympathy.

The General caught Sheena's arm, just as she was drawing back for another blow. "That's enough! This isn't one of the girls." He looked at Keane and sighed. "I see my best operator getting soft." He pointed to the trussed and helpless Ruth. "Last night, this little beast must have thought she'd died and gone to slavegirl Heaven." He shook his head. "Then, Sheena tells me you decided not to whip the new slave before she was branded."

Then Ruth cried out:

"No! No! Please! Leave him be."

"Whip her!" The General didn't even turn his head.

Instantly, the room was reverberating to Ruth's agonised cries and the crack of leather biting flesh, as Sheena slammed the whip into the sensitive skin on the inside of the girl's thighs. The whip curled itself right around the meaty part of Ruth's left leg. Sheena pulled back on it, tightening the loop, before releasing it and drawing back for another blow.

The red weal left by the whip encircled the quivering thigh, and Sheena moved across to the other side, changed hands and slashed into the right leg. Another shriek of agony as Sheena raised another garter of red, just above the knee. Then Sheena stepped back and the whip thundered down into the exposed vee of the defenceless girl's thighs, slashing down into her sex-lips, extracting an ear-shattering wail.

Ruth's hips lifted a good two feet clear of the mattress as the blow landed, and she began to buck and writhe in her agony, trying to wring the pain from her body. Her fingers clenched and unclenched, as she tried in vain to reach the hurt with her hands, and her face contorted, her tears pouring down her cheeks. Then Sheena landed a slashing blow into the tight rounded bottom, raising another fearsome welt across the crease of Ruth's buttocks.

Keane was forced to watch the shackled girl; her futile struggles as she tried to evade the lash; Sheena raining another three or four blows into the offered buttocks. Keane shut his eyes, wishing also he could shut his ears. Then he bellowed out. "Leave the girl alone. For Christ's Sake, leave her!"

"Enough Sheena!"

With her breathing heavy and loud, Sheena stepped away from Ruth, sneering. She ground her thighs together and groaned again, a soft grunt of pleasure, as she watched the wretched girl trembling in her chains, sobbing, trying to bear the agony as best she could. With the beating finished, Ruth lay gasping, her head on one side as she sobbed into the sheets. Still she tried to get her hands to the burning parts of her body; where her buttocks and thighs were a mass of welts.

"You see Nick!" the General said, "You're getting soft."

"Damn you bastards!" Keane exploded. "There was no need for that!"

"Oh! I see." The General grinned. "You'd rather Sheena took the whip to you?"

"Fuck off!"

The General shrugged off the expletive. "Nick!" he said, "I don't care what you do with the girls I provide. If you want to pamper them, that's your affair." He flashed a cold smile. "In fact, it increases their fear, when they come back to me." He dragged up another chair and straddled it backwards, facing Keane. "What bothers me, Nick, is that you might fall down on the job out there." He poked Keane's chest with his leather bound cane. "And that can be dangerous for all of us."

"You know damn well I've never let you down!"

"So far, no." The General took out a pocketknife, and opened it slowly. "But the signs are there." He cleaned under a fingernail with the knife. "I thought it was time to remind you, we can't afford mistakes."

Keane's pulse quickened.

He and Brice had similar sexual tastes.

But only broadly so.

Keane knew himself for what he was.

He had undergone Psychoanalysis in prison. He had been

told that, whilst not a homosexual, he didn't really like women. Sure, he would have sex with a woman and enjoy it. But, to him they were mere sex objects. In short, he got the same satisfaction from a good wank. If there was a woman present at the time, so much the better. Something to wank over. When he shagged them, he did it mainly for the sense of power and control it gave him. Underneath, his sadistic urges would be at full pedal, and he would want only to subjugate them, subject them to bondage or, better still, inflict pain upon them.

But his sadism was always sexual. He only got his charge from hurting a woman. Preferably a dolly, and even better, on one who had spurned him; the main reason for his hatred.

Brice was different.

Man or woman.

It made no difference.

And he didn't inflict pain just for sexual pleasure.

He would torture for pleasure alone.

He was a pure sadist.

Compared to the General, Keane knew himself to be a baby.

If the bastard took that knife to him, it might be goodbye gonads. Keane buried the thoughts. "You don't have to worry about me."

The General chuckled, as he held up the knife, allowing the light to glint off the blade. "Of course not Nick!" He returned to cleaning his nails. "Prison isn't really a holiday is it?" He examined the four-inch blade. "And, if you go again, it will be for life." He shrugged. "After all, every time you take one of the girls here, you are committing rape." He grinned. "Or is that too fine a point for you to appreciate?"

Keane clamped his teeth angrily. "No need to draw pictures!"

"I thought not!" The General leaned back. "Of course, it applies to all of us, but in your case..." He pulled a doubtful face, and inclined his head towards Sheena. "Now, Sheena for instance..."

"You bastard!"

"Actually yes! I am illegitimate," the General said. "But we were discussing Sheena." His grin was wolfish. "Perhaps you should think about pampering her a little." He regarded Keane with an intense stare. "You won't have to rape her, we know, but she could be persuaded to say you did."

Sheena gloated. "Think it over Nick!"

"Bitch!"

The whip slashed again, cracking a hair in front of his eyes, close enough for him to feel the draught of its passing. He drew back sharply, his breath hissing through clenched teeth.

Sheena glowered at him. "You don't need eyes for sex Nick!" She came up close. "And I can take them out as easy as—as easy as winking!"

"Bitch!"

The General chuckled. "She is, isn't she?" He reached out for the woman and pulled her close to him. "That's what makes her so interesting." He allowed his hand to wander up and down Sheena's thigh. "Now, you do see where you're going wrong Nick!"

"Okay! Okay!" Keane swallowed his anger. Since the General had become more involved in the real white-slave trade, Keane had been reluctant, nervous even. Shipping girls abroad was too risky and would, one day, land them all in the shit. But the General was right. It would be so easy to fit him for rape and that was definitely something to be avoided. Like it or not, he would have to carry on with the job.

The General turned to Sheena. "Watch our friend doesn't do anything silly." He leaned forwards, and slid the knife beneath the cords around Keane's ankles. The razor-sharp blade sliced through them like tissue paper, and the General sat back. "Be sensible Nick, and I'll free your hands."

"Just cut the frigging ropes!"

The General shrugged, and handed Sheena the knife. She cut through the ropes, allowing her hand to trace down his body and along the inside of his thigh, dwelling by his crotch as she straightened up. She breathed a kiss beside his ear. "I love you Nick! You know that don't you?"

Keane sighed and shook his head. "D'you know what the word means, Sheena?"

"All right then," Sheena grinned, "I lust you! But I still want you to fuck me!"

Keane stood up, rubbing his wrists. "Yeah! Well, we all know where we stand." He didn't bother to add that he could hoard a grudge like a banker hoarded cash.

Sheena stepped away, a wary expression in her face.

The bitch knew.

As though she could read his mind.

And the thought seemed to bother her.

It should, he thought, for he always repaid with interest.

He stored the fact away.

A nugget of satisfaction to savour later.

He turned to Brice, but the General smiled. "Come on Nick! Leave it." He nodded towards Ruth and handed Keane the leather switch. "Take her legs down." He jerked a sadistic smile onto his face. "Let's see you mark those breasts. Just so they match her arse!"

Keane drew in a deep breath. "What for? She's done nothing!"

The General shook his head. "Just show us you haven't forgotten how."

Keane swallowed sour bile.

He had to do it.

In some ways he was as much subject to the General's will as were the girls. With reluctance, he took the whip and stepped over to the chained Ruth.

The girl's shivering had gone into overdrive, her fear widening her eyes into bright orbs, as she looked up at him.

She didn't say anything, asked for no mercy, but he could see the pleading in her eyes.

An almost imperceptible shake of his head. He was sure she knew.

He was just going to do what he had to. For once, he wasn't going to enjoy this. He leaned over the helpless girl and slipped the chains, lowering her legs until they were spread wide. He bent over her and again shook his head, allowing sadness to show in his face, as he secured the chains again. He drew back the whip, and slashed it down across her breasts, but, at the very last, pulled the blow a little, so it did the minimum of damage.

Even so, Ruth's hips lifted clear of the bed and she screeched her agony. Soon, she was twisting her head from side to side, rolling her hips, trying in vain to evade the lash as blow after stinging blow landed across her tender breasts, raising vivid red slashes across the nipples; nipples which suddenly became turgid as the nerves, deadened by the assault, ceased to feel any further blows.

Keane stopped. Pointless going on. She'd had enough. Much more and she would be unconscious.

The General took the switch from him. "You were pulling it a little Nick, but it will do." He leaned over the girl. "She's tendered up nicely." He peered at her sex-mound. "I said you were good Nick! She's juiced up like a squeezed fruit. You should take her away and have more fun."

Keane swallowed his anger and bent to the sobbing girl. He released her and, almost tenderly, lifted her trembling body in his arms. He felt the surge of guilt as he looked at the mess he had made of her gorgeous breasts, but bit back on the feelings. There was no point. He had brought her here and he was responsible for everything that happened to her. This was the life he had chosen. He had to carry on. He turned to face the General. "I reckon this little bitch has earned a rest."

The General shrugged. "As you wish. I've grown tired

of her anyway. She will suit Sheik Malik. I think she will pull an oar well." He grinned at Keane. "Enjoy her while you can!"

Keane wanted to call the General all the bastards under the sun. The little turd knew how much this girl meant. But it was best to keep quiet. There was always the possibility he would change his mind, for he often forgot his threats from one day to the next.

Nick turned away and carried his sobbing, soft-skinned burden from the room, taking no notice of the giggles from Sheena.

Sheena could wait!

The General could wait!

They could all wait!

One day soon, something was going to happen to them all.

And that something, or rather someone, was Keane.

Oh Yes. Keane was going to happen.

***

Keane stood by his bed. Ruth lay naked before him.

Why was his mind in a turmoil?

He was supposed to hate women.

Why then did he feel tenderness and sympathy for this poor unfortunate creature? He looked at her, his brow creasing into a frown.

She had stopped crying, but she was clearly still in agony. Her eyes were closed and it looked like she was praying.

She may well have been.

The girls needed all the help they could get.

Although there was not much chance of Divine intervention.

Not much chance of any kind of intervention.

Knights in shining armour didn't get this far.

He stepped across the room and sat on the edge of the

bed. He reached for her thick dark hair and allowed his hand to run through the strands.

Instantly Ruth drew in a gasp of breath. Her eyes opened and she cowered from him.

Expecting a beating of course.

That was the way most guests on the Island started the night's entertainment. Generally, they finished it that way too. Often, that was all there was to the entertainment.

He let his hands rest on her shoulders, then traced them down over the curve of her back, lingering for a moment at her waist, and then back up to the elegant curve of her neck, deliberately avoiding the bruised and swollen areas of flesh.

Her body shook and he heard her soft sigh.

Smiling to himself, he repeated the manoeuvre.

She sighed again. He could almost read her mind.

Tenderness was a novelty for her.

He lifted her to a seated position.

She was like a doll. Light, delicate. She always had been.

But God, did she know how to make love!

He pulled her close and began to rock her gently. He didn't want to hurt this girl any more. Did he?

He knew he hadn't really changed.

That was more like the truth.

Not all this sentimental crap, stealing up on him.

He had to watch that.

Sure, he wanted to hurt her.

His frown deepened and his mind lapsed into near turmoil.

Yes he wanted to hurt her, yet strangely, he wanted to be the only one to do it.

Inflicting pain on this woman was the only way he could really express his feelings for her. The more he was attracted to a woman, the more he wanted to hurt her; the more he desired her.

The more he loved her?

But wasn't love supposed to be allied to tenderness?

You didn't hurt the one you loved.

Or did you?

Keane shook his head. The hell with it. He was confused.

He laid her down on the bed again and she stiffened as her body touched the coverlet. She began to tremble slightly. Then she spoke. "Nick? I know."

"What do you know?"

"That you love me."

The shock pulled him up sharp. What was with this girl? He'd just beaten her almost senseless and here she was, telling him he was in love with her. And the way she was saying it, she felt the same about him.

She didn't wait for any reply. "I know. I knew the other day in the bathroom. You weren't like the others." She smiled slightly. "And I want to be your slave Nick! You're my real Master, not the General."

He groaned to himself, and let out a resigned sigh. The General had worked his magic on her. As he'd suspected the last time, she wasn't Ruth any more, but just another slavegirl. Another submissive.

She said nothing, just looked at him, a sad little smile playing on her lips, her eyes journeying about his features. "I know what you're thinking." She winced as pain lanced into her again. "But I really am yours." She tried a shrug. "The General didn't make me like this you know. He just made me see it for myself. But I know who I want as my Master." Her fingers tried to intertwine with his. "And I knew you were pulling the whip just now." She shrugged. "It was bad, but not unbearable. I had to scream for the General's sake." She traced her fingers down his face. "I can stand so much you know. Especially from you Nick, my real Master!" She looked right into his eyes. "Are you going to take me away from here?"

God! Yes! He did want to, but how?

"I can't."

Her body slumped then. "I didn't think so." A tear started from her eyes. Letting out a heavy sigh, she turned her head away.

He shook her then, as some of his anger returned. "Three bloody years Ruth. For what? Just making love to you, when you wanted it that way."

"Father made me give the evidence, Nick! He threatened to throw me out without a penny."

"So you said." He slumped and let out a frustrated sigh.

She let her hand rest on his thigh. "Father would have seen to it you went to prison anyway. He is a Magistrate after all."

"Oh Hell! It's all in the past! Maybe I really should think about getting you away from here, getting both of us away. And me out of this business."

She massaged his thigh. "Nick! Just forget it for now!" She smiled, rolled onto her right side and looked back at him. "Make love to me. Properly."

He looked at the offered buttocks, the soft skin, the elegant curves of her body, and felt his hormones begin to trudge. The trudge became a march, a run, as in near frantic haste, he stripped off.

I can do as I wish with you, can't I Ruth?"

"Yes Master!" Her voice went quiet and her face was clouded as she clearly expected the usual beating.

But he just squeezed her buttocks again. "Then get ready for a rearguard action."

She shivered, then squealed with delight, as once again, he entered her.

13: THE ROUND ROOM

The circular room was cold. The walls were covered with white glazed tiles. Fixed to the wall near the metal door was a stainless steel sink, and next to that a long wooden rack. The rack was festooned with coils of rope, more lengths of dog-chain, collars, whips, manacles, leather hoods and other bondage devices. The floor was carpeted with a deep pile sheepskin material, except in the centre, where there was a round patch of brown floor tiles, about ten feet across.

In the middle of this tiled circle there was an old-fashioned leather birching-stool.

Shivering with the cool air on her flesh, Tristie knelt beside it, sobbing to herself.

She felt muzzy, half-drugged.

Hardly aware of what she was doing here, or even who she was.

She shivered in revulsion as she remembered the branding and her passing out. Then she moaned to herself, as she recalled what had happened afterwards.

They had awakened her with a jet of freezing water, unshackled her and, for what had seemed like eternity, they had played a fierce jet of water over her, pushing her helpless body all over the place. Then they had taken her for a bath. Or what they had called a bath. It had merely been another sadistic ordeal.

Telling her she was to have her first lesson in submission, they had brought her to this room, shackled her to the glazed wall and hosed her down, this time with hot water. Then they had cleaned her body with soft soap and an antiseptic fluid, scrubbing her flesh with stiff bristled brushes as they would an animal. After another hosing down they had dried her off with a wash leather, before covering her body with a liberal dusting of talcum powder. The only part of the proceedings that had been anything near normal was the way they had washed her hair and blow-dried it, before brushing it out into its normal silken beauty.

Then they had fitted the beauty chains to her body, before winding a length of chromed dog-chain twice about her neck. They had padlocked the chain in place and manacled her hands behind her back, with her arms forced upwards and secured by her wrists to the rear of the neck chain.

Then, after smearing more Vaseline over the brand on her left thigh, they had carried her to the centre of the room, dropped her on her knees, and left her in chained nakedness—to wait, they had said, for a guest.

So here she was, waiting, her head lowered, her arms aching from being secured so high up her back and her lovely hair brushing the cold tiles beneath her knees.

Tristie was still bewildered, her mind a whirl of fearful anticipation of the unknown, but slowly coming to terms with her situation.

She stifled another sob as she admitted to herself how stupid she'd been to trust Lisa to take her to that awful club in Soho.

Her body trembled again.

Anyone could whip her as and when they wished.

Her heart jumped then as she heard someone come into the room, but Tristie dared not look up. She waited until she could see a pair of bare feet in front of her.

Then a sudden gasp was wrenched from her as a hand twisted in her hair and yanked her head upwards, so that she was looking into the half-masked features of a middle-aged woman. The woman was naked but for a leather waistband from which hung a quirt, brushing against her shapely thigh. In her right hand she had a riding crop. Her tanned flesh had a healthy glow under the light from the overhead lights and she smelled of expensive perfume. She had a fine figure and, from what little Tristie could see of her face, was rather attractive for her age.

Something familiar about her?

"What is your name?" the woman demanded, brandishing her whip.

Tristie's fear returned and she began to gabble. "Please, please, please, don't hurt..."

The woman ignored her, shaking her shoulders. "Your name, you stupid girl, what is your slave-name?"

The sobbing Tristie cowered from her, shaking with fear, trying to understand what was happening to her. "I—I haven't got a slave name..."

"Your number then!"

Tristie shook in fright. "S-s-Seven."

The quirt slashed into her naked back. "I asked you a question girl."

The whip slashed into Tristie's buttocks, extracting a howl of pain.

"Tell me properly!"

"Number seven, Mistress."

"Better! You're a new slave aren't you, Seven? You have some tricks to learn, I think!"

Tristie had no idea what the woman meant, but she knew what she had to say. She bowed her head again. "Yes, Mistress!"

"Well, one thing's for certain. You're not at Greenacres now." She chuckled, and slowly peeled off the half mask.

Tristie looked up, frowning, her eyes puzzled, then her jaw dropped in amazement. God! It was Miss Hayward! Her Head Mistress at Greenacres. Lisa's, too, of course. But how? It couldn't be! Surely?

"Miss Hayward? Is it you?"

The woman laughed. "At last the bitch recognises me!" Still laughing, she bent to Tristie and cradled her chin. "Here you must call me Mistress. You know that much don't you?"

"Yes, Mistress."

"Lisa arranged your abduction, didn't she?"

"Yes, Mistress!"

"You must be so frightened, little one."

Again Tristie frowned, her mind in a whirl at this sudden change of heart. Why was Miss Hayward being nice to her? Tristie shook her head. "Please! I don't understand. I want to go home. Please. Let me go..."

Miss Hayward's hand clamped over Tristie's mouth. "Shush, now, little one! I can't let you go. That's up to the General." She caressed Tristie's cheeks, then turned her attention to Tristie's flanks. "You'll get used to all this, but you must learn to obey, or you'll be whipped, even by me." She caressed Tristie's cheek again. "I don't think you'll be difficult though. You were always such a compliant little thing at school." She continued caressing Tristie's body. "That mustn't change. You understand?"

Tristie was becoming more bewildered by the second, even though she knew Miss Hayward was right. She had always preferred to do as she was told rather than risk punishment. She tried to hide her bewilderment and the sudden wish to submit completely.

"Yes, Mistress."

"Good!" Miss Hayward stroked Tristie's soft hair. "That makes worthwhile all the risks taken in getting you brought here."

Tristie knew she could do no more than agree, try to please this woman, whom up until now she had always trusted. She nodded slowly. "Yes Mistress." She looked up. "Please Mistress, why me? What did I do? Why did you have me brought here?"

The woman smiled lazily. "Come now, Seven. You must realise you're not the first girl I've sent here?"

"But Mistress, I don't understand."

"Running that school was getting expensive, until Lisa told me a little secret which gave me an easy way to pay some of the bills and enjoy myself into the bargain." She cracked the whip. "Enough of all this. It's time for some fun!"

Tristie bowed her head, her mind in turmoil. All that time

at the school yet not knowing what was going on. Until she found out, the hard way. Oh God! Why? Why? Why?

The whip cracked again and disturbed Tristie's thoughts. The woman stroked the leather across her back. "You may call me Mistress Hayward!"

"Yes Mistress Hayward."

Miss Hayward gave an approving nod, and walked over to the birching-stool, where she stood, quietly looking at Tristie. "What do you think of the Round Room, Seven?"

"It frightens me, Mistress."

Miss Hayward chuckled, and nudged the girl with her toe. "Well that's good, because that's what it's meant to do." She leaned towards Tristie. "And, as a new girl, you've every reason to be frightened. You don't know what to expect, do you?"

"No, Mistress."

"But you know you're a slave, don't you?"

Tristie bowed her head miserably. She didn't want to play their game, but she knew what would happen if she didn't. And she couldn't take much more of the whip.

"Yes, but…"

The whip whistled through the air again, this time slashing into Tristie's upper thigh, curling about her legs and cutting into her buttocks. Screaming, the helpless girl fell to the floor and tried to roll away. Hopeless. The stinging, cutting whip laid into her flesh and she rolled herself into a ball, screaming as the whip slashed across her buttocks, thighs and shoulders. Without the use of her arms she was unable to rise properly and every time she tried to get up the whip would slash into her, forcing her back to the floor. Screaming and shrieking, she rolled about in a huddled ball as she tried to ride the blows tearing into her skin.

Then the rain of blows ceased and Miss Hayward went to her, helped her upright, and hugged the tortured body close. "Oh little one! You really must be a good girl. Then I shan't have to whip you so much, shall I?" She cracked

112

the whip again. "Now, little one, lie across the birching stool and show me those gorgeous buttocks."

Shaking in terror, wincing at the agony of her bruised and burning skin, Tristie struggled to her feet and approached the stool awkwardly, barely able to keep her balance. Wobbling a little, she lowered her body over the stool, snatching a breath as the cool leather made contact with her breasts and belly. Lying across the stool now she closed her eyes and held her breath, not daring to move, as she anticipated the agonising kiss of the whip.

Miss Hayward laughed. "You're shivering, Seven. Why are you shivering?" Her voice had a taunting quality now.

Tristie wondered just how much more degradation she could take. "I'm frightened, Mistress." Still she waited for the sting of the wire whip.

Nothing.

Her trembling increased as she waited to suffer for the woman's sadistic pleasure. Sadly, Tristie realised that mental torture was as much a part of things here as physical punishment.

Then the woman's hands were suddenly on Tristie's buttocks and, gently, they began to knead the firm flesh. Her strong fingers invaded Tristie's vagina, her thumb pressed against the tight ring of her anus. Tristie winced, fighting back the sobs as this new humiliation tormented her soul.

The woman finished her perverted caressing. "Now, turn and face me."

"Yes Mistress!" Tristie stood up. She almost overbalanced as she turned, and instinctively lowered her head before her tormentor.

"Kneel before me!"

"Yes Mistress." Tristie sank to her knees on the brown tiles.

"Wait there!" Miss Hayward walked across to the side of the room where there was a stainless steel sink, and filled a metal bowl with water. She came back and set the dish in front of Tristie.

"Drink."

Tristie's mind recoiled.

She did want a drink.

How she wanted a drink!

But, trussed as she was, she would need to lap like a dog. Miss Hayward couldn't be so cruel as to make her do that. She shook her head...

The whip whistled down across her back and she screamed, jumping back, trying to avoid the lash.

"You must obey, little one."

Swallowing her dignity, Tristie moved forward to bend towards the bowl. Without warning, the whip slashed into her flesh again and she screamed, straightening her body in agony as the whip aggravated the welts already scarring her soft white flesh.

"Too close. Move back."

Obediently, Tristie shuffled backwards a foot or so and tried again.

"Wait." Miss Hayward pulled Tristie upright again, then, going over to one of the racks on the wall, she took down a long length of elasticated rope. She swished the elastic through the air. "Just imagine what it's going to feel like when I whip you with this!"

Tristie began to shiver again. She felt her bowels loosen and, frantically, she held back the need. That really would earn her a whipping. Holding her breath in fear, Tristie waited as her Mistress edged towards her.

Coming close to the defenceless girl, Miss Hayward caressed her long hair again.

"Stand!"

Tristie staggered to her feet, teetering as she stood upright. Miss Hayward began to move her hands over Tristie's shapely thighs. "Don't worry little one," she said, "I'm not going to whip you just now." Her hands fluttered about the swell of Tristie's delicious sex mound. Then, as easily as if she'd been tying a parcel, she wrapped the rope around Tristie's waist and pulled it in tight, taking the free ends down between her trembling thighs. She pulled the rope hard into the cleft between Tristie's buttocks and pulled the elastic upwards, until it was at full stretch. Then, with some difficulty, secured the elastic to the back of Tristie's neck-chains.

Tristie was squirming in agony as the stretched elastic cut into her tender flesh and her cries filled the room.

"Come now, Seven. Anyone would think I was whipping you!"

Tristie couldn't stifle her sobs as she tried to stand the pain of the cutting strands. But the worst was to come. Miss Hayward pushed Tristie's head downwards. "On your knees and drink! Lap it up, like the little bitch you are." She pressed Tristie's head lower. "Move further back and stretch for it!"

Moaning her agony, Tristie lowered her head, moving back another foot or so. Now she had to strain her head and neck forwards. She pushed her tongue towards the dish and began to lap the water. Fully stretched, the vicious rubber strands cut deep into her flesh, burning her skin, chafing deep into her groin and between her buttocks. Tristie continued to lap at the water, squirming as she tried to ease the pain caused by the bonds.

Miss Hayward bent down and began to run her hand along the graceful length of the girl's extended neck and over her full taut breasts, groaning with pleasure as Tristie winced when the contact aggravated the hurt.

Slim strong fingers forced their way between Tristie's thighs, kneading the flesh, extracting further moans of agony as they caused the elastic to cut even deeper. With difficulty, the woman eased her fingers past the elastic, and entered the warm moistness of Tristie's vagina.

Tristie was still moaning. Her back and buttocks were

burning with the pain of her whipping and the elastic strands were digging into her flesh. Also her neck chain was cutting deep into her throat, as she tried to ignore Miss Hayward's perverted caress.

Then Miss Hayward released the cutting elastic strands and her fingers began to slide faster in and out of Tristie's sex, her thumb pushing against the tight lips of the offered anus. Tristie began to wriggle her hips, trying to ignore the massage.

Despite herself, however, Tristie began to feel excitement mounting, and forgetting even the pain and discomfort of her chains, began to moan in ecstasy, forcing herself down onto those persistent fingers as they pummelled her body.

Miss Hayward started to moan now and she slid down onto her back, forcing her head from the rear between the girl's shapely buttocks. Then her tongue began to explore Tristie's sex and suddenly Tristie realised she was no longer play-acting. God this was delicious! It was a woman's caress, yes, but it was a caress; far better than the beatings she had experienced since she had been brought here.

Tristie arched her body backwards, screaming both in passion and pain as the tongue slid in and out of her vagina and soft skin contacted Tristie's lashed and burning body.

Miss Hayward panted. "Turn round, Seven... dribble your saliva on my belly!"

"Oh Yes Mistress!" Tristie's mouth trembled with ecstasy as she twisted herself around to face Miss Hayward's feet. Then, leaning over Miss Hayward's body, she allowed saliva to run out of her mouth onto the woman's belly.

Miss Hayward began to rub Tristie's saliva into her tanned skin. Then she reached upwards and grabbed the girl's hair to pull her body down on top of hers. "Kiss me! Lick me! Kiss me there... suck me until my juice runs over your face. Come on my little one! Come on! Let me feel that sexy little tongue inside me!"

Again Tristie turned about and obeyed, allowing her

tongue to slide in and out of the dripping vagina. Tristie began to moan as she felt her own juices flowing in response to Miss Hayward's tongue. Then she tasted the woman's juices and, greedy now, began to lap at the silken crotch. Soon Tristie's neck and breasts were covered in the love-juice as it flowed like water from Miss Hayward's body. Together the pair rocked, thrusting against each other's hips, as their passion mounted; overflowed, in a tide of their juices. Lapping and sucking at each other's parts, they flailed about the floor, moaning and screaming their passion.

Tristie knew she was beginning to think like these people. They were winning. Perhaps she was finished. Maybe she should accept she was their slave and behave as they wished her to. Become a sex-slave; perform whatever depraved and perverted acts they demanded of her...

Somehow there was a strange delight in her mind as she savoured the raw female smell of this delightfully formed woman. Tristie experienced a sudden rush of sexual pleasure and she clasped the taut body to her and pumped her tongue hard into Miss Hayward's moist sex-hole.

Then, suddenly, the enormity of what she was doing struck home. She pulled away sharply, beginning to sob.

Miss Hayward stood up, her face contorted with fury. She picked up the whip again and she spat onto Tristie's breasts. "You disobedient little bitch! You dare to disobey me. ME! YOUR MISTRESS!"

The whip slashed down again and again and, screaming in agony and frustration, Tristie was obliged to roll away from the demented attack. It was hopeless. Screaming and shrieking, she huddled against the birching stool, as for the second time, Miss Hayward laid a protracted beating into her flesh with the whip.

Screaming for mercy, Tristie rolled into a tight ball. "Oh! Please Mistress! I beg you! No more Mistress! Please stop Mistress! Please, PLEASE STOP!"

Miss Hayward stood over her. "You get no mercy from

me," she snarled. "You're my slavegirl! I paid for your body. I want enjoyment from you." She rolled Tristie onto her back, and laid the whip into the offered stomach. "And, if you don't perform as I want, then this is another way I can enjoy you!" She slashed the girl's body again.

"Mistress! No more!" Tristie gazed at the floor, tears running freely. "I can't stand any more!"

Then Miss Hayward stooped down and pulled Tristie close to her again. With a gentle rocking movement she cradled the helpless girl against her breasts. "Shush, now, Seven. Cry if you wish, but don't complain." She kissed the girl's temple. "Or I have to whip you like that, and I don't really want to do it."

She looked into the confused girl's eyes, and then kissed her forehead again. "Now I have to go and leave you here for the General." She wiped the tears from Tristie's face. "And he will be very cruel if you disobey him." She kissed Tristie again. "Do you understand?"

Tristie understood.

14: TRISTIE MUST SUBMIT!

Tristie had been stripped naked again and was now suspended, horizontally, face downwards, secured by her ankles and wrists between four steel poles set in the concrete floor of the well-lit room. Her genitals and mouth were at the General's waist height; her arms and legs stretched to their limits, so she was fully accessible, should the General choose to enter her in any orifice.

Her quivering body was stretched taut, her skin shining with the sweat of her torture, and she was whimpering, her breath coming in gasps as she struggled against her bonds.

Barely conscious, Tristie hung her head in total submission.

The General and Keane were standing near her, the General with his switch in his right hand. "It seems Nick, we must teach this animal a lesson," he said, moving towards the unfortunate Tristie. Stooping a little, he pushed the handle of his switch beneath her chin and jerked her head up. He knelt to gaze into her tear-streaked face.

"We could physically force you to do what we wish, but I pride myself I can train my slaves so they will do anything of their own volition and without hesitation." Smiling at her, he continued. "Of course, some girls disobey because they like to be punished. Then there are the girls I reserve for guests who like to play with unwilling slaves; to hear genuine screams of agony."

He removed the whip, allowing Tristie's head to drop forward again. He stood up, turning his gaze to Tristie's whip-lashed body. "You may well have served such a purpose." He walked around the stretched girl, and began running his hands over her body, a sadistic smile on his face, as she whimpered. "However," he continued, "I want no further truck with you. I shall sell you to our friends in North Africa." He chuckled as his words caused Tristie a fit of even more violent trembling.

"Evidently that frightens her, Nick."

Keane's smile was cold as his gaze wandered over the naked body. "So it should General, though it would be a waste."

"Maybe." The General sauntered around Tristie. Ignoring her futile struggles, he allowed his fingers to slide in and out of her defenceless sex, sneering as his helpless victim moaned at yet another invasion of her body. "Yes, I agree, but they do so like blonde white girls out there. I always get a good return for them." Again he grinned, as Tristie's frightened shaking became more convulsive, her breathing more ragged with terror. "I think though, she will need a few weeks to recover." He ran his hands over the bruised body again. "At the moment her hide is worth little, but, we can at least show her what happens to disobedient slaves."

He clapped his hands and a curtain at the side of the room moved as a gorgeous young girl emerged and walked towards him, her sexy hips swaying in a delicious come-hither way.

This girl's figure was of ample proportions, but no fat marred her delightful curves. Her smooth flawless skin was honey-gold; matching her straw-coloured hair; full of health, shining in the light. She was not exactly naked, although she had on no clothing. Instead, she wore a wide, stainless-steel collar, with a silver chain stretching from beneath her chin to the ring in her pierced left nipple. Another silver chain ran from there to her right breast, where it was again clipped to a nipple ring. The effect was completed with a tiny silver slave-bell attached to each nipple.

But the most striking part of her 'clothing' was the silver link chain-mail 'skirt'. It was no more than a loincloth, but a most unusual one. The finely made mat of silver links lay gracefully on her stomach. The mat was triangular, its widest part stretched right across her hips, with the point just covering the fuzz of hairs at the base of her slightly rounded belly. The mat was about seven rows deep and each link in the top two rows was joined to its neighbour, whilst also being set into the girl's pierced flesh. Attached to the point of the triangle, a further silver bell tinkled as she walked. Her body swayed in a hypnotic, sinuous dance.

There was another triangular mat fixed into the flesh of her lower back, this one lay enticingly over the smooth slope of her gorgeous buttocks. The point of the triangle, with its small bell, was precisely in the centre crease of her bottom, brushing against the velvety skin with every step. A much larger silver ring had been set into her flesh where the top of the two triangles joined at her hips, to support the weight of the metal cloth.

The whole thing was a delightful accentuation of the well-formed swell of her hips and abdomen, a sexually charged sight, the fine mat barely covering her shapely rear and the erotic swell of her unshaven sex. The exotic garment allowed enticing glimpses of her long, upper legs, and the oak-leaf brand on her left hip. As he watched her sway across the room, Keane felt an erection beginning to surge.

The girl shimmied up to the General. "You summoned me, Master?"

The General pulled her towards him and embraced her, allowing his hands to trace downwards, over the velvet skin of her back, over the silver links, to fondle her buttocks. Then his hands came around to her front, his fingers lifting the silver mat, to wander among the fine, almost invisible hairs. His hand disappeared into the crease between her legs, and she moaned, leaning against him. "Oh! Master! Your caress is so wonderful!"

"Ahh, my slavegirl Kim," he said, "You look delectable." He lifted the girl's chin and planted a kiss on her full red lips, then stroked her cheeks. "I have work for you." He pointed to Tristie. "Take this slave to the Discipline Suite. Show her what happens to girls who disobey, then come back here and go with Master Nick." He grinned and pointed to Keane's obvious erection. "He seems to need a slave for the rest of the day."

The girl sighed, moved across to Keane and smiled enticingly. She touched Keane's neck with her lips. "Oh Master, it is my pleasure."

Keane showed another cold smile. "You won't be giving in too easily, I hope?"

She lifted her head and licked her lips. "I will do whatever Master wishes." She wrinkled her nose, and smiled at him.

The General broke in. "It will be very unfortunate for you if you don't." He took a handful of the flesh at Kim's rounded buttocks and squeezed hard, grinning as he looked into the suddenly anguished face. "Nick can be very cruel."

The slavegirl turned towards Keane. "You have a good whip-hand Master? Perhaps I should misbehave on purpose?"

Keane's eyes gleamed as his gaze wandered over her delicious body. "Oh yes! Am I going to enjoy you!"

"I will promise you that, Master." She turned to the General. "Master, I go to do your bidding." She bent to her knees and kissed his feet. "I will be back soon!"

The General smiled down at the prostrate girl. "Just do as I ask for now. I will see you tonight, when Nick has finished with you. I am sure further discipline will be necessary."

The slavegirl kissed his feet again, and then got up slowly, and kissed his mouth. "I wait to do your bidding Master!"

The General smiled at her and took a key from his pocket. He handed it to the girl. "Unchain the bitch and take her away."

The slavegirl Kim smiled at him and then went over to Tristie. For a moment she stood in front of the chained girl, before going behind her to lean forward and grab at the rounded swell of the wretched girl's sex in a vicious full handed pinch.

Tristie squealed in agony and Kim sniggered. "Just remember, bitch! I am the Mistress for a while now." She spat onto Tristie's body. "Slut!" She unlocked the chains, grabbing hold of Tristie's hair as the half-conscious girl fell towards the floor.

As she stumbled after Kim, Tristie was shaking violently, her mind wrestling with the question of what horrors she would undergo in the Discipline Suite. No matter, she resolved to herself. They would never make her become a lesbian. She gagged as she thought about it. Whatever they did to her, she would rather die than be forced to kiss another woman like that.

Kim grabbed Tristie's genitals in another savage squeeze and slammed her against the wall. Her other hand went to Tristie's neck and squeezed her throat. "Before we go to the Discipline Suite," she said, "just remember that beating you will be a pleasure. So be sure you obey me." She sneered at Tristie and reached towards a rope whip, one of many which hung on the walls at regular intervals.

Kim was revelling in the fact that she, for once, could inflict pain on another, and she threatened Tristie with the whip, a sadistic grin on her face.

Tristie flinched and slid down to her haunches, cowering before the girl: just another slavegirl, but one who, for the moment, was her Mistress. Tristie knew her place. "Please Mistress," she begged, "don't hurt me."

"You are learning," Kim looked at Tristie scornfully. "Well, you have good reason to beg of me. After a few minutes in the Discipline Suite you'll be begging to obey anyone, rather than be kept there."

15: In the Discipline Suite

"Turn left," said Kim.

Tristie obeyed. Her stomach gave a nervous flip as she saw a green metal door with a soundproof legend painted across it. She hesitated, pulling back a little, but Kim pushed the door open.

"Listen!"

A girl was screaming; wailing, pleading to be released, begging for mercy. Tristie felt her insides churn as Kim shoved her into the room.

It was another circular room, but gloomy, and with grey rock walls. There was a brazier in the centre of the room and scattered round the walls were several naked girls, chained to iron rings, their feet suspended above the floor.

Tristie's eye's widened in horror. Her insides turned to water and her knees began to wobble. Horrified, she looked down at the floor where there were several circular gratings in two straight rows. Above each grating there was a heavy inclined timber cross. She began to whimper as she gazed, in terror, at this Bacchanalian scene.

Miller was there, standing by a wall-rack full of metal collars and chains. He selected a collar and belt and came across to Tristie. "This is a discipline collar," he said. He held it under her nose. The device was evil, made of flexible stainless-steel, about three inches wide, with a forest of wicked quarter-inch spikes sprouting from the inner circumference. It had two snap rings, so it could be parted into two halves.

Tristie nodded fearfully, knowing he was going to put the awful thing about her neck, and knowing she could do nothing to resist. She suddenly had a deep realisation of her position. These monsters could do just as they wished with her.

With a deft movement, Miller opened one of the snap rings and slipped the collar about her slender neck, fastening it at the rear. He sneered as Tristie cried out, the spikes lancing into her skin. "Don't move about too much slave, or the spikes will rip your neck to shreds!" He grinned at her again. "It will come off when the General thinks you are ready!"

He walked away to stand over one of the crosses. There was a naked girl roped to the cross, her limbs stretched out, so she looked like a fragile starfish, her body completely vulnerable, available to Miller for whatever he decided to do to her, and although she had stopped screaming she was still sobbing.

Tristie was reeling, hardly able to believe her eyes. She moaned and swallowed, just managing to hold onto consciousness as Miller turned towards Kim.

He worked an evil grin onto his face, and pointing at Tristie, spoke to Kim. "Take her back to the General. Remind the bitch that she'll be in here herself if seeing it doesn't work." He stepped over to Kim and grabbed her, pulling her to his body, allowing his hands to slide about her bottom, his fingers seeking the crease of her buttocks and the wet lips of her vagina.

"Have you work to do today, Kim?"

Kim lowered her head. "Oh Master Zach! I have to serve Master Nick, and then the General."

Miller squeezed her buttocks again. "In that case, when the General's finished with you, you will beg to be brought to me, my pretty little slave!" He looked at the steel link garment she was wearing. "There's something about that metalwork that turns me on!" He grinned and pulled her to him.

Kim rubbed her hips against him. "Oh Master Zach! I will do as you say." She licked his face gently, and her tongue played about his lips.

"And what will you do to please me?"

"Anything Master wishes!"

Miller chuckled and lifted her breasts by the silver chain,

grinning as she winced at the hurt. Then, lifting the chain-mail at her rear he slapped her buttocks playfully and pushed her away. "Go, before I rape you here and now!" He stepped over to Tristie, who had been looking miserably at the ground. Savagely he grabbed a handful of Tristie's pubic hairs and dug his fingers into the soft swell of her genitals. He hissed into her pain twisted face.

"Take note, you little bitch! That's how a slave behaves in this place! Sooner or later we'll have you beggin' to be like her." He pushed Tristie to the floor and turned back to Kim. "Take this creature back to the General!" He grinned then. "And remember what I said. I want your body in my bed as soon as possible!"

"Oh Master! I hope you will bind me well, when you take me. Master, you are the best!" Then she dropped to the floor and kissed his feet.

He looked down at her in contempt. "I'm not going to shag you, you stupid bitch! You like it too much!" He grinned. "I have other plans for you. One or two new games to try out!"

Kim nodded, and fear showed in her face as she swallowed. Evidently, she had experienced Miller's attentions before. She whispered. "Whatever Master wishes. I am your slave Master!" She got slowly to her feet, keeping her head low. "Now we must return to the General." She straightened up and went across to Tristie. Grabbing her hair, she yanked Tristie along behind her. "Come on!" she said, "or it won't just be you who will be sold to Sheik Malik."

Tristie felt herself stiffen with horror. Did that mean she really was going to be sold to Sheik Malik? She had not yet met the man, but everything she had heard was enough to strike fear into her.

Minutes later, Kim dragged Tristie into the General's suite and, putting her hands on her shoulders, she pushed Tristie headlong into the room. Tristie sprawled full length in front of the General's chair. For a moment the wind was knocked out of her and she lay there, gasping and moaning. She could feel her terror mounting, as her mind spun with thoughts of Sheik Malik and what would happen to her if she were sent to him.

Then Kim came over to her and pulled her to her knees in front of the Master. She pushed Tristie's head down, causing her to gasp in pain as the spikes in the collar dug into her.

"Lower your head in the presence of the Master!"

The General was sitting in his huge armchair as usual, and he had his switch in his hand. He was running the thin leather through his fingers, caressing the switch, as he looked down at Tristie.

"I have reached a decision."

He leaned forward and placed the switch beneath Tristie's chin, tilting her head up, causing her to screw up her face in pain from the discipline collar. He looked at her with contempt. "You are of no use to me." He shrugged. "No problem, of course. I can easily replace you. I am quite sure my friend Sheik Malik will soon have you brought to heel." He chuckled. "In more ways than one!" He rose from the chair. "Stand!"

Tristie obeyed. Her heart was leaping about like a caged bird as she tried to come to terms with the dread his words had placed in her mind. She had little chance of escape, she knew, but at least while she was still in England there was always a remote possibility. But, once she was out in the Middle-East, she would vanish without trace.

She knew enough to believe what the General had said about the cruelty out there. She was a Christian and they would go out of their way to be especially cruel because of that. At the best, she would finish up in some hellhole of a brothel. At the worst, well, who knew what? She had no doubts that Nick Keane had been telling the truth when he told her of girls being used as horses, or chained in teams to huge oars and forced to race...

The General had begun to caress her breasts. "Such a pity, but there it is!" He turned to Kim. "Take her to the Despatch Room."

16: THE VIEWING ROOM

They had removed the discipline collar from Tristie, and fitted a hood over her head, buckling it tight about her throat, blinding her. Her hands had been manacled in front of her, with about a foot of chain between her wrists. Someone prodded her buttocks with what felt like a whip handle and she realised she was being taken into a warm place.

Someone grabbed her shoulders, spun her around and pushed her down to her knees. Her breath whooshed from her body and she cried out as she felt herself slammed back against a wooden post. She grunted in pain and shock as her arms were snatched upwards, one wrist released, so her arms could be pulled back behind the pole. Her free wrist was shackled again, and she felt the chain between her wrists being yanked upwards and hooked over something, stretching her torso, forcing her breasts out and her buttocks into close contact with the pole.

She groaned in agony as her body weight pulled on her wrists, her knees short of the floor by about four inches. Then further pain, as her legs were splayed wide and pulled back, pressing the pole even further into her back. She gasped into the hood as she felt manacles being fastened to her ankles, preventing her from pulling her legs forward at all.

Then a sudden squeal of shock as the hood was unbuckled and snatched away from her head. The bright lights made her blink and squint. In moments a wide collar was placed about her neck and she heard the click as it was locked in place. Finally, a tight chain was placed about her waist, squeezing her stomach and pressing her back tightly against the pole.

The back of her skull was also hard against the wood, for the collar, tight and unyielding, prevented her from dropping her head without choking. Slowly her eyesight adjusted and she took stock of her position.

She was in a large room; wooden walled this time, a long rectangle, with a line of heavy wooden posts at six feet intervals all down the centre. Five of the posts were occupied by a naked collared girl. Each of them, like Tristie, was on her knees, with her back to the posts. The steel collars were fixed to the poles, and were clearly for the express purpose of keeping a girl's head upright.

Each girl, just like Tristie, had her arms shackled to rings at the back of the poles, well above their heads. Pert, shapely breasts pushed forward into full view. A taut chain was wrapped about each waist and fastened behind the pole, to pull in the belly, so the hollow of the back was held right against the timber. Their legs were spread wide, pulled back, right behind the posts, pressing the pole into the crease of their rounded buttocks, and their ankles were secured with chains, so their thighs were spread wide, displaying their shaven sex-mounds.

Like all of the General's slavegirls, their breasts, ears, noses and bellies were pierced and fitted with rings. However, the usual golden rings had been replaced with stainless-steel ones, no doubt just to keep the piercings open. These girls were for sale. Golden rings were for the girls the General wished to keep.

But there was something Tristie couldn't quite understand. All these girls, items of merchandise, as the General liked to call them, seemed to be remarkably clear of whip-marks. Then she realised. If they were to be sold, they would have been allowed to recover and heal. Certainly, Tristie could see they had been washed and scented. Each girl's body had also been covered with a sweet smelling oil, so the skin shone enticingly in the low light. It was quite hot in the room and their bodies glistened with running sweat, as they suffered at their posts, awaiting the arrival of whoever was to inspect them.

But none of this had been done to Tristie. By comparison, she looked a mess, and she still had her golden rings in her body. Did this mean she wasn't to be sold after all?

She sobbed then.

Who was she kidding?

It was pointless trying to make sense of anything these monsters did. All she could do was wait and see. In the meantime, try to shut out the sobbing and moaning of the other girls, as, with fear in their faces, they all watched Miller standing in front of them. He had a switch in his hand and an evil smile on his face.

"Some of you lot are going to be especially lucky," he said. That obviously amused him. "You'll be chosen to go on a holiday in the Middle-East. Perhaps you'll learn a few new tricks out there. They specialise in a certain kind of pleasure." He sliced the switch through the air, making a swishing sound. "Although, you won't be getting much pleasure. You'll just be the ones who are supplying it to others. As for sex, forget it. Like as not, you'll be sewn up, to keep your energies for pulling a trotting-rig, or an oar in a racing cutter. No doubt the Arabs will find other ways of using your bodies for sex."

He grinned maliciously.

"You thought we were bastards, but we're soft compared to that lot out there. Real sadism is the name of their game. Ah—here they come..."

The door banged open and Tristie caught her breath as the General walked in, accompanied by a tall distinguished man dressed in flowing white robes. His face was half hidden by his Arabian headdress, but she could see he was swarthy, with a hooked nose and a dark beard. Cruel black eyes glittered beneath thick dark arched eyebrows as he looked about the room.

Tristie had never seen a more cruel looking man and she shuddered, her heart racing with panic. God help her if she was sold to him.

The two men went to one of the poles and stood in front of the wretched girl on display. The Sheik forced his fingers into her mouth, causing her to squeal as he opened her lips wide. "Strong teeth. They will bear the bit well." He went on to poke and prod the girl's thighs, arms and stomach muscles. "She is well muscled General. You are to be complemented on your training methods." He stroked the girl's hair. "Ah! This one is not quite so blonde as the others." He turned to the General. "Is this slave not a Christian?"

The General smiled. "She is, but she has been dyed, Sheik Malik. It's growing out now." He pointed to her face. "Look at those blue eyes." Then he smoothed his hand over the girl's exposed unshaven sex. "As you can see, she is truly blonde."

The Sheik smiled and nodded. "Good. She will look well between the shafts of a gig."

Tristie was beginning to boggle at this exhibition of disregard for human dignity. They really did treat women as though they were beasts, showing no more consideration than if they were buying cattle.

Sheik Malik caressed the bound girl's ample breasts. "Such fine breasts, General. They will jiggle most enticingly, when she trots." His hand reached out to grasp the soft globe of her left breast and his fingers dug deep into the flesh. Another sadistic smile split his bearded face as the girl shuddered and moaned. He ignored her discomfort, and caressed her belly and hips. "She will also be good to play with, I think." He nodded. "I will take this one General." He took a marker from the pocket of his robes and scrawled an Arabic symbol on the girl's belly. "Now what else have we?"

He looked about, and then his eyes widened as his gaze fell on Tristie. "Ah! General! This is the one you told me about!"

Tristie's heart sank. She was to be sold to this awful man after all. Oh God! No! She began to tremble as they came towards her.

The Sheik stopped right in front of her and began caressing her body, allowing his fingers to probe her vagina and knead the flesh of her thighs. He forced his strong fingers into her mouth. "Good teeth again, but this one looks to be more suitable for training as a Pleasure Slave. The teeth may have to be removed." He grinned into Tristie's face. "Unless we can convince her it would be foolish to bite."

Tristie sobbed in shame and degradation as she was forced to suffer the evil caress of this man, his hands wandering all over her exposed flesh, paying particular attention to her buttocks and thighs.

"Yes. I think so."

He stroked Tristie's long hair and stared into her eyes, "Such a mane of fine hair was meant only to grace a pillow and this fine, fine body was made to find itself writhing and moaning with pleasure beneath that of a real man." He stepped back and then took out the marker pen once more.

He was interrupted by the General. "Ah! Sheik Malik, I'm afraid this slave is to be auctioned. She is exceptional. It is only fair to give others their chance."

The Sheik frowned and his expression darkened. "But you always give me first choice, General."

"Sheik Malik, you are a valued customer, but this time I have to offer her at auction."

The Arab nodded. "Very well General." He ran his hands over Tristie's body once more, "I shall bid then, for I intend to have her!"

Tristie quivered with bewildered fear and she was trying to stifle her sobs, knowing it would probably earn her another whipping. She was to be sold. Sold like a piece of merchandise in a market. She was going to become the slave of an Arabian Sheik, who clearly didn't like Christian women. The fact that she had never been particularly religious didn't matter. To the Sheik she was a Christian and she would be made to suffer for it.

The Sheik and the General moved away and Tristie watched in fascinated horror as the Sheik examined the other girls, selecting just one more. Then the General said:

"You may as well have your slaves taken away now Sheik."

The Sheik nodded, and looking towards the doorway, snapped his fingers. "Abasi! Kadar!"

Two huge shaven-headed Lascars came into the room. They were wearing white tracksuits and large gold earrings, and carried thin leather quirts. In concert, they marched towards the Sheik, halted and bowed their heads.

"Effendi?"

The Sheik indicated the girls he'd marked. "Take these to my boat!"

"Immediately Effendi!"

Minutes later the two men had unchained the two girls, who began to wail and protest. But, switching them into silence, each man picked up a girl and slung her over his shoulder. Then they marched out, carrying their struggling wailing burdens on the start of a journey which would end in the sweltering heat of the Middle-East.

The General turned to the Sheik. "Shall we go to my office? We can get the financial side of things sorted out and have a drink."

The Sheik moved towards the door. "Certainly, my General." He smiled. "But for me, something soft. Alcohol is a curse!"

The two men left the room and Tristie began to shake as she reflected on what was about to happen to her. She was going to join the two unfortunate wretches who had just been carried out of the room. Her life would be Hell from now on.

Then, Miller was in front of her and he grinned into her face, holding up a pad of cotton-wool. Tristie could smell the ether and she groaned as Miller placed the pad over her nose and mouth. In moments, she slipped into unconsciousness.

Miller was looking through the observation hole in the door of the cell where the slavegirl Tristie was lying on top of the small bed. The girl was partially clothed now—buyers liked to see a new slave stripped on the auction block before their eyes—and her breathing was deep and rhythmic. She stirred, shook her head as she woke, then enjoyed a lazy smile, as her hands explored her clothed body.

Miller chuckled to himself as he heard her murmur. "So it was just a nightmare after all..." She moved a little and then caught her breath as the jingle of chains sounded.

Miller smiled, at the cruel joke played on her.

Tristie sat bolt upright, her hands flying to the thick brass collar about her neck. The chain was fastened to it and led to a ringbolt in the wall. Miller watched, fascinated, as Tristie began to explore the skimpy clothes in which he had been told to dress her. The garments were dirty and barely fitted. A thin nylon blouse, torn and tied together over her navel, exposing her small waist and the swell of her belly. She also wore a diaphanous skirt, which was rucked-up and did nothing to hide the narrow bikini-bottom which was pulled tightly into her groin and the crease of her buttocks. The skirt exposed her legs and thighs, and the waistband was held by a small button at her hip.

Miller felt his loins stir. She looked real sexy this one; dressing her unconscious body had given him a real buzz. It had taken him some time, and his hands and fingers had explored the superb flesh and secret places at will.

A horrified expression came over Tristie's face as she looked at her thigh, and her fingers flew to the crescent shaped mark as if checking to see if it really was there. Her head drooped and her shoulders rounded into a ball of misery as her body began to shake.

Miller opened the door and Tristie sat upright again, wiping the tears from her eyes. Then the freezing draught hit her and she shook with the sudden cold as weak sunshine streamed into the tiny room for a moment. The glow was blotted out again as Miller entered and stood looking at her. Then he sneered.

"Welcome to the market, bitch!" He took his whip from his belt. "I'm the Auctioneer! Aren't you lucky?" He nudged her with his toe. "And remember, I have the whip!" He reached for her collar and dragged her to her feet. He ignored her struggles and unshackled her from the bar. He cuffed her twice, and waited until she was still. Then, keeping hold of the chain, he dragged her out through the doorway into a small, circular yard.

17: Sold from the Block

The air was clear and sparkling, but it was freezing and Tristie immediately began to shiver as the cold went through her light clothing. She stumbled, and Miller pulled on the chain attached to her collar.

Tristie bowed her head, accepting the hopelessness of her situation, and staggered after him, feeling more bewildered than ever as she glanced about her.

There was a circular area, about thirty feet in diameter, surrounded by a twelve-foot high stone wall, and every few feet there was an entrance like the one they had just passed through. In the centre was a raised stone platform, surrounded by a crowd of people, all dressed against the cold. Then Tristie's eyes widened in terror as she noticed, all around the platform, heavy iron rings set in the stone—and some of these rings had naked girls chained to them, all crouching against the wall.

On top of the platform there were two more girls, both quite lovely, but with the familiar look of despair and hopelessness in their faces. The same look that Tristie knew would be on her own face. The look that said they realised they were all slaves, prisoners for whom there could be no escape.

The one on the left was a raven-haired beauty, naked and kneeling on the stone flags. She was bent low, her face almost touching the stone, due to the short iron bar running from the front of her collar to the large ring set in the floor.

The blonde girl on the right was not quite naked, having been dressed in leather bondage straps, wrapped about her neck and criss-crossed in a cruel weave all about her torso and legs to emphasise the shapely curves of her body whilst displaying all her obvious attributes to the onlookers. Her arms were shackled in front of her body, but her wrists were secured to the large ring set in a wide belt just below her breasts, so that the delightful swell of her belly and shaven

137

sex was well displayed. A steel chain, also wrapped about her neck, led to the pole in the middle of the platform. She was shivering, her teeth making an audible chatter, as she looked in awe and fear at the small crowd, most of who were slavering over the erotic sight she made.

Tristie began to pull away from the horrors of the block, but Miller tugged her towards the platform.

She resisted desperately, trying to go back to the yard, but Miller growled and pulled her to the floor where he laid three short strokes across the top of her buttocks. "Up on the block!"

Sobbing, Tristie got to her feet and began a slow ascent of the stone steps. Without being told, she sank to her knees in the centre of the block.

There was an appreciative gasp from the watchers. Eager whispers bounced about the area.

"Stand!"

Tristie raised herself, cowering from him as he pushed her between the two other girls on the block and chained her to a free ring on the pole.

"Stay still."

He turned to face the crowd.

"Good morning ladies and gents..."

Tristie began to sob again. "Oh no! No, no no!"

The blonde looked at her angrily. "Shut your face you whining bitch, or we'll all get the whip!"

"They can't do this!"

"You stupid bitch!" the blonde said. "We're on an Island, miles from anywhere. They can do as they like with us! They're going to sell us! We can't stop them! We have to accept it! We're slaves, you stupid cow!"

Then Miller turned from the crowd and growled in anger. "If there's any explaining to do, I'll do it!" Still angry, he pushed Tristie aside and unfastened the blonde from her ring. He dragged her away, down off the block and across to one of the entrances, pushing her through to the waiting attendants. "Sort her out!" he said and turned back towards the block.

The crowd howled with delight at this and turned towards the entrance, to savour the whistling of the lash, the sound of thin leather slashing into bare flesh and the squeals and screams as the girl suffered her whipping. There was more screaming before the bondage leathers came sailing out into the yard. Then, sobbing and naked but for a heavy steel collar, she was herded back out into the arena, her head down in defeat and submission as she was chained to one of the rings at the side of the block.

But not for long.

A beefy red-faced man in tatty jeans and a donkey-jacket stepped forward. "I'll give you five hundred for her!"

Miller displayed a wolfish smile as the tall man sorted notes from his wallet. "Seven hundred!" Miller said.

"Six!"

Miller shrugged. "Six-fifty."

The man nodded. "A deal!"

Miller took the money. "Hope she serves you well."

The man raised his whip above the cowering beauty. "She'll soon learn!"

Miller chuckled and unclipped the girl, handing the length of chain over to the man. The buyer stalked off, dragging his new possession behind him to a pick-up truck, where he slung her onto the flatbed and chained her down before driving off.

Tristie stared at this exhibition. Then the sudden crack of leather on her buttocks made her cry out and she realised she had been daydreaming. She shook in nervous anticipation as the crowd began to shout out.

"Strip her!"

"We want to see her naked!"

Miller turned to Tristie and grinned. "No problem, folks!" He reached out and removed Tristie's neck chain, then he grabbed her blouse and ripped it from her shoulders.

The crowd shouted their approval as Tristie reeled away from him, her breasts swinging free. Immediately she began to shiver violently. "No! No! You can't!" Then, realising, she was being ogled by everyone there, she blushed and tried to cover herself.

Miller switched her buttocks, grinning as Tristie's hands flew away from her breasts and went automatically to the hurt. He grabbed her wrists. "Arms behind you."

Tristie stood trembling mutely on the block, knowing she must obey. She sobbed, and her head bowed in shame.

Miller began to fondle her breasts, lifting the rounded globes up, pulling on her nipple-rings, and sneering as Tristie winced at the pain. He turned back to the crowd. "How's that for a pair of tits? Come on lads, wouldn't you like to get those in your teeth!" He turned to Tristie again and dragged the thin skirt from her waist. The tearing of the cloth was loud and Miller grinned as he pulled the bikini down also. A gasp of admiration went up as Tristie was finally exposed in complete shivering nudity.

Miller pushed her forward. "Not a virgin." He sniggered. "Well, she might have been when she arrived, but you know how temporary that state is!" He waited for the crowd's laughter to quieten down. "She's been freshly branded, too. So, who'll start me off at a hundred!"

A thin, bearded man raised his arm. "I'll go there!"

Then a severe faced woman said: "And fifty!"

"And fifty again!" came from another woman.

Miller looked disappointed. He raised Tristie's head with the handle of his whip. "Come on ladies and gents! She's gorgeous! Who'll give me another fifty?"

A bald headed man raised his arm.

"Thank you sir!" Miller said, looking around for more bids.

"And another hundred!" It was the severe faced woman again.

"Any more?"

Silence.

Miller held the whip in front of Tristic's face, and whispered fiercely: "Kneel!"

Tristie obeyed.

Miller untied her hair, allowing the golden mane to fall about her abused body. He waited again as the crowd's admiring gasps diminished, then he shook the whip in front of Tristie's face. "Come on slave!"

Tristie was puzzled. "Please, what..." She screamed out as the whip lashed into her breasts.

Miller growled at her. "Hurry! I won't wait for ever!" Again he shook the whip in front of Tristie's face, so close she caught the scent of the leather.

Then Tristie understood what he wanted her to do, and, blushing and trembling with shame, she leant forwards and placed a soft kiss on the butt of the whip.

The crowd gave a roar of delight, and Miller draped the whip around Tristie's neck and stroked the lash across her back, allowing it to slide over her breasts like a snake. "See folks! Untrained, but she knows the whip! A natural slave!"

Miller then coiled the whip and stuck it in his belt. He bent over Tristie and cradled her chin in his left hand. His other hand went to her genitals and he started a gentle massage of her sex-mound. His fingers found her clitoris and she began to tremble as she tried to shut out the sudden tingling inside. She didn't want this animal to make her juice, but it was so difficult not to. Her face screwed up with shame as she realised she was failing and her juices began to flow.

Miller drew away and pushed her aside, cleaning the juices from his hand by using her hair as a towel. He nodded to the severe faced woman. "Step up Madam. Feel her yourself! She's a natural!"

Then Sheik Malik came into the arena, shouldering his way through the small knot of people. He stepped up onto the block and Tristie caught her breath, feeling her bladder contract with fear. The Sheik had a cruel sneer on his face and he leant over Tristie and slid his strong slim fingers into her sex.

Tristie gasped in shock and pain and tried to pull away from him, but, clearly well practised, he held her still by the hair. Ignoring her struggles, he massaged Tristie's parts for a few moments.

"Show me your teeth!"

Tristie obediently opened her mouth, allowing the Arab to shove his wet fingers inside, obliging her to taste her own juices.

Then he stepped back, and looked thoughtful.

"Sheik Malik," Miller interjected, "you'll like her. I guarantee it. Strong, too. She'll pull an oar well."

The Arab pondered for a moment, then nodded. "All right, my friend. Five hundred then!"

Miller beamed again and then stroked Tristie's quivering body and face with the whip. "You already kissed it slave! Now kiss it like you mean it. Like you want to. Let Sheik Malik see what you're worth."

Tristie reached for the whip and pulled it to her mouth. Her actions became lascivious as she began to kiss the whip; sucking and licking; sliding her tongue over the leather; groaning in mock ecstasy; behaving as though the whip was a huge, male organ. She moaned. "Oh yes Master!" Twice more, Tristie kissed and sucked at the whip, whimpering in abandon, trying to deny the wetness of her juices as, once again, they flowed of their own accord.

Sheik Malik gave an impassive nod.

"SOLD!" shouted Miller.

The Sheik looked at Tristie. "Now my little Christian slut," he said slowly, "we take you away. Soon, we really see how well you entertain." He snapped his fingers and his attendant, Abasi, forced his way through the crowd. He was holding a coiled dog-whip in one hand and held a black leather hood in the other.

"The hood Effendi?"

Sheik Malik nodded.

Abasi pushed Tristie's head down and slipped the hood over her hair. He aligned the eye slits and then, taking the neck chain, lifted her onto his shoulder, his arm about her legs. He pulled the neck chain taut, so that her upper body was stretched down his back. Then he stepped easily from the block and walked across the arena into one of the tunnels.

Outside the arena, Tristie could just make out the limousine parked in a large open area of gravel. Abasi walked to the car, leant through the window, and pressed a switch. The soft top at the rear slid silently open and he dumped her onto the rear seats as if she were a sack of potatoes. As she sprawled across the leather upholstery she clipped the end of the chain to one of the door handles, and then closed the soft-top again. He turned, as Sheik Malik came up behind him. Abasi bowed his head.

"We go?"

Sheik Malik nodded. "Yes Abasi, we go." A cold smile. "When we reach the yacht you whip the Christian bitch, well! Then shave and circumcise her, ready for sewing." A sadistic grin split his features as he watched the helpless Tristie begin to shake with fear, obviously hearing and understanding him, as of course, he had clearly intended her to do.

"I think she will soon begin to wish she had not been born a white Christian, yes Abasi?"

"Indeed Effendi!"

18: Tristie Finally Submits

Tristie woke in a dank cell. She was filthy and her heart dropped. She moaned to herself, disgusted, as she realised she hardly noticed the rank, human, body-smells any more. She did no more than wrinkle her nostrils now. Still half conscious, she shook her head as she realised just how easy it had been for her to get used to the stench.

The jingle of metal startled her, but only for a moment. Chains were something else she had got used to. Since she had been abducted, she had, more or less, been kept in permanent bondage of one sort or another. She was now accustomed to the heavy brass collar fixed around her neck and she realised, with some surprise, that it seemed a luxury to be chained only by the neck and to have her hands and feet free.

Then she became aware that she had been half-dreaming. Far from having her hands free, she was in extreme bondage. She was indeed chained by the neck and the collar was still there, but that wasn't all!

She was on her back and bent painfully at the waist, her legs stretched backwards over her body, manacled, with thick steel bands encircling her legs just above the knees, at her calves, and at her ankles. Her limbs were held straight. Fixed. Immobile, and kept that way by thick steel rods, one each side of each leg. Her thighs were spread by two chains which ran from her ankles to vertical wooden stakes behind her head.

Neither could she move her arms, for they were stretched sideways, bound tightly to ring bolts in the table-top, which she realised was some three feet high. The effect was that her naked and vulnerable buttocks were raised and stretched taut, exposing her sexual parts to anyone standing over her.

She ached all over, and her back, thighs, buttocks and belly were aflame with the stinging pain of the whip. She began to sob. Why didn't they just kill her and get it over with? She struggled for a moment, but soon realised it was hopeless. Just like everything else about her life since her abduction.

It was futile to fight it.

She was a prisoner and couldn't ever get away.

There was no one to help her.

No doubt now.

She was in the clutches of Sheik Malik.

Defenceless and at the mercy of monsters, in a strange land.

If she didn't do as they wished, they might well kill her. And she didn't really want to die! She ought to see sense. Maybe then they would stop beating her. She would have to play along with them. Convince them she was willing to do as they wished! Anything to end this torment!

Still sobbing and twisting in her bondage, she began to shout.

"Please! Please someone let me out! Please! I promise I'll be good! Let me into the warm! Please! I'll be a slave if you want, but please unchain me! Please!"

She didn't know how long she had yelled for attention. She didn't know how long she had endured the torment, or if indeed anyone had heard her, but suddenly the door opened.

Miller! It was Miller!

Tristie gasped in surprise. She was still on the island, wasn't she? Or had Miller come out to the Middle East as well? Perhaps to 'train' her, as they had put it.

She had no time to wonder further, for Miller stepped across to Tristie and grinned at her.

"Ready to submit?"

Tristie nodded frantically. "Oh Yes!" She knew she must sound convincing. "Please Master! Let me out. I'll behave and obey you!"

"Of course you will," Miller said as he leaned forward and unshackled her from the rack. "Stand up." He stepped back and waited as, easing stiff limbs, Tristie got to her feet.

"On all fours!"

Tristie sank to her knees, placing her palms on the floor.

Miller sneered into her face. "Ever kept a dog?"

Tristie frowned. "Yes Master. When I was little I..." The whip slashed into her buttocks and she yelped her pain, cowering from him.

"Save the chapter and verse," he snarled. "Just answer the question!"

"Yes Master!"

"Was it well-trained?"

Tristie nodded, lowering her head. "Yes Master!"

"And could it do tricks?"

"Yes Master."

"So you know what dogs have to do?"

"Yes Master!"

He bent to her then, and clipped a chromed chain to her collar.

"Sit!"

Tristie sat back on her haunches, her hands down between her thighs. She felt foolish and her cheeks warmed as she blushed.

Miller was delighted. "Oh Yeah! You're really learning." His hand went to his belt and he pulled out a plastic bag full of lumps of cooked ham.

"Hungry?"

Tristie felt her mouth water. The meat was cold, but they had given her mostly fruit and vegetables since her arrival and she had been feeling real hunger. She nodded, eager for the food.

"Oh! Master! Please yes!"

He grinned, and looked down at her. "Beg for it then."

Feeling ashamed and humiliated, Tristie sank back on her haunches, holding her hands in front of her.

Miller pulled slightly on the chain, and held up the meat.

"Want it?"

"Yes please, Master!"

The whip slashed into her body and she screamed.

"Since when could dogs talk?" The whip slashed her again. "Dogs can't talk!"

Forcing back the tears of shame, Tristie lowered her head. "Woof!"

Miller grinned and jerked the meat upwards a little, and again, Tristie knelt upright, and yapped at him.

Miller threw the meat towards her mouth, and she tried to catch it. Hopeless. The meat dropped on the floor and Tristie waited for the expected whipping.

Nothing came except: "Eat!"

Obediently, Tristie bent forward to pick up the meat in her teeth. Hiding her shame, she chewed on the meat, until hunger overcame her and in the end she wolfed it down, her degradation forgotten. It was remarkable what one would do when necessary. And it was necessary. Oh Yes! To avoid that whip it was necessary.

Miller grinned at her. "What do you say slave?"

Understanding dawned and Tristie barked again. "Woof!"

Grinning, Miller threw more meat on the floor and watched, sneering, as Tristie scrabbled for it.

When she had eaten all of the meat, Miller jerked on the chain. "Heel!" He dragged and pulled Tristie after him, forcing her to crawl forwards.

Tristie scurried to her place alongside his left calf.

"Sit!"

Tristie sat, as much like a dog as she knew how.

"The General wants to say goodbye," Miller said. He jerked the chain taut. "Heel!"

Tristie's heart missed a couple of beats. Goodbye? So she was going to Sheik Malik after all. But what could she do? She was helpless. She lowered her head and went to his left calf. Then, as he walked forward, she crawled after him along the rough concrete floor of the corridor.

They didn't go far before Miller stopped. Tristie didn't stop soon enough and Miller thundered the whip into her buttocks. She let out an ear piercing shriek and pitched onto her face, her hands reaching for the hurt.

Miller just grabbed her hair and pulled her backwards.

"Back on your knees, slut!"

Sobbing and struggling against his grip, Tristie tried to obey him, gasping with the effort as she tried to get to all fours again. Her buttocks were aflame where the whip had slashed into her flesh and she was trembling with the agony.

They were near to another red painted door, which was ajar, and Tristie was vaguely aware that beyond there was a gymnasium.

Miller nudged her buttocks. "In there!"

Tristie obeyed and, still crawling, went into the room.

Right in the middle was a vaulting horse, placed beneath a trapeze that hung from the high ceiling.

"Get over there and climb onto the horse!"

Tristie did as she was told, wincing in agony as the effort of climbing onto the horse aggravated the wheals from the sting of Miller's whip. But she managed to get herself astride the leather horse. The crossbar of the trapeze was just level with the back of her neck, and she wondered what she would have to do now.

She didn't have to wait long, for Miller came up to her, flicking her thighs with his whip. "Kneel on the horse!"

Quickly, Tristie knelt so the trapeze bar was now in the small of her back.

Miller grinned at her, then opened a cupboard and took out a pair of manacles with a longish chain between them. He came back, holding up the manacles for her to see. "Arms over the bar!"

Tristie's heart began to race as she realised what was going to happen, but she knew she had to obey. Shaking, she hooked her arms over the bar. She shuddered with fear as Miller came closer.

"Hands in front of your belly!"

"Please Master..."

The whip silenced her. "Haven't you learned yet, bitch?"

Tristie lowered her head in defeat and placed her hands in front of her body. She grimaced as Miller fastened her wrists in the manacles, tightening them so the chain dug into her stomach and the bar pressed hard into her back, just below her shoulder-blades.

Then Miller snatched the horse away from beneath her!

Tristie dropped, squealing in agony as all her weight fell upon her upper arms. She wailed as the bar almost dislocated her shoulder-blades, and gasped as she slowly swung to a stop. Her toes were about three feet clear of the boards beneath her.

Then she saw Miller uncoiling his whip...

As Tristie regained her senses she realised she was still in the gymnasium, and still suspended from the trapeze. But now she was cross-trussed with a chrome dog-chain and they had fastened her arms in front of her body. The bar of the trapeze still lay in the crook of her elbows, across her back, her weight causing it to press into the points of her shoulder-blades. It also forced the chain between her wrists to dig even deeper into her stomach, bending her spine into a slight backwards arch. Her legs were hanging free, but were now held apart by a wide bamboo pole secured between her ankles.

She could feel the ball gag which had been forced into her mouth, and her whole being was aflame with pain where Miller's whip had seared her flesh.

If she hung motionless; feigned unconsciousness, they might leave her alone for a while...

It didn't fool them.

Through half-closed eyes, she saw that the General was there. He came close. "She's shamming! Give her a taste of the goad Nick!"

It was Keane with him then, not Miller.

149

Keane stepped over to the suspended Tristie and looked up at her. He was holding a cattle-goad in his right hand. "Come on, little Tristie!" he said. "Wake up!" He reached for the bamboo pole between her ankles and held her gently swinging body steady.

Tristie felt terror as well as despair as Keane lifted the instrument towards her. The end of the goad touched the inside of her thigh and he inched it upwards, towards her sex-mound, to let the brass tip rest against the tight chain which was spreading her labia. Then he looked at her with a strange light in his eyes. Sympathy? In this place? From these perverts?

Surely not!

Her back arched and her eyes started from their sockets as Keane forced the goad past the tight chain and deep into her passage. Every muscle in her body spasmed, and she screamed into the gag as he forced the chains aside and pushed the goad deep inside.

Then he switched the goad on.

Three times he passed a surge of current through her, gazing intently at her, as she screamed and bucked against her bonds. He then held her steady as he removed the goad and pulled her down to the floor. With her toes just brushing the tiles, he left her suspended, while he took a riding-crop from his belt

The beating began and Tristie babbled into her gag, screaming and writhing as the leather cane cut into her exposed flesh. Soon the room was full of her futile screams as her defenceless body was abused once more.

Finally Keane stopped and stepped over to her. He lowered her down a little and removed the gag from her mouth. "Now," he said, "are you ready to serve as a slavegirl should?"

Tristie's heart sank. She was finished. Really finished, this time. Oh yes, they had won!

She had suffered enough.

Couldn't stand any more torture.

Submit; agree to their demands.

Be their slave.

Whether she liked it or not, she had to obey.

"I'm ready Master! I'm ready! You know I'm ready!" It was even easier to use the words.

"What are you ready for?"

"I am ready to serve as a slavegirl, Master," she whispered.

"And what does that mean?"

"That I will do anything my Masters wish!"

"Willingly?"

"Willingly Master." Strangely, she felt somehow relieved. Maybe it was true. After all, she couldn't deny the attraction she still felt toward this man, this strange one, who, cruel though he could be, occasionally showed tenderness. Maybe he was the one who had awakened some hidden desire in her; a wish to be dominated; to be a slave to him. It didn't matter. Either way, it would help her through the trials to come. She nodded, almost by instinct. "I am a slavegirl. I will obey. Always."

Keane smiled. "Reckon she's ready, General!" He slapped her buttocks gently, letting his hands wander over her hips and belly, before reaching up to massage her breasts. Then his fingers teased her nipples, and he leaned forward to kiss her sex-mound, his tongue flicking about her lips. He pulled away, looked into her eyes, and smiled.

"Juicing up nicely, aren't we?"

"Yes Master." Tristie was trembling, half in pain, half with desire; sudden desire for this man. This man who had the message in his eyes; the message for her? And why not? She was their slave now. It didn't really matter any more, but it helped to think he cared, in his strange way.

Keane stroked her buttocks. "And it's better now, isn't it?" His voice was soft.

"Yes Master." She knew he was right. She did feel better. She almost relished the knowledge that she was their slave.

The General stepped forward himself, and he too stroked her waist and buttocks. "We have a new slavegirl in our flock," he said, "ready to give pleasure to anyone. Anyone! Is that right?"

Again Tristie nodded. "Yes Master." Even him? Yes, even him. She was totally theirs now.

The General patted her buttocks. "Then welcome to your new life, Tristie... Nick, take her to the recovery suite." One more pat on her buttocks, and the General turned away and left the room.

Keane stepped forward and unfastened her from the trapeze, steadying her as her feet touched the floor. His arm went around her waist gently. "Come on sweetie," he said. "I have a treat in store for you."

Tristie shuddered then, and allowed her head to fall to his shoulder.

He didn't say anything. He just let her use his body as a crutch, as they left the room.

19: Tristie Accepts Enslavement

The General had sent for Keane. It was urgent. That puzzled Keane. Everything was so laid back here. Few things were urgent. Except the need to satisfy sexual urges.

When he got to the office, Tristie, the slavegirl number Seven, was standing just behind the crystal-bead curtain. He glanced at her casually. They had tidied her up. The General knew what looked good on a slavegirl.

Seven was naked, except for her gold collar and its slave-bell, with the golden chain hanging in its graceful arc between her pierced nipples to brush gently against her lower rib-cage. A heavier chain of chromed steel, each link having small raised protrusions welded on, ran from the front of her collar, down between her gorgeous breasts, to disappear between her thighs. The chain had been pulled tight into her sex-cleft, taken up her back, stretched taut and clipped to the rear of the collar. Her wrists were manacled, again with a good length of chain between them, and this had been clipped to the ring in her sex-mound. Today, there was also a slave-bell fitted to the ring.

She looked delectable.

Smelled good too.

The General looked across towards Tristie. 'Come here, Seven.'

She scurried over, submissive now, her slave-bells and wrist chain, tinkling.

"On your belly."

Tristie obeyed, lying down on the smooth marble floor. She shivered as her belly touched the floor and the bell at her collar clinked; a dull sound beneath her body.

The General stood over her, nudging her trembling form with his toe. "Palms down!"

Trembling, the slavegirl, number Seven, placed her palms flat against the tiles, her elbows jutting upwards. She winced as the chain between her wrists cut into her belly.

"Ten push-ups, number Seven!"

For a moment she hesitated, clearly puzzled.

But only for a moment, as the whip slashed into her buttocks. Tristie began to do the push-ups. But the chain between her wrists restricted her movements and, as she raised her body, it pulled on her belly-ring, causing her further pain. The taut chrome chain was also pulled tighter between her labia and soon she was struggling to obey, her face twisted with pain as her enforced movement caused further agonies.

Tristie had managed only four push-ups and was struggling with a fifth, when the General pushed her hips to the floor with his foot. "Not very fit, are you?"

Gasping, remaining on her belly, Tristie managed to answer: "No Master."

"But you are ready to submit?"

Still gasping from her efforts, Tristie nodded, her bell jingling. She wondered if she had been spared at the last from being sold to Malik.

"Yes Master."

"You don't sound very convinced, Seven." The General leaned over her. "You wouldn't be trying to fool us again would you?"

Tristie she shook her head emphatically. "Oh no. No Master. I am ready to submit. I want to serve you, Master."

"That's what you said before."

"But Master, I didn't know the truth about myself then. Now I do and I want to be a slavegirl."

"Don't push your luck, bitch."

"What do...?" Tristie was almost gabbling.

He silenced her with a kick in the ribs. "You're overdoing it. You sound just a little too eager." He lifted her head up by her hair, ignoring her grunts of pain. "You're taking me for a fool." He twisted her hair in his huge hand. "The auction and the viewing room were just a demonstration of what can happen to you, if you try it on." He shook her again, "What WILL happen if you don't see sense." He rolled her onto her back with his foot and sneered down at her. "This is your last chance. Next time, I really will let Sheik Malik have you. You wouldn't like that, would you?"

Tristie shook her head. "No Master!" Then, in a moment, Tristie was screaming in agony as the General's switch slashed into her flesh. To evade the lash, she scrabbled around the floor, but it was futile. All she could do was scream and bear the pain until, finally, the General stopped. He stood over her, impassive; silent for a moment. "I mean what I say!" He screwed her hair into his fist. "For now, think yourself lucky. The next time you become difficult, I won't relent. Do you understand?"

"Yes, Master." Tristie felt something like relief run through her body, although why she didn't know. She was still a slave, still had to obey these madmen.

"So your training continues." He smiled at her. "For now, I will use your own name as a slave-name. Now, what is your slave-name?"

Completely degraded and subdued, Tristie bowed her head in submission. "Tristie, Master."

Keane could see it in her face.

Realisation.

She was a slave and the Master had spoken.

The General sneered at her. "We're getting there. You're beginning to understand." He pushed her away and shook his head. "It will become second nature to you!" He leaned over her. "WON'T IT!" He shouted.

"Yes Master!"

Keane knew what would be going through her mind. It was obvious she feared the whip. All the girls did. She would also be fearing the prospect of becoming part of Sheik Malik's stock.

But she still seemed to have some pride left.

Well, Keane thought, she'd have to bury it.

Pride was no defence against the whip!

She had to obey.

She was a prisoner and she wouldn't escape from here.

She must have realised that her very survival depended on obedience; that as long as she resisted, the whippings would continue, until she gave in or died! Like all the others, she must know now this was no game.

It was reality.

Her reality.

It was happening to her and submission, complete submission, was the only thing which might end the whippings.

Keane grinned to himself. Might was the word. The General did have a habit of whipping a girl just for the pleasure of it. Oh! And then there were the shows for new members. That was another excuse to get the whip out.

Tristie's body language was clear. She seemed to push dignity aside, looking up at the General, pleading. "Please Master. Believe me. I understand. I'll obey, but please, don't hit me any more."

The General showed his evil grin. "The bitch sees sense!" He looked at his whip. "But then, sooner or later, the whip ensures that!" He stroked the whip handle across her thighs and nudged the blunt end against the swell of her sex. "Doesn't it Tristie!"

Tristie hung her head in defeat.

She must know she couldn't win!

They could do as they wished with her.

She stifled a sob. "Yes Master!"

Again, the General massaged her vagina with the blunt handle of the whip and Tristie groaned, a sound of pleasure almost.

The General chuckled. "You really are a natural slave, Tristie! And your talents will be used to the full. You will soon learn the ways of a Pleasure Slave. Then you'll be ready to serve our guests and give them full enjoyment!"

His smile was cold now, as Tristie's face registered the

defeat she was feeling. She shook her head. "I can hardly believe…"

He raised the whip. "From now on Tristie, when you speak you are restricted to four responses." He moved the whip slightly, "Those responses are, Yes, No, Please and Thank you, all followed by the word Master—or Mistress, of course. The only time you say anything else will be when the requirement is obvious. Understand?"

Tristie understood, only too well. "Yes Master."

"And you are a slavegirl?"

"Yes Master."

"An obedient slavegirl?"

"Yes Master."

"You're getting juiced up, aren't you, Tristie?"

"Yes Master."

Keane could actually see the moistness showing itself.

The General chuckled, and stroked her breasts with the whip handle, allowing it to trace the chrome chain towards her vagina again. "You see, little Tristie? You're a natural! I knew you would soon realise I am the Master!" Suddenly then he spat on her, grinning as she recoiled, unable to avoid the globule of saliva splashing into her face. "Now, once again Tristie! What must you call me?"

Tristie trembled and murmured. "I must call you Master!"

Keane could see she was beginning to mean it.

The General grinned again. "And you are a slavegirl," he said, emphasising his words with digs of the whip in her breasts. "What are you?"

"I am a slavegirl Master."

"And what can I do with you?"

Tristie was being conditioned more and more, Keane could see. They were finally breaking her spirit. The girl lowered her head and answered the General. "Anything you wish, Master!"

The General smiled, then leaned forward to lift her chin with the whip. Then he held the wicked implement up before her face.

Puzzled, Tristie looked at the whip and frowned.

The General shook the leather quirt slightly.

Still Tristie frowned.

The General shook the whip again. "I shan't wait for ever girl!" He jerked the whip in front of her face.

Tristie frowned still, but then, remembering her enforced performance on the auction block, realised what the General wanted. She blushed, then leant forward and slowly and seductively kissed the whip.

The General let out a satisfied sigh. "I think we do have a natural slave, Nick!" He leaned towards Tristie. "You really are beginning to understand, aren't you?"

"Yes Master!"

"And it's better this way, isn't it?" He caressed her cheek with the whip.

"Yes Master." Tristie barely suppressed a shudder. This time, Keane realised, it was a tremor of excitement. She would be moist and warm down there, and suddenly he wanted her badly.

Even as she spoke, Keane could tell she had accepted that she was a slave. And not merely because she was a prisoner, or just to avoid the whip. Quite simply, she was demonstrating her submission. Well, the General was that kind of man! Even Keane had to admit that.

"Excellent!" The General spoke softly and then glanced at Keane. "Persuade the bitch a little more, Nick."

Keane stepped forward and in moments Tristie was scrabbling about the floor and screaming for mercy as the curtain-wire whip slashed into her. Finally Keane tired and, breathing heavily, he leaned over the whipped slavegirl.

"Just remember, Tristie!"

The General went over to Tristie, grabbed hold of her collar, and dragged her to his chair. "Now! Once more. Do you accept you are a slave? A mere animal, who will obey without question?

158

"Yes, yes!" Tristie sobbed. She grabbed his arm and began to kiss his hand, frantic to avoid more punishment. "I accept I am a slavegirl! Your slavegirl! But please! Don't whip me any more!"

The General shrugged, and in answer to her plea, merely slashed her across the back with the whip. "You are forgetting. You say nothing except yes, no, please or thank you, and you call me Master! Now do you remember?"

"Yes Master!" she sobbed, as she rolled to the floor, sprawling in front of him.

He stooped to lift her to her knees in front of the chair. "And you are not going to be difficult?"

Tristie lowered her head, her crying subsiding. "No Master!"

He chuckled. "Of course you aren't." He sat down and leaned back into the chair. "You will shortly be taken across the Island, where you will serve as a pony-slave until I decide you really have submitted to us. If you fail to please, then you will be sold. And Sheik Malik really has taken a liking to you." He stroked her face. "I had difficulty in persuading him you were to remain here. Even I don't know exactly what happens to the girls I send to him."

Tristie had begun to shake with apprehension again and the General lifted her chin with the handle of his whip. "Now do you understand your position and do you submit. COMPLETELY!"

Tristie nodded, fearfully. "Yes Master! I do know my place Master! I understand and I submit to you, Master!"

The General nodded and turned to Keane. "I thought this one was going to be awkward, but it seems I was wrong. The bitch is ours." He pointed to the door. "Take her away Nick."

Keane nodded, bent to the prostrate Tristie, and pulled her by the hair to her feet. Ignoring her wails he then frog-marched her from the room.

Outside, in the corridor, he said:

159

"Turn left and keep walking." He flicked her buttocks with the whip. "Don't dawdle!"

Tristie squealed as the whip stung her again. She increased her stride, the extra pace pulling the chrome chain deeper into her sex-lips as she walked. The torture lasted for about five minutes before another slash of the whip brought her to a halt outside a thick steel door.

It was another dark granite-walled room, nothing more than a dungeon. Keane followed her in and took the chains from her body. He left the collar in place, securing it to a ring in the wall by a short steel chain. Then he unfastened her wrists and placed her arms behind her, before clipping the manacles back onto her wrists.

He bent to her and took something from his pocket. He showed her his open hand. There was a small yellow tablet in his palm.

"Put out your tongue!"

She shook her head. "Please, no more drugs."

"Take it." He gave her an almost imperceptible smile. "It's just to help you sleep." He caressed her upper arm softly. "Help you recover and heal your skin!" He squeezed her arm, gently. "I promise you. Just this once to help."

There was a strange light in his eyes, and he seemed to be trying to tell her something. The message wasn't clear, but there was no threat at the moment. She sighed and did as he said.

He placed the tablet on her tongue and then put a cup of water to her lips.

She swallowed the tablet, wanting to talk to him, but not daring to.

He bent forward then and kissed her forehead softly. "Sorry, but I have to leave your arms behind you." He caressed her cheek. "I'll be back for you. Just sleep."

He slammed the door behind him.

Tristie slumped against the wall and slid to her haunches. She just couldn't understand that man. One moment he was

160

a cruel sadist, the next he was all sweetness and light. Or was he just that way, because it was his form of mental torture?

She sighed again, what did it matter? She was stuck here and she had to accept everything or be constantly beaten. She shuddered and lay down in the straw. At least it was clean straw and smelled quite pleasant. Soon, despite herself, she drifted off to an uneasy sleep.

But not for long.

Two of the overalled attendants had come into the cell, waking her. One put a plate of fresh vegetables and fruit and a large dish of milk beside her. "Eat," he grinned. "I should enjoy it while you can. Pony-slaves live on oatmash and water." He turned away and left her to it, slamming the door behind him.

Tristie dragged herself over to the food, knelt in front of the plate and stooped to eat, like the animal they were turning her into.

It was difficult, especially lapping up the milk, but eventually she finished the meal. At least it had been good and fresh and it had satisfied her hunger. When she had finished she crawled into the corner of the room and sat down, her back against the wall. She sighed, pulling legs up to her breasts. Lowering her head to her knees, she began to sob. But there was no one to hear and her cries merely bounced off the uncaring walls. Soon, tiredness overcame her and she fell asleep again.

20: Tristie is Saddled

Tristie woke, it seemed just moments later, and wailed as she felt the slash of leather across her thighs.

"Wake up!"

Tristie screamed, rolled away and opened her eyes. She then had to close them tightly against the glare of the lights as she fought her confusion at being jerked awake so brutally.

As her eyes adjusted to the glare she huddled against the wall, cowering from the man standing over her.

Miller! With a dog whip!

Tristie shivered and moaned as she adjusted to reality, recalling how to behave. "Please Master! Don't hit me any more!"

But then the door opened and Sheena came in. She was also carrying a dog-whip and a long piece of hempen rope. She looked at Miller and smiled. "Give her a good whipping Zach!" She licked her lips. "Let's hear her scream!"

Miller grinned, and began to beat the naked Tristie, ignoring her frantic screams for mercy. Finally he tired and, panting and sporting a huge erection, he looked at Sheena. "Right now she'd make a lovely shag!" He grinned, wolfishly. "What d'you reckon?"

The woman moved close to him and pressed her leather-clad body against his skin. Her hand slipped down and she caressed his huge penis. "Why waste that on a slave!" She squeezed the fearsome weapon, then sank to her knees in front of him and took the massive weapon deep into her mouth.

Miller groaned with ecstasy and grabbed Sheena's hair, pulling her head close to his groin.

Sheena moaned as she licked and sucked at his penis. She caressed his thighs and buttocks, her tongue flicking at and around the thick stem of his shaft. She swallowed the swollen head of the penis, taking it deep into her throat.

His hips began to thrust at her willing mouth and soon he was ramming his penis deep into her throat, jamming her face hard into his groin and slashing at her buttocks with the whip.

Sheena was wriggling, squirming, gurgling in her passion. Her hands scrabbled at the open slit of her leather suit, her fingers plunged deep into her own body as she sucked and bit at the weapon. Her hips were gyrating now and she shuddered each time the whip landed on her body. Soon she was in a frenzy. She masturbated herself with one hand, whilst clutching at Miller's buttocks with the other and swallowing the thick length of his member.

Miller ceased his whipping and his movements quickened until, with a roar, he lunged deep into her mouth, clenching his buttocks as he climaxed, his seed jetting into Sheena's mouth.

Sheena held on for a moment, sucking every drop of semen she could from the huge weapon. Then she pulled gently away and went over to Tristie.

Tristie had been watching in fascinated bewilderment, but had been aware of a warmth and tingling in her own vagina. She turned away in embarrassment, but Sheena stooped down and grabbed Tristie's face in her one hand, then forced open her mouth. She bent to kiss Tristie, forcing her tongue into her mouth.

Tristie moved away momentarily, but then realised she would be whipped, and so suffered the perverted kiss instead. Then suddenly, she tasted the warm sperm in her own mouth, as Sheena forced Miller's discharge from between her lips into the back of Tristie's throat.

Tristie tried to pull away but it was hopeless, for Sheena clamped her lips shut and held her as she was forced to swallow, ignoring the heaving and retching. Sheena held Tristie's mouth shut until the vomiting reflexes had passed and then, wiping stray spunk from her own mouth, she smeared the droplets across Tristie's face, grabbed Tristie's chin and forced a hard deep kiss on the girl. Her tongue reached down into Tristie's throat. Then she pushed her away and stared at her. "Don't say I never share anything with you!"

Tristie trembled, hiding her disgust. "No Mistress."

Sheena patted Tristie's cheek. "There's a good little slave!" She turned to Miller, bent to kiss his softening penis, and then straightened to kiss his forehead. Softly, she caressed his taut belly and chest, her fingers teasing at his light body-hair. "Your body... It's gorgeous!" She unzipped the front of her leather suit, allowing her tits to fall free, and rubbed them against him. Her right hand clasped his already firming member.

"Oh Zach! Why don't you go and whip another slave? Really pump up this gorgeous thing! I'll see you in my rooms when I've finished here, and you can bang it up me!"

He squeezed her tight leather-clad buttocks and kissed her cheek. "I'll be ready when you are!" Then he turned away and left the two women alone.

Sheena stood for a moment and looked down at the lashed slavegirl. Then she grabbed Tristie's hair and pulled her towards her. Ignoring the slavegirl's cries, Sheena unclipped the collar and chain from Tristie's neck and replaced it with the rough hemp, tightening the rope under her chin. Then, jerking on the rope, she dragged Tristie across the room towards a smaller alcove.

Sheena switched on a dim light in the wall and Tristie could see that inside the alcove there was a six foot square pit full of a steaming black liquid. Sheena yanked Tristie to her feet. "Time to turn you into a brunette!" She deftly pulled the rope downwards to wrap it tightly about Tristie's arms and body. In moments Tristie was trussed with the rope and she began to sob.

Sheena prodded her forward to the lip of the vat of steaming liquid. Then, still holding the rope, she pushed Tristie into the vat, laughing as she screamed.

Coughing and spluttering, Tristie struggled to the surface. The hot dye stung her eyes and lanced into the injuries on her body. The pit was quite shallow, but with her arms secured to her side, Tristie was panicking. She struggled frantically to the edge, pleading to be let out. But she was merely pushed under again by Sheena. Three times she tried before Sheena finally dragged her out by her now black hair, and unwrapped the rope from her body. Then, jerking Tristie upright again, Sheena pulled on the rope.

Tristie was still spluttering, spitting out the bitter taste of the black dye, as she was dragged back to the stall. Her soft white skin was streaked with the dye, and her long hair was slicked about her shapely torso. She screamed as Sheena shoved her into the stall, before bending to remove the rope. Totally naked now, Tristie cringed against the wall of the straw littered room and sobbed.

Sheena merely laughed aloud and hefted the wire-whip which she was holding in her right hand. She allowed the coils to fall loose and took her hand back, cracking the whip. A loud report bounced about the room.

Tristie was screaming now. "NO MISTRESS! PLEASE DON'T WHIP ME ANY MORE!" She sank to her knees and cried. "I'll do anything, Mistress..."

Sheena cut her short with an evil chuckle. "You certainly will! You're just a slave, a piece of worthless female flesh which will be used as we see fit." She shook the whip again. "You think because you were a glamour model you're something special." She spat on the floor in front of the shaking girl. "Well, you're nothing. Just a sex-slave."

With contemptuous ease, Sheena curled the flex through the air, so it landed on Tristie's shoulders. The impetus wound the flying end of the whip tight about the slavegirl's collared neck and, laughing now, Sheena dragged the helpless girl towards her.

Sheena pulled Tristie upright. "Don't ever back away from me again!" Sheena squeezed Tristie close for a moment, and then shoved her to her knees once more. "Now, kiss my sex. Lick it and suck it until my juice runs into your lovely little mouth. Then you swallow my love juice! Just to show me you beg forgiveness." She grabbed Tristie's throat and hissed in her face. "And you had better do it as though you mean it!"

Trembling, Tristie caressed Sheena's hairy love-mound with her cheeks and then, opening her mouth wide, she pushed her tongue deep into her Mistress's vagina and began pumping her head back and forth, whilst her other hand began to caress Sheena's buttocks and thighs. Soon Tristie's mouth was running with saliva as she lubricated the woman's parts, and her hands were fluttering about Sheena's waist, teasing the soft flesh.

Tristie knew she had to play her part well and she began to moan with mock pleasure as her soft tongue slid in and out of the woman's genitals. Her tongue darted about the moist orifice, and she nuzzled her head close into Sheena's belly as she tongued the woman's clitoris, bringing her Mistress to a frenzy.

Then, screaming her pleasure, Sheena grabbed both ends of the improvised whip and pulled Tristie's head hard into her body, ramming her hips against the helpless girl's face. Heedless of her cries of anguish and her choking, Sheena ground Tristie's face deep into her body, wriggling her hips as Tristie's ineffectual panic-stricken slaps landed on her Mistress's flesh. Sheena began to pant and scream. "Come on you sexy little slave. Fetch me off with that tongue of yours. Suck me! Suck me! Suck me!"

Then a final scream as the woman came. She continued to press her groin into Tristie's face, ignoring her struggles and her frantic efforts to breathe. She pulled Tristie's tongue deeper into her running wet slash, forcing her to swallow.

Eventually Sheena drew away. "I'll let you finish the job later, slave!" She sighed and pushed Tristie to the floor, pulling the whip away with a jerk so that the girl rolled over and away from her.

Stepping across to the prostrate Tristie, Sheena stooped and lifted her by her hair. Ignoring her protests, she frog-marched her captive over to a wall, where in moments she chained her wrists to a large ring in the stonework. She spread Tristie's legs and shackled her ankles together with a long iron rod. She then stood back and admired her handiwork.

She ran her hands along Tristie's shapely flanks and pinched a handful of flesh at her buttocks. "The General wants you as a pony-girl, and what the General wants the General gets. So now you're going to be fully saddled. Permanently. And I'm going to enjoy this too." The evil woman patted Tristie's rump. "You're going to make a fine pony!" She pointed to a wooden rail. There was a strange riding saddle draped over it. "See your saddle, slave! It's been made to fit your sexy little waist!"

Tristie looked at the object and trembled. It was much like a normal riding saddle, except the back was raised right up, and shaped like a seat. Tristie could see how it would be fitted to her body and she groaned to herself.

Sheena went across to the rail, picked up the saddle and brought it across to the horrified girl. She dropped it to the floor and then sorted out a wide leather strap with a huge buckle. Stirrups were attached at each side and there were two large rings stitched into the leather at the back and front.

The belt was placed about Tristie's slender waist, and nipped tightly so that it rested at the generous flare of her hips. After adjusting the stirrups to hang down each side of Tristie's legs, Sheena fitted two smaller straps to the front of the belt, and pulled them down through Tristie's legs from the front, to be secured to the rings at the back of the belt.

Tristie gasped as the belts were pulled tight into her labia. They rested one to each side, cutting into her genitals, stretching her sex-lips wide apart.

167

Sheena chuckled as she slid her hand past the belts and into Tristie's vagina. "Have to keep you ready for sex!" She grinned into Tristie's face. "Just because you're going to be a pony-slave doesn't mean you won't be serviced now and again!" She giggled cruelly. "And again, and again!"

She straightened the stirrups again so they lay flat against Tristie's flanks, then caressed her thighs. "In fact, you will be used by some unfortunate guests who have trouble making it. It'll be up to you to cure their problem, or you'll be whipped. Some of them would rather torture you than have sex anyway! In fact, some of them just can't get a hard on so they can't do anything else! And of course, there'll be the women like me. They'll ride you hard! None of them need lessons in torture either!"

She ran her hands down Tristie's flanks again.

"Or maybe they'll race you against other pony-slaves. Who knows? They can use you as they wish. If they do race you, you won't be fit for anything afterwards." She lifted Tristie's chin. "Most of our guests like to win. Otherwise, you know what will happen!"

Tristie had begun to shake more and more. Now, grinning into the terrified girl's face, Sheena picked up the saddle and fitted it to Tristie's back. She grinned at Tristie as she clipped the hooks into the rings on the belt. At the front of the saddle there were two thick leather straps, and at the end of each strap there was a length of dog-chain. The straps were taken over Tristie's shoulders and both ends were crossed tightly between her breasts, taken around her back and then brought to the front again, to be secured beneath her breasts with a padlock. The saddle was now tight around Tristie's waist and the rear of it jutted outwards from her back.

Sheena slapped Tristie's trembling buttocks and caressed the naked flank again, allowing her fingers to slide around her captive's thigh. Her thumb slid into Tristie's tight little anus and she pushed her saddled captive forward against her shackles, grinning into her pain-wracked features. Then Sheena took her hand away and went across to a large cupboard set in the wall.

Sheena opened the doors and a strong smell of leather pervaded the room, as she took out a bundle of straps and chromed metal pieces; some kind of riding tack. She came back to Tristie and stood in front of her. Grinning broadly, she reached for Tristie's head, grabbing her hair as she tried to avoid the grasp.

Deftly she slid a leather helmet over Tristie's head, pulling the thick material down tightly, so all that could be seen of Tristie's lovely face was her eyes, nose, lips and ears. Still chuckling Sheena picked up a bridle and put it in place over the mask.

Tristie struggled briefly, but it merely earned her another cuff around the head. "I said keep still, or this won't be pleasant at all." Sheena secured the bridle behind Tristie's head and then picked up a shining chromed bit.

Sheena forced the bit between Tristie's teeth, and clipped it to the rings on the bridle, fastening the reins to the bit at the same time. She yanked Tristie's head back against the collar and tightened the strap behind her head, pulling the bit back, hard into her jaws.

Tristie had thought nothing could hurt her any more, physically or mentally. But she had been wrong. Now she was sobbing, both in pain and shame, as she realised fully that they considered her as no more than an animal.

Sheena cuffed her along side the ear. "Silence!" She unshackled the iron rod from Tristie's ankles and then reached up to release her arms. "On your knees, mare!"

Tristie knelt and Sheena mounted her, settling into the saddle. Digging her heels into Tristie's thighs, the woman slashed at Tristie's right buttock.

"Up!"

The helpless girl squealed with pain, and felt the despair of shame. But she struggled upright, wobbling as Sheena settled her weight into the now horizontal rear extension of the saddle.

Grabbing the reins, the woman forced Tristie's head back and brought the quirt down wickedly.

Tristie stepped forward, and soon began to trot as Sheena urged her on, laying the quirt again and again into her naked flanks and digging her heels into her thighs. Before long Sheena was riding the wretched girl round the large room at a fast run, shouting with glee, lashing her with the quirt, urging her to go faster and faster.

Finally, Sheena tired of her sport as Tristie began to totter from exhaustion. She dismounted and pushed Tristie into a straw littered stall, and shackled her collar to the wooden partition.

Then she left Tristie to her private misery.

21: HARNESSED TO A TROTTING-GIG

Tristie was becoming fit. Since she had first been saddled, it had been necessary to tighten her harness four times as weight had come off her. She had become lean, but was still shapely, with the sleek, well-toned look of the fit athlete. Tristie found no pleasure in that. What good was it all, if she wasn't free? The chances of that were nil, for in all the time she had been kept as a pony-slave, she had hardly left the bowels of this awful place. And whenever she did, she was always under close supervision.

The pony girls were treated as animals, and were expected to behave like animals. They were kept in a proper stable and each had her own stall. Whenever they weren't being used, they were chained to a large ring attached to the front of a feeding trough and could move only a few feet from the wall of their straw-lined stalls. The only time they were unshackled was once a day in the early morning, so they could clean out their stables and lay fresh straw.

Then, if they were lucky, they were allowed to clean each other with the hoses. The water was freezing cold, but at least it got them clean. But it wasn't really enough, and Tristie was becoming disgusted with the rank stink of her own body. She was forever pestered by flies, being obliged to shake her head, so that her long matted hair acted like a horsetail, flicking away the bothersome insects.

She had to feed like an animal, having to lap at the mess of oatmeal mash which was poured into the trough twice a day, trying to shut her ears to the grunts and moans of her fellow pony-girls in the adjoining stalls as they, too, tried to lap up their share of the mash. Then the even more frantic wails as they tried to lap up the faster flowing water, which was thrown down the trough to clean it and provided their only liquid intake.

Only rarely were they permitted to rest for longer than a few hours, and the only time they were completely divested of their harness and tack was when they were given to a guest for sexual games. Even then some of the guests liked to have their slaves tacked up in harness, so they could ride them into exhausted submission.

Sex came in all forms, and in the past weeks she had been taken like an animal on all fours. She had been bound to posts, shackled to walls, roped to benches, and suspended from chains, often to be screwed by two, even three men at one time. She had also been used by perverted lesbians who usually beat her when their filthy sessions were over. And she had been tortured by pathological monsters, who never bothered with sex, but inflicted pain just for the pleasure that gave them.

It was all part of the conditioning process.

They treated pony-slaves as animals.

They expected them to regard themselves as animals.

But it was the pure fact of being a pony-slave which was the worst part of it. All of the girls on the island were treated as if they were of no account, but the pony-girls were abused more than any of them. Tristie had soon learned that the status, if it could be called that, was reserved as one of many forms of punishment awarded for disobedience.

Mistress Sheena had told her she was lucky.

Being a pony-slave was nothing.

Compared to being one of Sheik Malik's slavegirls.

Neither would it last forever.

If she obeyed them.

That didn't help Tristie.

Having lost track of time altogether, she had no idea how long it had been since she had first been saddled, much less how long it would be before she was taken away from the stables.

Until then, she had to suffer.

Most days she was ridden almost to exhaustion by sadistic people who slashed their riding crops into her buttocks; unmerciful; forcing her to carry them around the passageways of the complex. It was so bad, Tristie barely noticed a normal cropping and she was beginning almost to look forward to a hard rider because it meant that the following day she would be given a rest, to allow the bruises to fade.

Then, as if that hadn't been bad enough, some of the guests had made it known they liked to see Tristie, in particular, harnessed to a trotting-gig; they seemed to like the way her long hair streamed in the wind and her excellent breasts and buttocks bounced and jiggled as she ran. So she had been introduced to the trotting-gigs, to be used almost exclusively for the barbaric sport of trotting.

Three times a week, at least, she was taken up to the grass-track at the northern end of the island, where she was harnessed to a gig. Naked except for her harness, complete with bits and reins, she was made to race against other girls, dragging the aluminium trotting-gigs under the whip, wielded by cruel drivers.

For the winner there was always a prize of extra food and time free of the harness, and maybe even a bath. For the losers, there was punishment, which consisted of two weeks serving as a draught-slave, harnessed, naked and sweating, into teams of four or six-in-hand, pulling heavy carts, moving stores, or behind ploughs. Not for growing food, which was all bought-in, but merely as a punishment.

Now Tristie knelt, miserable and cold, huddled into the corner of her straw littered stall, waiting to be taken up for yet another trap-race. A few minutes before, one of the attendants had come into the stall and bound her arms in the regular fashion for moving slaves about the complex. Her wrists were lashed together and tied to the back of her collar, leaving the buttocks exposed to the whip.

She groaned with discomfort and tried to lie down in the straw, wishing they would hurry. At least when she was harnessed into the gig, her arms were not tied in this agonising way. Then a rattle of the latch on her door startled her. Her heart missed a beat and she felt herself drop into deeper depression. She sighed as a rather ugly female attendant, dressed in the now familiar red nylon overalls, stepped into her stall.

"On your feet, mare! We've got a treat in store for you!"

Having long since learned the futility of resistance, Tristie got up and stood submissively, just wondering what perverted things she would have to do now.

The woman cackled and, none too gently, unclipped Tristie's chain from the ring and led her out of the stall, to walk her along the passageway. She was led only as far as the mouth of the tunnel, where Keane was waiting.

Keane took hold of Tristie's neck-chain and led her onwards through the tunnel to the tack room.

In the tack room, he pulled Tristie close to him and caressed her rump, smiling at her, almost fondly she thought. Then he gave her a light kiss on the lips and unfastened her arms, unclipping the chain from her collar. "Let's get you ready," he grinned. "Race day today sweetie!" He slid his arm around her waist and led her over to a shower in the corner. He turned on the water.

Then, quickly, he stripped himself and picked up a bottle of shower gel. Smiling, he held the bottle up. "Bath time, little Tristie!" He flipped the top of the bottle, and poured the liquid soap over Tristie's head, working up a lather in her hair. Then he began to soap both their bodies.

Tristie could hardly believe what was happening.

She had to grit her teeth.

Not because she didn't want his hands on her body.

Not because she didn't want to feel his hard maleness close to her.

Not because she didn't want his skin against hers.

But because she had to avoid showing that she was enjoying it. Harsh as this man was, there was something different about him, something she hadn't found in the others. And, of course, he was handsome. She knew she had harboured a secret desire to make love with him ever since she had first seen him.

Now, though, the need to prevent herself from juicing was important, for if he thought she really was enjoying this, he would stop—probably he would just beat her and wash her down with the hose. So she stood mute, squeezing her thighs together, trying to deny the tingling thrill that his closeness, his sudden tenderness, induced in her.

He wasn't fooled.

She could see that.

But he didn't stop.

He just smiled in that funny way he had; that attractive, lop-sided grin, his eyes shining with genuine pleasure as he massaged the soap into her skin.

He lifted her chin. "You're too classy for this place. You know that?"

"Master?"

Then he scowled, as if angry with himself, and pushed away from her. He turned on the hot water, rinsing her down, then handed her a towel. "Dry yourself!" He nodded towards the corner where there was a stool, on which lay a large toilet bag. "There's a portable hair-dryer and brushes there. Make sure you get yourself looking good!"

He was still frowning as Tristie stepped out of the shower. He grabbed her arm and stopped her, to gaze into her face. "There's fresh fruit and bread in the toilet bag."

She blinked, surprised. "Master?"

He placed a finger across her lips. "Just shush and eat the stuff!" He held her shoulders and looked her up and down. "A body like yours needs looking after. That mash they give you is crap. You're getting thin." He smiled, affectionately almost. "I'll give you fruit whenever I can, sweetheart!"

Tristie felt a sudden blush come to her cheeks and a lump swelled in her throat. What, a kindness?

Then she felt fear.

Was this just another way of torturing her?

Teasing her?

Would someone say she had stolen the fruit?

Then would she be whipped?

Well, what did it matter? She would be whipped anyway shortly, as she struggled to pull some overweight beast of a man behind her in the trotting-gig.

She lowered her head. "Thank you, Master!" She allowed him to turn her round and propel her towards the stool.

As he towelled himself dry, she picked up the bag and opened it. There were two apples, an orange, and a couple of bananas, together with some new crusty bread. She turned to him, but he silenced her. "Just eat it and then get yourself ready." He was dressing himself now. "And you tell no one!"

Keane sat down and watched, half amused, as she ate the food and dried her hair. Then he watched her brush her glorious mane into its usual shining state.

Finally, she stood up. "I'm ready Master."

He nodded and came over to her. He tilted her head again, and ran his hands through her soft hair. "You look gorgeous. That stinking dye is growing out of your hair, too. It's getting back to its proper colour." He kissed her lips again. "Nice?"

She frowned at him, puzzled. "Master?"

He gave her rump a playful slap. "Never mind." His arm went about her waist, and he pulled her close, kissing her lips again. "Now come on. The hard bit is due to start!"

Minutes later, Tristie was herded out of the main building onto a large grassed area outside. Sheena was waiting for her, whip in hand. "Come on slut!" She picked up the leather racing collar, a three-inch wide brass-studded affair, and fastened it around Tristie's neck. Then she clipped an aluminium bar to each side of the collar. At the end of each bar there was a shackle for securing them to the shafts of the trotting-gig, and just clear of the ends there were wide metal bands, into which Tristie's wrists would be shackled.

Sheena slapped Tristie's stomach. "Forelegs out sideways,

mare!"

Tristie lifted her arms and stretched them outwards. The aluminium bars had been made to fit her and when her arms were stretched sideways they were held out taut by the wristbands. Sheena clipped the bands around Tristie's wrists, then added a leather strap around each of her biceps, to ensure her arms remained stretched taut.

Then Sheena began the process of harnessing Tristie's body.

Tristie remained still as Sheena clipped the centre of a thick leather strap to the front of the collar, then brought the ends down to cross them between Tristie's firm breasts. Where the straps crossed, there was a series of horizontal loops worked into the leather. Sheena fixed a large steel ring into one of the loops, so that the ring lay directly over the point of Tristie's sternum. The ends of the strap were then taken behind, and secured with another large ring at the small of her back.

Now Sheena attached a chain to Tristie's belly ring and pulled it towards her breasts, stretching her shaven sex upwards. The chain was clipped to the ring on the straps between Tristie's breasts, causing her posture to become more upright, holding her head high and pushing her fine breasts even further outwards and upwards. Tristie grimaced with the pain as her sex-mound was dragged upwards, fully displaying her vulva and clitoris.

Sheena grinned at her. "Have to give the spectators something to see." She grabbed a handful of Tristie's stretched vulva and squeezed, grinning as Tristie yelped in pain. Then a thin chain was led from her belly-ring, down between her sex-lips, and pulled tight into her cleft, where it was clipped to the ring at her back. Finally, a bridle and blinkers were fitted over her head and a chrome-plated bit was forced between her back teeth.

Ramming the metal home, Sheena ignored Tristie's gasps of pain. She clipped reins to the ends of the bit, and draped the long leathers backwards over the gig. She tapped Tristie's right thigh. "Lift your foreleg!"

Tristie stifled a sob of shame, but obeyed. Her stomach flipped as Sheena put a pair of running-shoes onto her feet and then slapped her stomach. "Back, mare!" she ordered as she guided Tristie back between the aluminium shafts of a two-wheeled trotting-gig.

Shivering in the cool evening air, trembling with shame and degradation, Tristie stood silently as Sheena clipped the ends of the aluminium arm-stretchers to the ends of the shafts. Then she stood back, nodding with satisfaction, as she looked at Tristie, now a servile harnessed pony-slave.

Tristie was shaking now, knowing what was soon to come. She was going to be whipped into a trot, to run as fast as she could, and to get the gig moving across the uneven track that lay to the right of the harnessing area. She also knew that if the gig turned over she would go with it, and could suffer serious injury. The prospect frightened her and it was not only the cold which was making her tremble.

She groaned to herself, and her heart sank even lower, as she saw the menacing dark skinned man who walked towards the gig. She recognised Miller immediately. He was dressed in a black tracksuit, and he had a wicked horsewhip in his right hand. This race was going to be murder.

Miller came up to her and sneered into her bridled face. "Stop slobbering from the bit, mare!" he said. "I don't want the thing slipping out half-way through the race. And you better win or I'll shred your arse."

Sheena stepped up. "She won't win, Zach. But I'm sure you'll make her try hard enough!"

"We'll see." Miller climbed into the gig. He cracked the whip alongside Tristie's face. "Trot on!"

Tristie felt her insides curl with shame as she began to pull the heavy load, answering to each tug of the reins as Miller guided her around the parade ring that served as a paddock. Every few seconds he snapped the whip beside her ears, or flicked her exposed buttocks.

Tristie wasn't alone in her misery, for there were four other girls ahead of and behind her, harnessed in the same way. All were trying to keep in step, their breasts and buttocks jiggling erotically as they trotted around the paddock, displaying their abilities or otherwise to the watching men and women in the warmth of the hospitality cabins beside the grassy area.

Tristie realised that she too would look just as erotic as she trotted up, feeling her own breasts and buttocks bouncing about in time with her enforcedly exaggerated gait.

Whilst trying to concentrate on her step, she tried to assess the other pony-slaves. She knew she had to win, or a severe beating would be the result. Sadly, as she looked at the ease with which most of the girls pulled their gigs and noted their sleek fitness, Tristie knew that Sheena had been right; she didn't stand a chance.

The others were all experienced in trotting a gig and Tristie knew she didn't have the experience to beat them. There would be money wagered on her running, but again, she admitted to herself, she didn't stand a chance. She never had been able to run very well and to be expected to haul a pony-trap and a sixteen stone man was asking too much of her.

She would lose.

Then she would be whipped, blindfolded and given a forced run, around the heathland, in front of the pleasure complex, her arms strapped up to the back of her neck. Every time she lost her balance, or tripped over unseen obstacles, there would be another excuse to whip her as she struggled to keep going. She would be whipped on until she dropped. Then she would be beaten until she got up and started again.

She pushed the horrific prospect from her mind and risked

a glance to the side, hoping Miller wouldn't notice. Closer to the hospitality cabin now, she could just make out the people behind the windows, relaxing, drinking and eating their fill. It only made Tristie more aware of her enslavement, of how helpless she was, and of how uncaring these monsters were.

She glanced sideways to get a better look, but this time there came a growl from Miller. A stinging blow from the whip across her buttocks brought her to her task once more and she faced her front, straining at the bar, struggling to pull her load.

After some four circuits of the lawn, the whip cracked again and she was urged into a run. Miller twitched on her left rein and guided her towards the gate and the muddy track. A few minutes later and the girls were lined up abreast across the track, all trembling, waiting for the start.

A starting gun cracked and the whip smashed into Tristie's back, causing her to scream out as she started to run. The muddy turf was slippery beneath her feet, the spikes in the shoes ineffective, as she struggled to get the pony-trap moving. She dug her feet in. She heaved and hauled and grunted with the effort. But the trap barely moved and she groaned as the other girls began to pull away from her.

Then her mind was shattered as the sharp end of the leather whip slashed her naked buttocks again. Miller was roaring at her, slapping the reins, slashing at her vulnerable hide with the whip, urging her on. "Run! Run!" Miller hauled savagely on the reins, causing the bit to be rammed back into her mouth. She screamed as the metal ground on her teeth, her saliva spraying about as she tried to adjust the metal rod in her mouth.

At last the trap began to roll a little more easily and she realised it wasn't quite so hard. Even so, the whip still lashed into her back and buttocks, cutting into her thoughts. "Feet up mare! Knees bent! Trot properly!"

Again the whip cracked into Tristie's flesh, this time

across her bare shoulders, and she screamed out, but obeyed, lifting her knees high, wincing as the chain cut deep into the cleft of her sex, sobbing as the whip landed repeatedly on her naked buttocks and thighs. She was panting with the effort and her head roared as she began to accelerate, shutting her ears to the maniacal yelling of the onlookers, shouting on their particular wagers, willing their choices to win.

Soon Tristie's body was slicked with a slimy mixture of mud and her own sweat, as her breathing began to labour. The bit was grinding on her teeth, ramming her tongue to the back of her throat. Miller continued to lay the whip across her naked shoulders and buttocks, and her feet were constantly slipping and skidding about in the wet grass. She was slowing down now, well behind the others, with the finishing line in clear sight.

There was the sudden delighted roar of the crowd as the leading gig passed the winning line. Tristie's heart missed a beat.

She had lost.

She was last!

Miller cursed.

The whip slashed down across her buttocks and Tristie sagged in the shafts, sobbing as she fell to her knees in the mud. But the whipping continued. "On your feet!" Miller roared at her. "You might be last, but you'll damn well finish!"

Sobbing, Tristie raised herself and began to pull once more. She was screaming, her thighs and buttocks quivered with the effort, and her naked body was steaming with the sweat of her exertions. Finally, she got the gig over the line and collapsed between the shafts before Keane, who was waiting just beyond the finish.

Miller climbed down from the gig and walked towards the naked, exhausted Tristie. He gave her one more slash with the whip, before turning to Keane.

"She's useless Nick! Needs more training!" He handed Keane the whip. "I'll leave her to you!"

Keane nodded, and as Miller walked away, stepped up to the kneeling Tristie. He shoved the butt of the whip beneath her chin and lifted her head.

"On your feet!"

Tristie gagged as the bit dug even deeper into her mouth, and gasped as the pressure forced her jaws wide apart. She gurgled and more saliva ran down her naked front as she struggled to her feet.

Keane held the whip steady beneath her chin. "Seems you're not so fit as we thought. But not to worry, we'll soon alter that!" He released her arms from the aluminium stretcher and removed her collar. Then he took the bit from between her teeth, before guiding her clear of the shafts. He gripped the bridle and pulled her along towards the path leading from the track.

Tristie had no option but to follow as he led her towards the open heathland in front of the Pleasure Palace. Her soul cringed as she felt her feet sinking into the soggy grass, and she groaned as Keane pulled her towards the small building at the foot of the hill.

22: MALIK'S PROPOSITION

Keane had just finished stabling Tristie when Miller stopped him in the main corridor. "Hey Nick! Get your arse over to Malik's yacht will yer! He wants a chat!"

Keane wondered. It was unusual for Sheik Malik to bother with the minions of other employers. Was this something the General had cooked up? Well, he reflected, there was just one way to find out. He turned and walked back down the corridor, towards the far side of the island, where the Sheik's yacht, 'Salamander', was berthed.

Keane liked the Sheik, but even by his own standards, he found Malik's attitudes towards women a bit much. The Sheik made even the General seem like a mouse. Now, as Keane stepped aboard the huge yacht, he was still wondering what on earth the man had to tell him that was so important.

'Salamander' was a floating palace, and as Abasi led him through a maze of perfumed corridors below decks, Keane gazed about in awe. Then they arrived at a huge pair of mahogany panelled doors in a wide bulkhead which was covered in rare satinwood veneers. Abasi bowed and knocked on the door.

"Come in my friend!" The Sheik's voice sounded warmer than usual.

Abasi pushed the doors open and Keane stepped into the stateroom. Ankle deep sheepskin carpets covered the deck and the bulkheads were clothed with cured zebra pelts. Anything made of metal was of solid silver, and anything made of wood was crafted from the rarest available rosewoods, ebonies and mahoganies. Even after the General's excesses in opulence, Keane found the surroundings mind-boggling. The Sheik must have money dripping from every pore of his body. By comparison the General was a pauper.

The Sheik was lying on a raised bed and he was attended by a naked white slavegirl, yet another delicious blonde, who was massaging a glowing aromatic oil into her Master's skin, working the stuff into his thighs and around his genitals. Every so often, she would stoop and kiss his body, her hands probing deep into his taut flesh, her lips and tongue sliding over his erect penis, her slim fingers teasing the shaft, caressing his scrotum.

Slave bells on her wrists and golden collar tinkled with her every movement and the sunshine, reflecting off the water outside, flickered through the portholes, dappling a dancing pattern of light across her naked body.

As Keane walked further into the room there was a sudden movement at the edge of his vision. He turned quickly to his right, but there was no threat. Instead, he saw one of the most gorgeous blondes he had ever laid eyes on. He stopped short and gazed at this clear-skinned beauty for a moment. It was clear where the General had got his ideas about body piercing.

The girl was naked, but from her hips right up to her deliciously firm upturned breasts, her slightly rounded belly was completely covered in small silver rings, all set into her flesh. Each ring had a small pearl hanging from it, and Keane could see that this 'bodice' went completely around her middle, like a brocade belt. Around her neck they had riveted a silver collar about three inches wide, and this too was decorated with tiny pearls. It was an exquisite piece of craftsmanship, and it could hardly have looked more in place than it did around the slender neck of this delicious slavegirl.

The girl's nipples had also been pierced and were coloured with black rouge. From each nipple-ring hung a much larger pearl, so that it looked as if each breast was weeping a pearly drop of mothers' milk. It was a final touch of magic in an entirely magnificent effect.

As the girl sank to her knees before his gaze, the pearls shook and shimmered like the northern lights. Despite his feelings that body-piercing damaged the goods, Keane had to admit that this was a superb sight. He could enjoy playing

184

with this one, enjoy making her scream.

Sheik Malik chuckled. "She is beautiful my friend, is she not?"

Keane nodded, looking at the girl who had come to kneel before him. There was nothing he could add to the Sheik's description. "She really is beautiful, Sheik Malik."

Malik sat up, quickly pushing the other slavegirl aside, sending her sprawling to the deck, her slave-bells tinkling. He shrugged himself into a white robe, turned to Keane and pointed to the kneeling figure.

"I call that one Jumana, which is Arabic for silver pearl. She is yours. A gift from Sheik Akram Ben Malik, to his English friend, Mister Nick Keane." He smiled widely. "And I mean she is yours to keep, including the jewellery she wears. Take her back with you when you return to the Island." He clapped his hands and said something to the girl.

The blonde beauty lifted her head and smiled up at Keane. "I am for you Master!" She had a cultured English accent. It sounded like Home Counties, Keane decided. She opened her lovely arms and supplicated herself.

"Thank you for such a wonderful gift Sheik Malik. I shall treat her as you would wish." Then he gave way to the Sheik's own customs. "And may Allah shower bountiful gifts on you in return!"

"Ah! Nick. You are so kind. May Allah's blessing be upon you my friend." He pointed to the slavegirl Jumana. "As for the slave, she is no longer my property. Treat her as you would wish." He smiled. "I will have Abasi take her to the cages to await your departure." He held up a finger. "But please grant me one freedom?"

"Certainly Sheik Malik!"

"May I have your permission to have her disciplined before she leaves my care? Just so she remembers who first enslaved her, and how she must behave towards you."

Keane knew the Sheik would be insulted if he didn't

agree. He tried to hide his disappointment as he nodded. "Of course, Excellency, but please no marks on her flesh."

"Ah! Nick! Do not worry. We have other ways of disciplining the girls, without recourse to the whip. Few of them show any trace afterwards." He clapped his hands and almost magically, Abasi appeared in the doorway.

"Take Jumana to the cages to await Master Nick's departure." He smiled cruelly. "And ten minutes of the 'Strappado' before she leaves us." He held up a warning hand. "Just enough to remind her. She must not be damaged."

Abasi grinned. "Yes, Effendi." He looked at Jumana and nodded. "Prepare yourself."

The girl began to shake, not without reason, and Keane hid his distaste as he thought about the Strappado.

The Strappado.

The girl would be strung up by her wrists, her arms wide apart. The ropes would be adjusted over pulleys and tied off, so her feet would be about twelve inches above the floor. For ten minutes, she would suffer the pain of repeatedly being hoisted up, then dropped, to be pulled up sharp, at the limits of the ropes. Done properly, it could wrench the arms out of the sockets. The slavegirl was fortunate. She wasn't too heavy and Abasi would not dare disobey the Sheik. Maybe it wouldn't be too bad on the lovely Jumana. Keane looked at her intently, and shook his head almost imperceptibly.

The slavegirl gave him the slightest smile of understanding. "I will suffer for you Master!"

Sheik Malik chuckled quietly. "Jumana has given herself to you completely it seems!" He beamed. "But then she knows what to expect if she stays with me." In good humour, he shrugged. "But what of it. She accepts you, so that pleases me."

He turned to the other slavegirl and shoved her head down with his foot. "As for you, there is much for you to learn in the ways of pleasuring a man. You shall have the whip!"

Malik turned to Abasi. "Twenty lashes, Abasi. Buttocks and thighs!"

The huge Lascar grinned evilly. "It will be done, Effendi." He made to turn away but was stopped by the upraised hand of Malik. "Oh! And the Bastinado! Twenty good strokes of the rod, across the soles of her feet." He chuckled. "A little time crawling on hands and knees will teach her her place."

Keane watched as the slavegirl, trembling and trying to keep from sobbing out loud, began to writhe, belly down and backwards, out of the room, clearly not daring to turn her face away from her Master. Again Keane had to smother a feeling of sympathy. This wretched girl was really going to suffer at the hands of Abasi.

Abasi stood waiting, one hand coiled in Jumana's hair, the other holding a whip. As the grovelling slavegirl came near to Abasi, he switched the girl's offered buttocks.

"Back to your cage."

The girl squealed and only now did she stand to walk away, followed by Abasi, dragging Jumana behind him.

There was the sound of leather against flesh again and another squeal from the girl, as Sheik Malik pressed a button beside his huge bed and the door closed. He waved Keane to a seat beside him and then poured wine from a jug. He handed Keane a glass.

"Now I can welcome you formally aboard my boat, Nick!"

"Boat?" Keane looked about at the luxury. "Some boat. Ship would be more like it, Excellency."

"Please Nick. My friends call me Akram." His swarthy bearded face split into a huge grin. "The Muslim equivalent of a Christian name. It means Generous One!" He laughed. "And I can be generous to my friends, as you have just discovered." He shrugged. "And you must now realise, I count you among my friends."

Keane smiled. "Thank you Akram!" He toasted the Sheik.

"And may I ask what Malik means?"

Another huge laugh. "It means, Master!"

Keane grinned. "That figures. But I bet your girls don't see you as a generous Master!"

The Arab shrugged. "The feelings of slavegirls do not concern me, any more than they do you." He smiled. "We share the same attitudes to women."

"I'm glad to say!"

The Sheik chuckled. "Because of my reputation for intolerance towards Christians, you mean?"

"Ah! Now I didn't say that did I?"

"No! You didn't." He swirled his orange-juice around the glass. "And I don't think you are the sort to be frightened anyway."

"I'm a Godless bastard, Akram. Why should I be frightened? Live and let shag, that's me."

Malik laughed out loud. "You are so refreshing Nick. I see we will get on. However, enough of the small talk." He sipped his juice. "I will come to the point. I know you are good at your job and I want people like you with me." He looked thoughtfully at Keane. "How would you like to be my agent, here? Supply me with the sort of female flesh that you find for the General?"

"You know I've worked for the General for three years?"

"Are you not a free agent my friend?"

"Not really." Keane shrugged. "Wish I could be. But there you are."

"Does that little—how do you say—does that little turd have something on you, Nick?"

"Turd!" Keane chuckled. "Hey! You're right there, Akram, but the little shit pays well." He pulled a face. "And why ask questions to which you already have the answers, Akram?"

The Sheik laughed loudly. "I said you were good did I not?"

"And loyal!"

"To the General!" The Sheik scowled. "A man like you must have nothing but contempt for such a creature. In fact he isn't really a General, is he Nick?"

Keane shrugged. "That's true." He smiled. "Not the genuine article, whereas you are."

"You see. We are alike Nick!"

"I would prefer your money to his, Akram. But…"

"There would be much more of it, my friend!" Malik sipped his drink. "The General thinks he is rich. Well, I suppose he is. But to me…" he waved an arm about the luxurious state room, "…well you only need look. This boat I use just for business trips." He shrugged. "My main vessel! Ahh, you should see her. I call her the 'Scimitar'." He smiled. "Like your 'Kukri', hey?"

Keane grinned. "But much bigger, I dare say."

The Sheik spread his arms wide. "Ah yes. But not so much." He grinned. "I use her for collection and transport." He displayed a sly grin. "I need hardly add, those from whom I collect don't give away their possessions. The 'Scimitar' is fast. We need to get in, collect our, er, cargo and get out. She is not so much an indulgence as a necessity."

Keane nodded and worked a slight smile. "You old pirate, Akram!"

Malik chuckled. "Once more, you display that you are no fool Nick!" He sipped his juice again. "Well, these days we do not wear eye patches, nor do we fly the Jolly Roger. I do not sanction killing anyone. I steal only that which is particularly desirable." His eyes twinkled. "As you may have noticed, I keep the blonde ones for myself. The rest I dispose of." Another small shrug. "So yes, as you say, we are pirates." His face filled with enthusiasm, and he leaned forward. "There are other ways of obtaining slavegirls, Nick, as you well know, but few of them are as exciting." His face was alight with pleasure now. "The 'Scimitar' makes a perfect raiding vessel. All she needs is a good captain." He looked at Keane. "You are a seafarer Nick! Would you not

189

like to command such a vessel?"

Keane swallowed. Christ! The man was asking him to become a pirate! Then he considered. The work was the same. Just a different scenario. No worse than the job he was doing for the General. He tried to keep his enthusiasm from showing. "Well, yes, Akram, of course, but..."

"I crew the 'Scimitar' with six of the most beautiful females, Nick. Not slaves, you understand. Well-trained female mercenaries, all expert seafarers." He sat back. "They are, however, far from reticent when it comes to relationships with men." His eyes glinted, almost mischievously. "Just think! You could be the lone male on a ship crewed entirely by beautiful compliant women!"

He held up a warning finger. "They have worked together for so long now and they have learned to rely on one another. I think it would take a real man to control them." He leaned back still smiling. "And Shara, the captain, now she is a real Tigress! She will give you a run for your money." He sat back and held his arms wide. "Can you tame her, Nick? Are you up to the task?"

Keane tried to keep his eyes from boggling. He knew Malik was into the white slavegirl trade in a big way, but this was a new slant. This would be living! Living with a capital L. Sailing the high seas. The excitement, the possibility of a few good fights. Raiding unsuspecting vessels. Kidnapping girls. Carrying them back and forth, worldwide. It exceeded the wildest imaginings. And, it certainly did make the General look like small beer. Picking up girls in bars and clubs was child's play in comparison.

Still trying to hide his delight, Keane looked at Malik. "And what do you want from me?"

The Sheik laughed and refilled Keane's glass. "I want the woman Sheena!" He snapped his fingers. "The General, he calls her his Madam, yes?"

"Sheena?" Keane almost laughed. "Akram, you just have to ask her. She'll whip your girls into shape for the love of it. Give her a whip and she's in heaven."

Malik shook his head. "I want that woman as a slave, Nick, and I don't allow female slaves to control anyone." He drew in a deep breath. "She will be used as a trotting-slave." The Sheik sighed again. "Such hair. I have rarely seen it's like anywhere in the world." He paused. "Except for that little trinket called Tristie." He shook his head. "That is another beauty, but sadly, not strong enough for a trotting-gig. Much more suited to the bed or the Discipline Chamber, yes?"

Keane nodded. "She's a sexy little piece of goods, that's for sure." He arched his eyebrows, enquiringly. "Do you want her as well?"

Malik shook his head. "I would only sell her on. Probably to our Sicilian friends. They would find her useful in their brothels. No my friend, if you bring that one with you, she is yours."

Keane frowned. "Why don't you just take Sheena? She might enjoy the novelty and the General couldn't really stop you. Not with guys around as big as Abasi."

"True Nick, but it would put me in, how do you say?"— He searched for the words for a moment—"in bad-books. Yes in bad-books with the General. I don't want that. Much as I dislike the son of a camel, he is a useful contact and he does supply good female flesh." He shrugged again. "Although, of course, that is due to your expertise Nick." He leaned forward eagerly. "I really must have that woman. She would be the cream of my racing stable. I would be the envy of all Karshina. Come, Nick, what do you say?"

Keane sighed deeply. Here was a chance to get away from the General, and still be doing what he liked doing. But the General really would drop him in it and he could never return to England...

The Sheik interrupted his thoughts. "Must I get Zach Miller to arrange it for me?"

Keane laughed aloud. "Zach? A great guy, but he couldn't

arrange flowers!"

"I may have him work for me," the Sheik grinned. "But you are right. He is not as good as you. He is weaker. I gave him just one hour with four of my girls and he was begging to be taken on."

"But you didn't offer the slave Jumana to me as a bribe, Akram? You gave her to me before you put your proposition."

Malik chuckled. "That's true and it is because I have more respect for you than that, Nick." He shrugged. "The slave is yours, to keep, whatever you decide."

Keane laughed. "You make it sound like I'm joining a book club!"

Malik frowned. "I'm sorry, Nick. I don't understand."

"Just my English sense of humour, Akram. Don't worry about it."

Malik smiled. "I think you would like to join my er... club though?"

"Yes!"

"But you would rather not get Sheena for me?"

"I didn't say that."

"Very well Nick!" He paused. "We must devise a way of persuading the General to co-operate. Do you think that could be arranged?"

"I'll think of something."

Malik smiled widely. "I don't wish to, how do you say, push my luck, Nick, but there is another woman I would like, if that can be arranged too."

"Oh! And who might that be?"

"I have seen her only once or twice, but she is much like Sheena." He smiled, "In fact I do not think she is a slave at all. You know who I mean Nick?"

"Ah yes! Lisa!" Keane sucked in a breath. "Dicey Akram! She's one of the General's suppliers." He shook his head. "A bitch! A real lesbian bitch!"

"Even better!" The Sheik sighed again contentedly. "It

would be such a pleasure teaching her other ways. Yes?"

Keane paused for a moment, considering. Then he shrugged. Why the Hell not? Maybe it was time Lisa's chicken came home to roost. He made his decision. "We get them both!"

"Ahh! Nick! My Friend." Malik poured out more wine. "You see. I told you there was a way."

23: Tristie Must Eat Grass

Miserably, Tristie knelt, huddled into the corner of her stall. Her arms, as usual, were strapped across the small of her back. She sighed and tried to lie down in the straw, just as a rattle of the latch on her door startled her—and then she groaned.

The ugly bitch!

She was back and she was holding a slave-saddle over her arm.

"On your feet!"

Tristie got up and stood, waiting obediently, just wondering what perverted things she would have to do now.

The woman saddled Tristie, none too gently, clipping the seat to her waistband and ramming the bit between her teeth. She drew a gasp of pain from her captive as she tightened the cinch between her legs. The leather strap spread her creamy thighs and stretched the soft lips of her vagina.

Then the woman clipped the reins to Tristie's collar and slapped her naked rump. "All ready, horsey!" She unshackled Tristie's tether-chain. "On your knees!"

Tristie did as she was ordered and waited whilst the woman mounted her. Knowing her place now, Tristie stood up as soon as her rider was settled.

"Trot!"

Ten minutes later Tristie was outside the Pleasure Palace, shivering slightly in trepidation, but, all the same, delighting in being able to take delicious breaths of the cool evening air. Her elation didn't last long, for after guiding her across the paved courtyard towards the damp sweet-smelling grass, her rider pulled up hard on the reins.

Tristie grunted in pain as her head was jerked backwards, and she stopped while her rider dismounted. The woman pointed to a small figure about two hundred yards away. "Mistress Sheena wants you! Have a nice ride!"

Tristie stood, shivering, her heart heavy, wondering what

was to happen to her now.

Sheena cracked the dog-whip she was holding and even at this distance Tristie heard the sharp report. "Come on, you mare! Move your hide! Get yourself over here!"

Tristie broke into a run, gasping as the leather tack rasped against her body, and trotted towards Sheena. She halted, panting and sweating, and stood trembling in front of the woman.

Sheena was wearing a thick fur coat pulled close about. For a moment she stood looking at Tristie. Then she stepped forward and lifted Tristie's head a little. "Let's get all this stuff off you. I want you stark naked." Sheena removed all of Tristie's harness, and her leather collar. She smiled an evil smile as she watched Tristie begin to shiver as the sweat began cooling on her naked flesh. She shoved the handle of the whip under Tristie's chin and jerked her head up.

"Cold is it?"

Tristie nodded. Her teeth were beginning to chatter.

"Roll in the grass then, slut!" The whip cracked. "NOW!"

Tristie needed no second telling. She dropped to the ground and began to roll over and over in the damp grass. It wasn't entirely unpleasant and not so cold as she thought it would be. In fact it seemed to be warming her slightly, and it was certainly cleaning some of the filth from her body. Sheena allowed Tristie about two minutes of this. Then she leaned forward. "On your knees."

Tristie obeyed and awaited her Mistress.

Sheena stooped and kissed Tristie lightly on the forehead. "Now I'll have to warm up your hide a little, won't I?"

Tristie began to shake in fearful anticipation, knowing that a whipping was coming.

But Sheena didn't do anything like that. She merely began to caress Tristie's breasts, and then opened the front of the fur, to reveal that she too was completely naked beneath. She held the coat wide.

"Lower your head and put it between my legs!"

Tristie was puzzled, but she obeyed, nuzzling her head between the woman's legs, so Sheena was virtually sitting astride her neck. Sheena gripped tightly with her thighs, and allowed her hands to wander over the offered back of her slavegirl. Then, casting off the fur coat, Sheena began to grind her hips against Tristie's neck. In moments she was slashing at Tristie's exposed buttocks with the whip, all the while grinding herself against the squirming girl's neck and shoulders. She ignored the screams of pain as the whip slashed into defenceless flesh.

As Sheena's movements became more frantic, her juices began to run freely over Tristie's body, and Tristie could feel the warmth of the fluid as it coated her neck and shoulders. Then, suddenly, Sheena stopped and moved away from Tristie. She looked down at her.

"Now, you can do something else for me, you sexy little slut!" She stooped to pick up the fur coat again, draping it about Tristie's naked body. "Start kissing my pussy! Sink that tongue deep inside me, deep as you can!"

Tristie groaned again, but she began to tongue the woman's sex-lips. In moments, Sheena was gyrating her hips again, sliding her sex-mound around Tristie's face, grabbing the long amber-blonde hair, pressing Tristie's face close into her vagina.

Tristie was soon gasping for breath, but she knew she had to keep on pushing her tongue in and out of the woman's dripping sex. Although she tried to fight it, she soon felt her own lesbian tendencies rising as she tasted the sex-juice, sweet and warm, trickling into her mouth. She hated this woman. She was a monster, but she tasted so sweet.

Then the whip slashed into Tristie's back and she was pushed to the ground.

Sheena wrapped the coat about herself again and looked down haughtily, at her cowering slavegirl. "You're getting to like women too much."

Fearing the woman was jealous and expecting a beating,

Tristie knew how to respond. "Mistress, it is nice only with you! I like it with just you Mistress!"

Sheena laughed. "I'm not worried about that, bitch!" She cut into Tristie's hindquarters with the whip, ignoring the scream of pain. "Don't forget, you have to satisfy men as well."

"Yes Mistress!"

The woman grabbed Tristie's hair and dragged her to her feet once more, pushing the butt of the whip beneath Tristie's chin, lifting her head a little. She put her face close to Tristie's. "You're also becoming a useful pony-girl, but you're not fast enough for the gigs, are you?"

"No Mistress."

Sheena grinned and pushed Tristie away. "That's why your training is to be stepped up, and to start you off we're putting you on a special diet." She grabbed Tristie's head and pulled it down. She re-fastened the leather collar about her slender neck, and clipped a chain to the collar. Tristie shook with apprehension, wondering what was to come now.

"We start right away. Back on your knees and eat!"

Tristie frowned. Surely not, she thought. "What must I eat, Mistress?"

Her answer was the dog-whip. Screaming, she dropped to her knees as Sheena lashed the handle of the whip into her unprotected buttocks. Twice she extracted squeals of pain, then stood, hands on hips, looking down at Tristie.

"What do you think you eat? What all horses eat! Grass!"

Tristie couldn't believe her ears. The perverted woman was serious. She expected her to eat grass. Oh God! What would they think of next?

One more blow of the whip shattered Tristie's thoughts. She screamed in pain and anger, and then bowed her head in submission. Like the animal she was being turned into, she began to graze at the soft meadow grass. The sickly taste made her gag and she knew she was also eating other things. But she had no choice. She carried on munching at the grass, her stomach heaving and wanting to vomit.

Then the whip lashed unexpectedly into her buttocks again. She rolled over, trying to evade the lash, but it was hopeless. Sheena slashed her four or five times.

"Eat as though you enjoy it!"

Sobbing, Tristie got back to her knees, and began to tear at the grass with her teeth; greedy now; ripping the green blades from the earth, chewing and swallowing the sickly stuff, her teeth grinding on the grit which came up with the grass. Her stomach rebelled again and she began to hope that Sheena would soon tire of this sport. But she knew her hopes were futile, for out of the corner of her eye, she saw Sheena open the fur coat again and begin to finger herself.

In moments Sheena was ramming her own hand into herself, sliding it deep into her dripping vagina as she watched her helpless naked slavegirl grazing like a beast.

She moved over to Tristie and, still masturbating, knelt behind her slave and leant towards her upthrust creamy buttocks. She pushed her tongue between the soft buttocks and began to lick around the inside of her thighs.

Soon Tristie too was moaning as she tried to resist the advances of the woman's silky tongue. But it was hopeless. She began to squirm with desire as she chewed at the grass.

Abruptly then, Sheena got up to stand astride Tristie's back and pushed her head lower to the ground. She rubbed her crotch against Tristie's flesh, and began to flick at her buttocks with the whip handle.

Sheena was gasping. "Come on you slut. Eat like an animal! Graze like the sexy little beast you are. Chew that grass. Swallow it, you sexy little bitch!"

The woman's juices were slicking all over Tristie's back again. The weight of her pushed Tristie's face into the grass as she tried to obey. Tearing at the grass, Tristie chewed it into a foul tasting mash, gagging as she swallowed the sickly stuff, feeling her stomach filling with wind.

The woman ground her hips into Tristie's neck. Harder and harder. "God! Oh God! Come on you gorgeous little slut! Come on! Fetch me off!"

Finally the frantic woman gave a wail of ecstasy and her love-juice came in a mini-torrent as she bore down on her slavegirl. The two women squirmed in an embrace on the cool grass and Sheena's tongue sank deep into Tristie's mouth as they cuddled in a love grasp, their passions cooling into the night air.

Eventually Sheena draped the big coat over both of them and gently caressed Tristie's body. She kissed the girl's forehead. "I think I'm going to persuade the General to take you out of the stables, my pet." She smiled in the dusk. "Your delicious body is wasted as a pony-slave. How would you like to be my personal hand-maiden?"

Tristie began to shake again, wondering what was really in the woman's mind; wondering what horrors would lie in store for her if she was to become the personal plaything of this female monster. But it couldn't be much worse than being used as a beast of burden for evermore.

"Whatever Mistress desires!"

Sheena smiled warmly and hugged Tristie to her body. "Then so it shall be!"

Tristie gave a hesitant smile. She had no choice anyway, so there was little point in resisting. As if she meant it, Tristie returned the woman's passionate kiss. At least for the moment there was tenderness.

Sheena smiled then and got up slowly, pulling on the fur coat.

"Stand up, my little slave!"

Tristie obeyed. Sheena came close, slipped her arm about the girl, and hugged her to her own body as she wrapped the coat about them both. "Come, my sweet." Sheena pulled Tristie gently along with her. "We'll go back inside now."

Tristie allowed Sheena to lead her back towards the tunnel, suddenly feeling relaxed and, for the moment, enjoying the woman's caresses, as they walked back towards the Pleasure Palace.

24: The Handmaiden

As she struggled to regain full wakefulness, Tristie could hardly believe the pleasurable sensation she was feeling. For a moment, still sure she was dreaming, she lay still, eyes closed, and explored her sensations. She knew she was naked and seemed to be lying on a soft fluffy surface. She felt warm, and although she could still feel the soreness where her body had been abused, most of the pain had gone and her fetters had been taken off.

The pleasant sensation continued. This was so different. The dreamlike sensation was being induced by soft hands which were massaging her body with a warm fragrant oil, and she was aware of the breathing of the person who was busy working the oil into her skin.

Then she woke fully. Now she understood.

Sheena! It was Sheena!

But she allowed herself to relax again, enjoying the soft waves of pleasure as they washed over her mind. If this was what being a handmaiden was going to be like, perhaps her life of slavery wouldn't be so bad after all...

Then Sheena's voice broke the silence. "I know you're awake my pet!"

Snapping her eyes open, Tristie lifted her head slightly and looked to her right.

A firm hand pushed her head down again. "Shh! No need to move my sweet!"

The massage continued and, slightly puzzled, Tristie allowed herself to relax once more, sinking gently back into the soft white terry-towelling beneath her naked body. She gazed at the shapely thigh beside her and then let her gaze wander upwards.

Sheena was totally naked, and Tristie's heart sank a little as she saw a small star-shaped brand on the thigh. Even Sheena was branded then! Was she just another slavegirl? Then another sigh, as Tristie noticed the fine chain slung about the woman's waist. Now she knew they were both slaves. Tristie also experienced a shudder of fear as she also saw the vicious wire whip, hanging from the chain to brush the firm thigh. A little sadly, Tristie began to reappraise Sheena.

There was no doubt about it. Sheena was beautiful; statuesque. She was an Amazon among her sex, at least six feet tall, but with a perfectly proportioned figure. Tristie experienced an unexplained thrill of pleasure as she looked at her beauty; beauty which seemed to be unaffected by the large rings in her nipples. On Sheena, the silver chains were definitely an adornment, their graceful curve emphasising her fine shape. Her face was exquisitely sculptured and her teeth were white and even. Her lips were fuller and her face soft. Long and silky, her fine corn-gold hair hung in a shimmering fall to the middle of her back and her honey-tanned skin gleamed with a light sheen of perspiration.

Sheena bent and kissed the nape of Tristie's neck. Then she spoke gently. "Welcome back Tristie! The General has agreed to give you to me. I had to give up my status as Slave Mistress. Like you, I am a slave. No longer a Madam!" She brushed Tristie's shoulders with her lips and tongue. "But, as it's still my job to help train you as a handmaiden, at least we can love each other when we aren't being used!"

Her hands drifted over the swell of Tristie's buttocks, the strong fingers sliding between the globes of flesh, massaging the insides of Tristie's thighs. Tristie shuddered and closed her eyes as Sheena's fingers slid easily into her love-slit.

Tristie squirmed away. "Please Mistress," she said, "don't hurt me."

In a blurred movement, Sheena's hand reached for the whip and lifted it high, bringing it down across Tristie's naked buttocks.

Tristie screamed and tried to roll away, but Sheena was too quick for her. Grabbing Tristie's arms she crossed them, forcing them up between her shoulder blades. She leaned over the squirming girl. "Don't struggle my pet or I really will have to hurt you."

"No, please Mistress, let me be."

Sheena grabbed a handful of Tristie's left buttock and began to squeeze, smiling softly into Tristie's contorted face as the pain took hold. "Listen to me. You have to accept that when you are not being used by a guest you belong to me." She released the grip on Tristie's flesh and stroked her hair gently. "Now that can be pleasant, or it can be painful. You are a slave on this island just as I am. But it happens that you are a masochistic little weakling! The ideal kind of girl for me to have."

"I'm not a masochist," Tristie protested. "Nor a weakling!"

"You are a snivelling little wretch." Sheena's tongue licked Tristie's lips. "You're a helpless little creature who needs to be punished, then have someone like me to care for her."

Tristie felt her heart pounding. Was this woman right? No! That could never be! She didn't like pain. But she had to admit just how lovely Sheena was and how nice it would be to feel the woman's bronzed skin against her own. She shuddered and lay back as Sheena continued to caress her body. She felt her juices beginning to flow. That she had lesbian tendencies she had known for a long while; even, really, since her teens. It had started at school, all those years ago, when she had felt a crush for the gym mistress.

But the feelings she had towards this woman were different. There was something about Sheena's imperious attitude which thrilled Tristie, as though she enjoyed being bossed around by this magnificent creature. And then there was the comparative ease with which she had accepted her slavery when she had first met the General. Yes, she had submitted, mainly to avoid whippings, but she still had experienced her juices flowing and a thrill of nervous pleasure as she had kissed that whip.

"You're finding out, aren't you my sweet?"

Tristie nodded and opened her mouth slightly, allowing her tongue to trace her lips. Reaching for Sheena again, she pulled the lovely body down onto hers and her lips searched eagerly for Sheena's mouth.

Sheena moaned with animal pleasure and lowered herself over Tristie's trembling body, grabbing the slender throat just below Tristie's collar, squeezing slightly, so that Tristie began to pant. It was exciting knowing that Sheena could squeeze the life from her. She slid her hand down to feel the warmth of Sheena's genitals, and then allowed her fingers into the moist wetness of her sex.

Sheena was bucking against Tristie's hand, rolling her hips and gasping between wet kisses. She grabbed Tristie's wrist and forced the hand ever deeper into her body, until, screaming and writhing, she began to ride on Tristie's slender forearm.

"Oh God!" Sheena gasped. "Oh God! Deeper!" Sheena was ramming herself down onto Tristie's arm and Tristie could feel the soft tissues inside as her hand was forced deeper into the willing body. Both Sheena's hands were around Tristie's neck now, and her hair hung down to brush Tristie's body. Sheena had her mouth open and was gasping, her saliva dribbling down onto Tristie's body.

With her free hand, Tristie massaged the saliva into her flesh, moaning with pleasure, thrusting her own burning sex up towards Sheena.

Then Sheena suddenly screamed and sat bolt upright, wrenching herself away from Tristie's arm, as a whip slashed into her body, knocking her flying from Tristie and off the couch.

Miller had appeared from nowhere.

He was wearing only brief bathing trunks, and he wasn't alone. The General and Abasi were with him, both of them also wearing bathing trunks. The General had his switch in one hand and a canvas bag in the other. He dumped the bag on the floor and nodded to Miller.

"See to the other one."

In a couple of strides, Miller was by the couch where Tristie still lay. He pulled her into a sitting position. "Now watch the General and see what happens to sluts who try to steal girls who are our property."

The General was standing over Sheena. He kicked her savagely in the ribs, ignoring her gasp of pain.

Sheena curled into a ball, gasping, the breath knocked from her by the blow as the General waited for her to recover her wind. Then he placed his foot on her chest. "You must remember," he said, "that you aren't my Madam any more. You're just another slave, and it seems you need to be taut a lesson."

"But General," Sheena began to protest, "Master Nick told me I could use…"

Her protest was turned to an agonised scream by the General's switch. He leaned over her. "First of all, you call me Master. Secondly, Nick Keane did not say you could use this slut. He told you to train her."

"Master! Please!" Sheena wailed, "Nick did say I could."

Her protest was cut short by another slash of the whip across her breasts. The General turned towards Miller. "Secure the other bitch!"

Miller reached for Tristie's hair and grabbed a handful. He dragged her over to the wall, where he shackled her neck to a large ring. Then he went back to the centre of the room where he and Abasi grabbed Sheena and held her still with her arms stretched out sideways.

The General gripped her chin and tilted her head up. "You can watch while I parcel up the slut you dared to interfere with." He chuckled evilly. "When we've finished with you, you can go back to her and entertain us! Then we'll entertain her ourselves." He stepped over to Tristie, unshackled her and, ignoring her scream of pain, pulled her to her feet by her hair and dragged her over to the opposite wall, where there was a rectangular metal frame about seven feet high. At six inch intervals there were small hooks welded to the inside edges of the uprights. He pushed Tristie against the granite, between the uprights, and pointed to the crossbeam of the frame.

"Arms up!"

Tristie lifted her arms and hung her head in defeat as she felt her wrists being strapped tightly to the crossbeam with leather strips. The General shackled her ankles to the floor, so her legs were stretched wide. Then, from a locker beside the frame, he took a roll of plastic cling-film and reeled off a long length. He wound the centre part of the strip about Tristie's neck, and then began to wrap the cling-film tightly about her body, following the curves of her figure closely, crossing the strip between her lovely breasts and about her waist. Then he took the ends between her legs, pulled savagely into her groin, dividing her labia and her buttocks, and wrapped them tightly about each thigh.

The General began to bind the film to the frame, passing the elasticated length of plastic over the hooks. Soon Tristie's naked body was bound immovably, like a fly captured in a plastic web. She was stretched out like a sacrifice, her head forced forward, so she was obliged to watch the two men who held the trembling Sheena.

The General was shaking with lust. He grinned as he ran his hands over Tristie's body, allowing his thick fingers to slip in and out of her exposed sex, grinning as he wiped her juices over her thighs. He chuckled. "Plenty of juice there! A natural! I said you were!" He ran his hands over her body again. "Now, you can watch what happens to slaves who try to enjoy themselves with our property."

The General turned and looked into Sheena's frightened face. "You lied to me. That was naughty." Shaking his head, he bent to the bag and took out a large reel of thin dog-chain.

"On your knees! Time to truss you in chains. It will be

quite a novelty for you." As he spoke, he was reeling off the chain. When he had about forty feet of the stuff, he took a pair of metal cutters from the bag, snipped the length off and dropped it to the floor.

"You know what to do!"

"Yes Master," mumbled Sheena. She leant forward and sorted out the chain, aligning the two ends. She picked it up and held it to the General.

"Stand!"

Sheena obeyed, still offering him the chain.

He took one end, hitched it through the ring on the front of Sheena's collar, and secured the centre of the chain there. Then he took the two ends down the front of her body, the close linked chain tinkling as he did so. Between her shapely upthrust breasts, he crossed the chains, then passed them around her back. Re-crossing the chains he brought them forward, and wrapped them tightly twice around her waist, before taking them down between her labia. He threaded the ends backwards, between her trembling thighs.

"Abasi!"

"General?"

"Pull the chains through please. Tightly!"

Abasi grinned and grabbed hold of the chains. He pulled them savagely, so that they parted the sensitive labia and dug deep into the tender flesh of her sex.

Grinning as Sheena wailed out, Abasi took both ends and draped them over her shoulders, so they hung over her breasts. The two ends were then passed through the rings in Sheena's nipples, and pulled back up, lifting her fine breasts outwards and upwards.

Sheena screamed as the chains dug into her flesh, but the General merely secured the ends of the chains to the rings on the sides of the steel collar.

The tortured girl twisted her face into a mask of pain as the chain dug into her body and pulled on her nipple-rings, straining her breasts into cones of pain.

"Hands behind your back!"

Sheena obeyed, and mewled out as Abasi clipped a pair of handcuffs tight up to the limit of the ratchet. Then her arms were lifted to the back of her neck where they were attached to the rear of her collar.

Abasi stepped back. "She's ready for the Gauntlet.

Sheena began to tremble at that, and shook her head from side to side frantically. "Oh No! No, no, no…"

Her pleas were cut short by the switch landing across her buttocks. "You say Master when you speak to me, slut!"

Sheena sobbed. "Please no Master, not the Gauntlet!"

The General ignored her. "Quiet. On your knees and over to that other slut. Suck her until I tell you to stop!"

Sheena nodded fearfully and began to hobble over to Tristie. She stopped in front of her and began to tongue her vagina.

In moments Tristie was writhing in her plastic bonds, her gasps of pleasure echoing about the room as Sheena's tongue slid in and out of her sex. Tristie's juices began to flow as her climax approached until finally, with an uncontrolled scream, she came, her love-milk running all over Sheena's face.

Then, abruptly, Sheena was pulled away by the General, who threw her to the floor and sat astride her chest. Grinning, he gagged her with a tube-gag. "Take the bitch to the Round Room." He stood and turned to Abasi. "The Gauntlet will soften her up for the Sheik."

Abasi nodded. "My Sheik tells me to inform you, he will thank you personally tonight, if you would care to come aboard."

The General gave a wide smile. "Indeed I shall, Abasi. Please convey my acceptance and regards."

"Mr Nick Keane is invited also." Abasi chuckled, a deep throaty sound.

The General laughed. "To a different sort of party Abasi. Yes?"

"Indeed my General." Abasi pulled Sheena upright by her hair, ignoring her muffled scream of protest, and dragged her from the room.

Miller and the General came across to Tristie, and grinned at her trussed form. Miller ran his hands across her bound body again. "Christ she was wet General! She really loves the girls does this one!"

"That is something Sheik Malik will soon break her of, I am sure."

Tristie had begun to shiver again and the General nodded. "Yes my little one! You may well tremble. I told you what would happen if you didn't please me." He turned to Miller. "Take her and hand her over to Keane. As Sheik Malik said, that bastard will come with us tonight. He can present the sluts to the Sheik."

Miller winked and grinned. "And the Sheik gets rid of Keane for us!"

"It will save me the trouble of arranging a further prison sentence." Then he leaned towards Tristie. "And just so you can't warn him…" He held up what looked like a hinged steel collar, with a clasp and lock on one end. On the inner side there was a ball-gag attached to the metal. He fitted the contraption around Tristie's face, forcing the ball in behind her teeth. Then, with an evil chuckle, he closed the hasp behind her neck and locked the metal gag in place. "There," he said, slipping the key into his pocket. "That should keep you nice and quiet. And to finish off, a nice leather hood, so you can't even speak with your eyes."

When he had hooded her, the General stood back and began to chuckle. "I would have had your tongue cut out, but Sheik Malik asked me not to, you need it to pleasure him with. So you see, he isn't so cruel after all!" He laughed at his joke as he slowly cut away the plastic from her body.

Tristie could do nothing but shake in terror.

25: THE GAUNTLET

When they reached the Round Room, the 'Gauntlet' was already in place. Around the circumference of the room, a ring of about fifteen people stood, all either naked or in skimpy revealing attire. They all faced inwards and each of them was holding some kind of whip or cane or strap. Inside this ring of people stood another, armed with more instruments of punishment. The people making up this second ring faced outwards so that, between them, there was a circular alley about six feet wide.

The Gauntlet!

Lisa was there too, and she chuckled as the door opened and Sheena was pushed towards the circles of grinning expectant people.

"Why hello bitch! My we have come down in the world haven't we?" Lisa was carrying a short but wicked looking switch and she slapped it against her leather-clad thigh. "Hope you're ready for this!"

There was a low growl from the crowd.

Sheena was still weeping into her gag and her knees were buckling as she shook in terror. But she could do nothing but obey as she was pushed towards Lisa.

Lisa grinned sadistically. "Me first then, General?"

The General chuckled. "Oh no Lisa! Not you." He nodded towards Abasi and Miller. "Now!"

The two men pounced on Lisa, knocking her to the floor. Her switch went flying and she screamed as she fell. Then, as they held her stretched out on her back, the General stepped forwards and took out his folding knife and held up the razor sharp blade for Lisa to see. "Time to get out of something uncomfortable, Lisa!" Smiling, he began carefully slitting the close-fitting leather slacks, so they fell away from her soft white skin like two opened pea-pods. Then he turned to her underwear. The flimsy bra went first. One slice of the blade between her breasts and the two cups dropped aside, freeing her firm bosom. He flung the scrap of silk aside, ignoring her wails of protest and ineffectual struggles.

Lisa was shuddering now, but her body went comparatively still as the general slit the front of her panties, grinning as the material gave way. He pulled the ruined panties down to her ankles, then cut them free and dropped them to one side. He was breathing heavily now, as he folded his knife away and stood over the helpless woman.

Lisa was revealed in her splendid nudity now, still held down on her back by the two men. The whole process had taken but seconds and the stripped beauty had barely had time to make a sound of protest.

The two men jerked her to her feet and the General came close. "It's a pity, Lisa. A great pity, but Sheik Malik has taken a liking to you." He caressed her cheek. "And he made me an offer I couldn't refuse."

Lisa had recovered her breath a little, and was struggling against the two men who were holding her. The General turned to Abasi and Miller.

"Tie her to the other slut and we can begin."

Lifting the naked beauty as though she were nothing but a sack of rags, the two men dragged her across to the bound Sheena. In moments they had strapped the two together, face to face. Both girls were now shaking in terror.

The General walked across to them. "I wonder which of you is best at running backwards?" he taunted them, as he pushed the pathetic couple into the lane between the two circles of people. Then with one shove he sent them on their way, Sheena almost falling over backwards, the pair stumbling between the lines of waiting people.

Instantly the room reverberated to the screams of the two girls, the sounds of leather against flesh, and the savage whoops of perverted delight from the torturers as the wretched pair struggled to keep upright, trying to run, but merely stumbling around the narrow lane between the two ranks of sadists. Every step took them into the path of yet more punishment, but to stand still would result in a protracted beating which would last until they fell unconscious.

So, they ran; or tried to. What they actually did, was stumble everywhere as they went around the narrow lane of the Gauntlet. Every step of their shambling journey was accompanied by a blow from one of the various weapons. As one or other of the girls turned to avoid a blow, so her partner was presented to another leering tormentor and a whip or a cane would slash into defenceless flesh again. Then that girl, in her turn, would present another part of her body to the people she had just passed, causing further pain to be inflicted on her.

Eventually, the two girls were merely shuffling along as the constant bombardment of blows reduced their stamina, until finally, they fell into an exhausted heap, sobbing, hardly moving. They no longer had the energy to scream, much less avoid the blows.

At last the General's voice rang out: "Enough!"

There were a few last-minute blows, then the onslaught ceased and the party broke up into small groups, standing around, pointing, jeering, even spitting on the pathetic pair of slavegirls sobbing on the floor.

The General looked at the small crowd. "That was a fine run, ladies and gents. Please now adjourn to the Pleasure Palace, where I have slavegirls waiting to satisfy your obvious appetites."

There was a mutter of approval from the group and they drifted towards the door, some of them already fondling a partner, as they walked towards an evening of sadistic delight.

When they had all gone, the General nodded towards the hapless girls. "Untie them, Abasi. Take them to the Despatch Room."

26: Given to the Sheik!

Lisa, Ruth, Tristie and Sheena, were in the 'Salamander's' stateroom. They were naked and kneeling in a semi-circle, their backs to the bulkhead. A short length of steel chain linked their leather collars at the side, forming them into a coffle, and they were each gagged and hooded. Their arms had been shackled high up their backs, fastened to the rear of their collars, and their oiled bodies glowed in the soft golden glow of the overhead lighting.

Tristie and Ruth, unlike the other two, had a narrow leather extension at the front of their collars, hanging down and pushing aside their upthrust breasts. The 'breast-plate' had a large ring at the end and from this ring leather straps had been taken behind their bodies to be secured below their shoulder-blades. Where the straps joined, another steel ring was stitched into the leather and clipped to the ring, and there was a coiled bunch of heavy steel chain resting in the small of their backs.

The Sheik, the General, and Keane, stood by a huge table which had been prepared for a sumptuous meal.

Sheik Malik waved an arm towards the coffle. "Fine merchandise General. You are to be complemented." He smiled, then walked over to the kneeling slavegirls. Tristie and Ruth were chained next to each other at the end of the small coffle. Malik stooped and detached Ruth's chain from Sheena's collar, then prodded Tristie and Ruth in the stomach.

"Stand."

The girls obeyed.

"Turn!"

Again the slavegirls obeyed, twisting away to face the bulkhead.

Malik grabbed the chain between the girls' necks and pulled both of them down towards the deck.

"Submission position."

213

As one, Tristie and Ruth knelt, lowering their heads to the carpet and pushing their taut buttocks up ready for the whip. As they did so, the two bundles of chain slid off their bodies and clinked to the deck.

"Stay."

Malik turned away and stepped over to Sheena and Lisa. He looked at them for a moment, then clapped his hands.

Abasi appeared, almost magically.

"Take these two to the cages."

A cruel smile crossed the General's face as the girls were led away. "I take it they will be settled in, properly?" he enquired.

"Oh Yes!" Malik answered. "They will be beaten. Then they will stay in the cages until we arrive at Karshina. Licking their wounds, so to speak."

"Good." The General chuckled. "The girl Lisa was a bit difficult, Sheik Malik. The stupid slut seemed to think she was immune to abduction herself."

The Sheik lifted his shoulders casually. "They will both learn their place soon enough, I assure you." He waved the subject aside. "Now General, can I suggest a little diversion before we get to business?" He pointed to Tristie and Ruth, still motionless, their soft, oiled buttocks presented. "I think these sluts could entertain us?"

The General chuckled, walked across to the hapless pair and picked up the bundle of chain attached to Tristie's waist. "I see you have had them readied for a tug-of-war, slavegirl style!"

"One of your better ideas General Brice," Malik acknowledged. "Highly original for an Englishman, might I add."

"Welsh actually, Sheik Malik, but I'll forgive you this once!"

"Ah! Of course. I forgot. Not all Britishers like to be called English... Now, Nick, would you care to get them ready for their performance?"

214

Keane nodded and stepped over to the slavegirls. He removed the chain from between their collars.

"Kneel!"

Both girls immediately straightened their upper bodies, thrusting out their breasts and spreading their knees wide. The bunches of chain behind them clinked again, settling to hang over their buttocks as they waited for the next order.

Keane undid the hoods and removed them. Then he unfastened the gags, allowing the girls a moment to gulp in deep draughts of air.

"Face each other."

Tristie and Ruth turned, still on their knees.

"One kiss!"

Both girls leaned forward and their lips met briefly before Keane cracked his dog-whip.

"Back to back!"

Keane unfastened both bunches of chain at their backs and sorted the links out into two twelve feet lengths. He then bent to each girl in turn, taking the long chain forward between their buttocks, threading the links through the ring at the bottom of the narrow breastplates. Then he took the end of the chain back through their legs, before shackling each end together.

"Take up the slack!"

Dropping to all fours, they crawled away from each other until the chain was taut between them, digging into the tender flesh of their genitals, spreading their buttocks apart. They remained still then, dreading the next order, tense and waiting.

Keane walked around them slowly. "Whoever crawls to the bulkhead in front of her first, wins." He chuckled. "You have to touch it, mind, but don't worry, we'll be encouraging you." He cracked the dog-whip, chuckling as the girls flinched. "The loser spends an hour on Abasi's rack... Are you ready?"

"Yes Master!" the girls answered together. Deep fear

showed in their tremulous voices.

Keane stepped back.

Malik and the General, each holding a thin, leather-covered cane, approached the girls. Malik turned to Brice. "General, you are my guest. You have the choice of girl!"

The General beamed. "Shall we have a wager Sheik Malik, just to make it interesting?"

Malik nodded. "Very well. Shall we say five hundred pounds?"

"Make that five thousand, Sheik Malik."

Malik nodded and shrugged. "As you wish."

The General nodded, then pointed to Ruth. "I'll take this one." He grinned at Malik. "Fitter, I think!" He positioned himself behind the kneeling Ruth, measuring off his distance from her buttocks with a slight tap of the switch.

Sheik Malik moved over and did the same thing with Tristie.

"Ready Gentlemen?" asked Keane.

The two men nodded and raised their switches.

Keane cracked his whip. "Go!"

Together the two men slashed their evil switches downwards so that they whistled into the unprotected flesh of the offered buttocks, and the two sadists began to beat their chosen girl with great enthusiasm, urging them onwards like beasts in the field.

Screams and wails of agony rent the air as, sobbing and screaming, the two hapless slavegirls scrabbled at the deck, straining for the bulkheads in front of them, each trying to overcome the strength of the other. As they pulled, so the chain became bar-taut, digging ever deeper into their tender parts. The chain continued to cut into their flesh as they fought against each other. Their rounded buttocks and their smooth oiled skin began to colour into wicked stripes of red and blue as the switches sliced into their flesh.

Tristie knew she was losing.

Just as in the trotting races, she wasn't fit enough. Nor

strong enough. She couldn't compete with Ruth. Screaming and wriggling her buttocks to ease the burning pain of the cane, she dug her nails into the carpet to gain purchase. She tried to ignore the pain as she suffered the agonising pressure of the chain in her genitals as Ruth, also screaming in her own agony, began to triumph, gradually dragging Tristie behind her.

Finally, almost exhausted, Ruth was able to reach out a desperate hand to touch the veneered woodwork on the bulkhead.

The moment the girl's fingers contacted the bulkhead, the two men stopped their assault, allowing the girls to slump into exhausted huddles. They watched the pathetic slaves impassively; uncaring, as sobbing and writhing, the unfortunate wretches tried to ease their agony.

"It seems you win General," said Sheik Malik ruefully. "I owe you five thousand pounds." He clapped his hands, and the double doors opened.

Again, Abasi materialised.

Malik pointed to the two sobbing beauties. "Take them below Abasi! Give that one an hour upon the rack."

As soon as they were gone, the General turned to Malik. "As I said, I am not a loser. Unlike our friend here." He gestured towards Keane and a sneer had creased his features. "He persuaded me to gift the girls to you. Unfortunately for Keane, Zach couldn't keep his mouth shut, so I know about your plans for disposing of Keane. That saves me the job of killing him myself."

Keane's face turned to a mask of anger. His fists balled and he made to go for the General, but Sheik Malik's arm stretched out and pulled him back.

"Wait," the Sheik said.

At that moment there was a noticeable shudder of the deck and a slight tinkling of crystal from glassware on the table. The General jumped to his feet. "Why are we under way, Sheik? No one said anything about leaving the jetty."

The Sheik placated him, gesturing towards the prepared table. "Please General, be calm. We go just for a small cruise. We discuss. We eat and drink and we use more of my female slaves." He smiled. "Then we return tomorrow morning, mutually satisfied. In all departments. Yes?"

"What's to discuss?"

"The future of Mr Keane."

The General's face was becoming suffused. "Zach told me you'd be disposing of Keane."

"Zach was misinformed!" Keane broke in. "Shall we say I've come to a crossroads in my career, General. Time I moved on."

The Sheik tried to intercede and he waved his hand at the table. "Let us start our meal and I will send for a few girls to entertain us."

But the General was becoming truculent. He started to pace up and down, and he shook his head. "No! Keane is for the chop!" He looked across at Keane. "You take care of that, Sheik Malik, and I go back to the Island."

Malik broke in. "I think you are right, Nick. The General won't see sense." He pressed a switch on the bulkhead beside him and the lights in the stateroom dimmed. Soft red lights came on, there was the whirr of hydraulics and a large screen in the bulkhead moved aside to reveal a huge square porthole looking aft.

Keane grinned into the General's face. "Take a look General!"

Almost in panic now, Brice stalked across to the porthole.

The Sheik and Keane went with him, and stared out across the stern deck of the boat.

The 'Salamander' was being closely followed by 'Kukri', Keane's boat, expertly piloted by a statuesque blonde woman. Beyond, a mile or so astern, the island was fast receding. But it was still possible to see the patch of light at the jetty.

To the right, a small fleet of eight or so launches were

approaching the Island at some speed. The occasional flash from bright Aldis Lamps bounced across the water. More ominous though, for the General at least, was the flicker of a blue flashing light on top of the leading boat.

"It's all over General," Keane said. "I was going to ask you so nicely, to just let me go. But, well, there you are."

Brice wasn't short on guts, it seemed, for he snarled at Malik. "Why all the crap? Just take me to sea and dump me overboard, like you intend to."

"General, I am not quite so barbaric as you seem to believe." Sheik Malik shook his head. "That wasn't the idea at all."

"Well what then?"

"Simple General. I was hoping to take you with me. My country has no extradition treaty with Britain. So, you would have been left to yourself, with a passport and as much money as you wanted. Or, you could have stayed. Karshina is a haven for foreign criminals, as long as they obey our laws. And for men with your sexual tastes, it is Paradise itself." He shrugged. "But as you were not co-operative, we will shortly drop you and Miller in a boat, with a radio beacon on it. It is quite calm and you will be perfectly safe." Again he shrugged. "As to your rescuers, well, the coastguard will see that you are cared for."

"And what about when I tell them of you?"

"That is a risk, yes, but by then 'Salamander' and 'Kukri' will be out of British territorial waters." He pressed a button beside the porthole and the screen closed again. The stateroom lights came up a little and the Sheik walked towards the double-doors.

"Abasi! Escort the General to his boat, and see he is pointing the right way when you push him off!"

Brice was fuming as he walked towards the door. "I'll have you both for this!"

"When you come out of prison, General," Sheik Malik said. "Maybe!"

The General ignored him and turned on Keane. "And you, you'd better not show your face in England again. I have friends and you're a marked man."

Malik closed the doors and gave a huge sigh, "That was unfortunate Nick. We could have used the General and his Island ourselves."

"There are other islands."

"And other Generals," the Sheik grinned, "and I have enough to buy both." He paused then, as the ship began to roll a little. "I think we have stopped. The General will soon be on his way." He turned to Keane. "Now, why don't you go to your suite Nick? Your girls await you!"

Keane smiled. "Why not, Akram. Why not?"

"You know the way?"

Keane nodded.

"And thank you, Nick, for Sheena and Lisa. The names have a certain ring, but numbers will suffice from now on." He grinned. "They will both look well, stripped off and harnessed to one of my racing-gigs. I am grateful to you, Nick." He lifted a glass of fruit juice. "Now, before you go. A toast to our future!"

Keane poured himself a brandy. "Yes Akram. A toast!"

They clinked glasses, downed their drinks, and Keane turned and walked out into the passage.

Minutes later he stepped into the reception lounge, where his three slavegirls, naked but for their bejewelled collars, knelt in a small semi-circle. Jumana still wore her pearl waistband and looked delicious.

Ruth and Tristie bore the wicked marks of their recent ordeal, but he could smell the soothing oils which had been massaged into their skin. They were still clearly in some discomfort. Tender care was indicated. Tenderness, just occasionally, was good for a slavegirl. It made her even more compliant; made her feel properly owned, and completely subject to her Master's will.

As he closed the door behind him the girls lowered

themselves, and touched the thickly carpeted deck with their foreheads. They spoke in concert: "Master! We are yours. We wait to serve you!"

The End